# THE *of* CLOCK HEAVEN

# THE CLOCK of HEAVEN

*a novel by* Dian Day

*inanna poetry & fiction series*

INANNA Publications and Education Inc.
Toronto, Canada

**Canada Council for the Arts**    **Conseil des Arts du Canada**      **ONTARIO ARTS COUNCIL** **CONSEIL DES ARTS DE L'ONTARIO**

We gratefully acknowledge the support of the Canada Council for the Arts and the Ontario Arts Council for our publishing program

We are also grateful for the support received from an Anonymous Fund at The Calgary Foundation.

Cover design: Val Fullard
Cover artwork: A. J. Gray, "Storybook Village," detail, mixed media on canvas, 8" x 20", 2003.
Interior design: Luciana Ricciutelli

Library and Archives Canada Cataloguing in Publication

Day, Dian
       The clock of heaven : a novel / Dian Day.

(Inanna poetry and fiction series)
ISBN 978-0-9808822-2-3

       I. Title. II. Series.

PS8607.A98C56 2008          C813'.6          C2008-906290-6

Printed and bound in Canada

Inanna Publications and Education Inc.
210 Founders College, York University
4700 Keele Street
Toronto, Ontario, Canada M3J 1P3
Telephone: (416) 736-5356 Fax (416) 736-5765
Email: inanna@yorku.ca
Website: www.yorku.ca/inanna

*for my children*
*Kao and Tove*
*everything*

*for my almost-children*
*Dana and Shayla*

*and for Piero*
*among the angels*

# Prologue

It seems that rivers come from nowhere, fully formed. A river runs its course over the distance of a few dozen miles with the opposite shore never receding or drawing nearer in any substantial way. Even the places where it widens to pools or narrows to rapids result in only small, and temporary, variations. It is bound by the earth and rock rising along its banks. The distance a small child can walk in one hour—stopping to pick up rose-coloured stones, or to watch river weeds run like snakes through the current, or to examine upside-down black beetles waving their legs in the air—this infinitesimal distance could not be said to generate any changes in the landscape at all. Rapids continue to rush over rocks. Trout keep turning in pools. The sun—if there is sun—still scatters leaf shadows and light across the water's tumbling surface. But where the river comes to the ocean and empties itself into that resting place of rivers, that river heaven, there the river's source has no meaning. The river is, finally, unbound.

Esa stood on the gravelly seashore. She'd walked along the river's edge from Gam's—it seemed to her a great distance, but if she turned and looked around she would see the house rise through the thin line of trees beyond the high tide mark and the steep sweep of the beach. If she looked very closely, she would see Gam seated in the press-back rocker on the front porch, turning the pages of the Sunday paper, and looking over the top of her reading glasses to gaze down the shoreline.

The sea was becalmed. Vast. Esa squinted her eyes, and looked down. She picked up a pink veined stone. A small thing, like the half-moons on her pink fingernails—how often did she look at those? How often were they scrubbed clean and *pink*, as they were now?

her father who had brought her to Gam's. He had not
ahead to announce their arrival. They got on the train in
city she'd never been out of, and they sat upright in stale seats
for an entire day and night, while the train clattered through the
green landscape. At least, Esa sat all night in her seat. Her father
was soon gone, Esa didn't know where. But when he came back in
the darkness he was whistling. He had trouble keeping his balance
as he walked down the aisles, and apologized too loudly, his voice
cutting through the night. Someone shushed him. Esa pretended
to be asleep. Later, her father lurched out of his seat and threw up
on the floor outside the tiny lavatory, and the porter had to come
with a mop. Esa kept her eyes closed as the familiar smell slipped
along the length of the carriage. When she opened her eyes again,
she could see a wispy moon through the dark window, pulling them
along like a surge of swelling water. In the morning, a woman in
a nearby seat with children of her own put oatmeal cookies and
a carton of perspiring milk on the once-again empty seat beside
Esa, but she didn't understand that the food was meant for her.
She kept looking out the window, because she did not know where
she was going.

Finally the train stopped and Esa and her father got out and
stepped into a bus, and then changed to another, bigger bus, which
put them down along a deserted stretch of road next to a boarded
up store. Beside the store stood a phone booth with a broken door.
Her father had to search all his pockets to find a quarter, and then
they had to wait a long time for the unmarked taxi. They rode
down long curving stretches of green, down a steep hill, up a little
one, and finally stopped at a tall, isolated house. Her father pulled
her from the seat and handed her the little suitcase he had hastily
packed. He paid the driver grudgingly, slammed the car door, and
marched up the flagstone walk to a weathered wood porch.

And at the end of the long journey, Gam answered her door,
surprised—but not surprised, really.

"Oh," she said, "*Burgess*." She said the word like she was saying
"turnips," or "collard greens." And her eyes shifted slightly to one
side, as if it was painful to look at him. Esa wondered if maybe

Gam preferred to look at the kitchen garden beside her door, to reassure herself that she could grow *something* useful.

From behind her father's trouser leg Esa watched her grandmother's lids narrow, taking things in: her father, herself, her suitcase. Gam took it all in quite well. Esa could not hide the suitcase, for although it was very little, she was even littler. Its metal corners poked the back of her bare knees.

Gam lived alone. Esa had never known that a person *could* live alone. All her neighbourhoods had houses crammed full of skinny children, raw-armed mothers, aging great aunts, reedy boarders, and drunken hangers-on. Gam's house was a huge, solid structure that creaked like a tree in the wind and had two floors and a narrow flight of steep steps with which to get up to all the bedrooms. Four of them. Esa was to have a bedroom, and a bed, to herself. The mattress sagged so much that it was impossible to lie anywhere except in the exact middle. She laid her little suitcase beside the bed and shyly tried it out, before she and Gam went back downstairs.

Her father was tipping his chair back, beside the Kemac, a cigarette between his thin lips—even though Gam had asked him not to smoke in the house.

"How old is she?" Gam asked.

"Seven," said Burgess. "I think. Are you seven?" He turned to Esa, who was settled on the red kitchen chair, kicking her feet against the top of the rungs where the paint was already worn. Esa picked at the hem of her shorts where the stitching was coming out, and said nothing.

"Where is her mother?" said Gam.

"Bernadine's out of commission," said Burgess, and he laughed nervously. "She's just out of commission for a while. The two older girls are with Bernadine's sister."

"There are *others*?" said Gam.

First thing, practically, Gam put her in the bath. Gam unwrapped a cake of brand new soap, without, it seemed, even thinking about it, and rubbed it vigorously on a cloth, which she then applied to Esa's skin. She had a clanky pot with a loose handle that she used to pour water over Esa's head. The water ran down, plastering her hair to her head, flowing across her face and tight-shut eyes, slipping around her neck and over her shoulder blades and across her thin chest. Esa too slipped and sagged into the warm tub with the run-off. Her ears were under water, her eyes still screwed shut. She didn't see the look on Gam's face, or hear her say, "Lord, you're *exhausted*!" but she did feel Gam's arms under her armpits, and felt herself pulled upwards. Esa kicked and sputtered, coughed up bathwater onto Gam's shoulder, and allowed herself to be wrapped in a stiff green towel that came down past her knees, round and round until she was only a pale aquamarine tube of a child, squeezed out.

Gam sat her on the lowered toilet seat—hard to bend in the middle with all that towelling—and cut her matted hair with a pair of yellow-handled scissors. Esa heard the sound of freedom and felt the falling hairs and watched the light on the three apple trees (the Three Sisters, Gam said they were called) she could see through the open casement window. Oh! the miraculous speechless self that looked out from the mirror over the basin, where Gam pointed her when she was done. Esa shook her head from side to side, feeling the ends of her hair sweep her shoulders. Later that first afternoon, with sun slanting through the trees, she picked up a branch of pine needles from the yard, just the size of her small hand, and ran it lightly across her cheeks and over her shoulders with her hair, and she could not feel the difference between mousy-brown and verdant green. But softness everywhere.

Her father didn't stay long. He didn't say goodbye, but that first evening as she lay in bed and watched the pale curtains billow inwards, and tremble outwards, like ghosts across the sills, she heard the front door slam below her, and noted the absence of his feet pacing the sea-swirled linoleum tiles of the kitchen floor. That is all she remembered of his departure: silence.

4

Next day, Gam threw out the meagre contents of her little suitcase and took her to the Sally Ann. There was a bell over the shop door that tinkled lightly as they went in, and an old woman behind the counter who smelled of crackers and fish chowder. Gam looked through the great bins and the circular racks—clack, clack, clacking the hangers along the curved rod, holding striped shirts and woollen sweaters across the back of Esa's shoulders.

"Do you like this one?" Gam asked, waving a small blue bathing suit in the musty air.

"What about this?" said Gam, holding up a bright red jacket with yellow piping.

"And this?" she asked. The collection of clothes over her arm grew, piece by piece, into an entire wardrobe.

Esa burrowed her way between the women's blazers until she disappeared from view.

On every windowsill of Gam's house, and in the corners of every room, and on the top of every bureau and desk and end table and sideboard, upstairs and down, there were piles of grey pebbles, moonlit shells, brittle brown seaweeds, and the legs of tiny crabs. It was as if the sea had crept in and scattered its salty treasures throughout the house, and Gam had gone about her business somehow without noticing. The air in the house was pregnant with salt, and every surface was powdered with sand dust.

"Do you want some more pudding?" Gam asked.

Esa stared down at her empty bowl, its chocolate-coated sides ribboned with spoon-marks. She turned the spoon over and over in her hand. It flashed diamonds up the wall and across the veined ceiling.

Esa walked along the beach. Ahead of her, in the distance, she could see a long wooden wharf run out into the water. The curve of the bay contained the wharf and the fisherman's huts and all the stones on the beach, and Esa herself. Her feet made only very small indentations in the gravel. The stones were mostly

5

grey, and grey-blue. On some days, like this one, the colour of the stones and the sea and the sky all ran together. Esa's thin frame walked in two dimensions, like a figure in a black and white photograph.

There were amazing things washed up on the beach, once-living things Esa had never seen. Deflated, gelatinous jellyfish, glazing the rocks underneath like fruit tarts gone mouldy. Long-tendrilled squid whose boneless bodies curled in crevasses when the tide ran out. Pried from their rocky anchors, barnacles like minuscule mountains with loose teeth—or little, silent volcanoes that never spewed lava. Dimpled sea urchin shells, shifting from green to purple, from prickly to spineless, now that they were uninhabited. Tesserae of purple-black clam shells, all that was left after the gulls dropped them and the rolling rocks pounded them.

And also the cast-aways of human life: An empty metal tube that once held toothpaste, still with an indentation where a thumb had pressed the last squeeze out of it. Esa fit her own thumb into the spot, and wondered at people brushing their teeth on the beach. Bits of frayed rope in bright colours: sunflower yellow, and the turgid aquamarine of her grandmother's car. Blue-violet fragments of glass, smooth and dusty with salt. Small green glass floats that fit in the warm palm of her hand, semi-translucent; thick bubbles that, when held to the eye, cast a dream shadow along the shore. The brassy keys from sardine cans that clearly had magical properties and seemed to be waiting for an opening; she tried them in the rusty locks on the doors of the storerooms on the wharf, but was not terribly disappointed when they didn't open. Empty tins of all description, razor lids still attached on one side, some with faded salt-stained labels still on—those were especially prized. A turned chair leg, with dog's teeth-marks up and down its length, as if it had been used over and over in a game of fetch—where was the chair? Broken over someone's broken arm like the one that they had at home?

"What *is* this?" said Esa, as she dug into her pocket and laid a hollow disc on the worn arm of the porch rocker. A five-petaled flower was inscribed on its pale surface. Gam stopped rocking, stopped sewing, looked closely at the speaking child. There was a hole in the centre of the disc's underside, and when Gam turned it over it made a small whisper, and grey sand sprinkled out.

"That's a sand dollar," said Gam. "Neptune's currency."

"What is this?" she said, and handed Gam a thin wedge with a row of sharp spikes on one side, their top surfaces split like tiny open mouths.

"That's a fox's jawbone," said Gam, "with teeth. A sea-fox. They have webbed feet, and can breathe under water."

"What is *this*?"

She began a collection of her own.

Esa sat under the wharf and watched the tide go out, an eclipse across the sweep of the beach like a dark crescent moon. Her new shoes and socks were wet. She watched the barnacles and limpets on the wooden pilings, their centres tiny mouths waiting to be fed and to grow eyes and ears and noses, then bodies and limbs, and break loose, finally, from their contained lives and run down beaches and up along riversides to houses where grandmothers *waited*.

Esa brought back a whole sea urchin shell, its byzantine surface still covered in hollow spines, and laid it on the kitchen table. Gam was impressed, stopped her reading to look.

"What a find!" she said, and Esa smiled.

It was her mother who came to fetch her home three months later. The Three Sisters were laden with ripening apples; that morning Gam sent Esa out to the yard to gather those that had dropped in the night—"before the worms get them," Gam said. Esa filled the checkered cloth with two-toned fruit, and dragged the bundle in to the kitchen table.

"Sister Jewett today, I think," Gam said, and her sure hands didn't hesitate as she sorted the Jewetts from the Cortlands and the Wealthies, though they all looked exactly the same to Esa. It was the day Gam had set aside to make pies for the community fair.

"Why do the sisters always have to be apart?" Esa had asked

her, and Gam had laughed and thought a while and said, Well now, she guessed they didn't.

So they made "Three Sisters pies" with three kinds of apples mixed together, the radio above the sink thundering fiddle music, the table strewn with apple peelings and flour dust and cut ends of pastry from when Gam ran her knife quickly around the edges of the uncooked pie crusts. Esa's head was bent over the brown sugar bowl, her sugared finger in her mouth, and Gam was saying, loudly, so as to be heard over the music, "Sugar! You'll turn into—," and they looked up and there was Esa's mother watching them through the screen door, her face faceted into tiny dark segments so it was impossible to read her expression. They looked at each other through the door, the three of them, and no one spoke or moved—except that Gam reached out instinctively and laid her floury hand on Esa's arm, on the soft, inside of her elbow where the blue veins ran.

Finally, Gam's hand dropped from Esa's arm, and she wiped the remaining flour and apple juice from her hands onto her worn apron. She crossed to the sink and reached out and turned the radio off. In the sudden, burning silence Esa saw all the places in the screen that Churchill the cat had clawed when he wanted to come in, small triangular tears that showed along the hemline of her mother's dress.

At the time it did not occur to Esa to question how Gam knew this strange woman was her mother; much later, when she was older and had left home for good, she searched the dim mirrors of her tenement rooms for any unwanted sign of maternal resemblance.

"Will you come in?" asked Gam.

Esa's mother would not.

"I've been knocking at the other door. I've come for Esa," she said.

"You *must* come in," said Gam, desperately.

"I'll wait out here," said Esa's mother. "I've a car out front."

They moved slowly. The air was suddenly watery and offered a resistance that required them to swim. They swam up the stairs, gasping for breath. Something had hooked them both, and was pulling them upwards against their will, beaching them. They floundered. Gam took Esa into her room and sat on the edge of the bed, one hand on Esa's boney shoulder, the other holding the bib of her apron, over her heart. The springs creaked. Gam stared straight ahead, but there was nothing there to look at but the shape of Italy where Esa had picked a small hole in the wallpaper.

Finally Gam shook herself, took down Esa's suitcase from the shelf in the closet, opened all the drawers in the dresser, began the journey from what was full to what was empty. She got the shoe box from Esa's new shoes, wrapped each of Esa's treasures carefully in tissue paper. The red marble. The knot-hole with pointy ends, like one side of a broken pair of eyeglasses. The three-legged, once-orange starfish, embedded with tiny grey stones. The liver-coloured bladderwort, the multitude of ribbed shells. The stones chipped from pink-toned rainbows. The whole, perfect sea urchin. Gam poked two holes in the side of the box with the yellow-handled scissors, and made a handle out of a piece of turquoise sea-washed rope, knotted at each end on the inside. She filled the box quite full, and then she taped it shut, wrapping it round and round with masking tape until the things it contained were sealed up tight.

Esa's mother was sitting in the car when they came around the corner of the house. From behind the wheel, she moved her eyes without moving her head. She looked rusty around the edges, like the car.

"Get in," she said. "What'd she do to your hair?"

Esa's mother pulled out of the driveway without looking back. In the back seat of the car, Esa held tightly to the handle of the shoe box on her lap, and bent her head down to the scent of apples that Gam had unknowingly left in the crook of her arm.

# Chapter 1

When Esa was in her third month of pregnancy, she stopped flossing her teeth. She kept brushing them, though. She didn't want to have bad breath, and she hated that stale taste first thing in the morning if they didn't get brushed. But flossing seemed like a lot of work for nothing. She couldn't imagine that she was going to be around long enough to get gum disease. She didn't want to think that far ahead.

Esa thought about having an abortion, but she never seemed to get around to it. The pregnancy wasn't a hard one. Esa never got sick, morning or otherwise. The only major change that occurred in her eating habits was that she couldn't stand to eat eggs, formerly a mainstay of her diet. It was as if their embryonic nature repelled her unconscious mothering instincts. She said afterwards that that was the closest her body ever came to having instincts that would guide her through this process. She didn't have a clue, she said, and that was obvious.

The weather that spring was uncommonly mild. There was a lot of rain, and the snow was all gone well before the end of March. Most days, the sky was the insipid blue colour of photocopy paper that has been at the back of the cupboard for years.

There was paper like that at Esa's office. Merle found it one day when he was looking for the copier instruction manual. The machine was always breaking down; the repairman spent hours there, interrupting the flow of work in the office so significantly, and making Merle so irritable, that often Merle told them they could just have the rest of the day off when the thing broke. That day in March when it broke down for the second time in one week, Merle decided he could do a better job of fixing it himself.

He dug out the instruction manual, found the ancient photocopy paper the exact shade of the March sky, and set about dismantling the machine.

"Take the rest of the afternoon off," Merle said from the floor of the copy room. "This isn't going to be pretty." Esa and Linda and Serge slowly put on their coats and filed out into the hall, trying not to look too eager. Merle's shirt was already smudged with copier ink. Outside the door, Linda giggled.

"His wife's not going to be happy!" she said. Serge looked at her narrowly, but he didn't say anything. Linda did a lot of giggling and making jokes about Merle's wife, who was actually a man and so was not, strictly speaking, a wife at all. Esa had asked Merle once why he bothered to tell people like Linda and he'd said, smiling, "I guess I just have an open-door policy on life," and he'd waved his hand carelessly at the empty door frames gaping like wounds around the reception area.

"I wish you'd put the doors back," she'd replied.

Esa suspected Linda of tampering with the photocopy machine whenever she had a date with her boyfriend, who only came into town sporadically, and never gave Linda any advance warning of his arrival. Esa noticed that the copier usually broke down within a half hour of Linda getting his call. She knew it was the boyfriend, because Linda always switched the call to the meeting room instead of taking it at her desk. Esa thought about telling Merle her theory, but she never seemed to get around to it.

The three of them went in single file down the narrow stairs, and emerged onto the deserted street like a failed explosion. They didn't say goodbye or wave as they parted, Linda and Serge to their cars parked along the roadway in opposite directions, Esa to stroll across to the park to sit on a bench and decide what she would do with the remainder of the afternoon. Linda's Neon shot out of its parking spot too close to the fire hydrant, and noisily climbed the hill. Another parking ticket, thought Esa.

Sometimes even now Serge offered her a lift after Linda had gone, but not today. Today he folded his long frame into his battered Volkswagen beetle, and drove off down the hill without looking in her direction, his head held slightly sideways so he wouldn't bang it on the roof when going over the potholes. His hands on the steering wheel were the colour of oak leaves that had over-wintered on the tree. Water splashed from underneath his tires as he bumped away.

Esa sat on the bench in the small park. It wasn't really a park at all, just a triangle of brown grass too small to build on. A path cut across the triangle from one corner to the middle of the opposite side, the concrete cracked and littered with paper coffee cups and silver gum wrappers. There was a small plot of earth on one side of the path. The bench, its paint a chipped and scarred apple green, was on the other. Across from her in the dormant earth she could see a few green heads of spring bulbs fighting their way up from underneath a chocolate bar wrapper.

"You're wasting your time, girls," Esa said to the daffodils. "Don't bother."

She looked around quickly, unsure of whether or not her lips had moved, but the streets remained empty. The wind picked up the torn wrapper and skipped it into the gutter, where it stuck in a puddle of black water laced with a dull, oily rainbow.

The cold seeped through the seat of Esa's jeans. She began to jiggle her legs to try to generate some warmth. A salty white van came slowly down the hill, its driver apparently lost. Esa tried to decide where to go. The bookstore? No point before payday. The library? The coffee shop? She lifted her jacket and patted her jeans pocket, feeling a satisfying bulge of coins. But she didn't know if she was hungry.

"Get up," she said to herself, but the cold had taken her over. She began to feel unwell. Her hands were ice, her belly fire.

"All *rise*," she commanded, but her limbs did not obey her. The March wind laughed its grey-blue laugh and spat a shredded plastic grocery bag across her feet.

Her belly fluttered. The heads of the daffodils seemed to shrink back under their litter protection. The white van turned into the street and came down the hill for the second time, its driver looking at her intently, and then looking around at the deserted street. He slowed down as he passed her this time, driving between her and her office door, and rolled down his window so she got a good look at his pallid face. Esa wondered whether Merle would hear her call from his place among the bits and pieces of photocopier. She imagined his ink-stained cheek turning to the curious noise of her screams, then returning preoccupied to *Do not attempt to remove this cover, call a qualified technician or warranty will be void*. But the van kept moving slowly on down the hill, the driver easily satisfied by the flash of wariness he had created.

She felt as if she had a small volcano inside her, and she rubbed her belly with her raw hands as she stood up, stiffly, anxious to be away. Something at her core tumbled as she stood up. Just hunger, she thought.

She knew she would have to leave work soon. She hadn't told anybody she was pregnant, and she wasn't going to.

"You don't look so good," Linda said as Esa walked in. Linda was at her desk, cracking gum and waving one bony hand in the air to dry the nail polish she had been applying.

"You don't look so good either," Esa replied. She hung her spring jacket on its hook and crossed the small reception room to slide open the single window behind Linda's desk. "Can't you put that stuff on before you get here?" Esa stood by the open window, the damp March air swirling eagerly into the grimy room.

"Jesus, it's freezing!" Linda scowled and shivered. She lifted a mirror the size of a pad of paper from the top drawer of her desk, her fingers with their cherry nails tentative on the edge of the frame. From behind her, Esa could see Linda's gaunt face searching for reassurance in her own reflection.

"And the mirror crack'd from side to side," quoted Esa.

"Huh?" Unfortunately, Linda was not really paying attention.

"So where's Merle?" Esa sighed. She left the window and leaned in the doorway of the office she shared with Serge. She didn't say, *Where's Serge?* She could tell there was no one else in, because she could see right in to each of the three offices and the copy room. Merle had taken the doors off their frames years ago and used them to replace the ones in his old apartment so he could get his damage deposit back. That was at a time when the business wasn't doing so well, and his previous relationship wasn't doing so well, either. Esa had been after him ever since she started working there three years earlier to at least replace the door on the copy room. When the machines were running, the oily fumes crept steadily into every corner of the office until they found Esa and the dead spider plant at her desk.

"Merle's got a meeting, Serge is sick," said Linda, and she got up to close the window, her fingernails tapping on the glass.

*What is he sick with?* Esa didn't ask. She sat with her elbows on her desk and the bottom of her palms held snugly against her closed eyes. She could see the dull orange imprint of the light against her eyelids, and beyond the box of light she could see Serge asleep in her narrow bed, his head resting on his outflung arm, copper-coloured against the pale flannel sheet. His left heel hanging over the end of the bed, his right knee, like a piece of exquisitely carved dark wood, emerging from the covers.

Esa's phone rang. She shook her head and the image faded. She could see Linda looking in at her, waiting with crossed arms to see if Esa would pick up the phone. Esa answered it on the fourth ring.

"CartoGraphie, ici Esa, Esa speaking," she said into the receiver.

Esa had a dream. In her dream the world wobbled on its axis, the northern hemisphere pulling outward as it turned. The land bulged and dipped in swelling waves. There were no stars, and the metallic ring around the beckoning moon was like a stain of gasoline in a dark puddle lit by a car's headlamp. The sky darkened, and Esa was flung into the sea by the rising ground.

She awoke covered in salt water and turned on the light beside her narrow bed. She pushed the covers away and sat up, feeling the stillness of the bed, the floor, the house, the world.

Esa put her hand under her t-shirt and rubbed her belly. She thought about her dream, and she thought about the seed the size and colour of a ripe acorn that was growing inside her. She remembered Serge's careless hand on her shoulder the evening they had gone out to eat after closing the office up for the holidays. And later, when he was a bit drunk, negotiating the Volkswagen around a corner with his hand on her knee, he'd said, "We might as well, you know, Esa."

And so when they'd arrived at her house she let them both quietly into her tiny room. Serge seemed surprised to find out where she lived, but he laughed when he discovered how far his feet hung over the end of the bed.

Afterwards, through narrowed eyes, he'd said, "Yeah, I thought we might as well," and he fell asleep squeezing her shoulder.

"But *why?*" asked Merle for the third time, his frustration rising steadily. "You can't just quit. You don't have any money. I *know* you don't have any money. I don't know what you do with your money, but you wouldn't live in that dump if you had any. Excuse me, that part's not my business. But this part is: You do a great job here. I thought you *liked* it." He paced his small office, sending adrift myriad small scraps of paper in the tangled air currents.

Esa sat in the orange chair and picked at the stuffing coming out of the arm.

"I just don't think I can stand it any more," said Esa.

"Stand what?" demanded Merle. "Stand *what?*"

Esa was intent on replacing a large cloud of yellowed cotton into a small hole in the orange seat cover.

"I don't know what there is to stand. I took you on three years ago and I trained you. I can't afford to lose you now. Business has really picked up, and I know that's largely because of you. We're all set for a major expansion, more staff…. You seem to be happy here—well, happy enough. You can't just say you can't stand it anymore and go!" Merle sat suddenly in the swivel chair behind his desk, the air in the seat escaping like a slow, soft moan.

"*What* are you *doing*, Esa?"

"Oh!" said Esa, and she quickly folded her hands between her

16

knees. The lump of cotton bulged like a cancer underneath the fabric.

"I don't mean the *chair*," said Merle, "I mean *you*. What are you *doing*?" He sighed all the air out of himself and, deflated, leaned forward and placed his forehead gently among the sticky notes on his desk.

Esa examined the spot on his head where the hair was thinning; there was a small point of smooth pink skin. She wondered why balding men seemed never to have dandruff. His ponytail was wrapped with the kind of thick elastic that came around the mail in the mornings. There was a long silence.

"You should get some hair bands at the drug store," she said finally, and got up and stood awkwardly by the door, her hand on the doorknob.

"I just have to go," she said. Merle did not look up as she left the room.

It was past quitting time, so Linda and Serge had already left, the coat tree in the reception area bereft of all the raincoats except hers, the green canvas kind with the bright yellow lining that she'd got on sale at Canadian Tire. She put it on, its cold embrace making her reluctant to go out into the evening rain. She glanced back at Merle through the doorway, his ink-stained arms motionless on his desk, then she thumped quickly down the stairs to the street.

When Esa got to work the next morning she unlocked the entrance doors herself, as usual. First the downstairs door, the grey scraped metal greeting her with *Elvis lives!* and *Tammy loves Jeff* and *call Gena for a sucking good time*. The stairwell light was out again, and she felt her way up in the near darkness to the top landing, groping for the keyhole in the office door. Underneath her feet she could feel the rumble of the presses starting up, and then stopping. She imagined Merle down there waiting for the first printing to come off the long machines, and calling quickly to Joseph and the others *Stop press!* when he saw how badly the colours came together on the maps. Esa went down to the print shop as little as possible. The echoing roar was like an endless train passing through a stone railway cut, and the men's hands were always black with ink.

Once inside the office she noticed right away that the door to the copy room had been replaced. Its closed face had been painted a yellow-gold, presumably to match the decor in Merle's apartment. She hung up her coat carefully, and then approached the door, running her palms along its smooth surface, placing her hand on the cool handle.

The copy room was empty. She examined the back of the door, which was a shade of olive green. She practised opening and closing it first from the inside, then from the outside. The hinges were well oiled.

She finally closed the gold and olive door and left it, smiling slightly at the *click* of the latch bolt as it met the strike plate. She rested her cheek for a moment on the top panel before crossing the reception room to open the window behind Linda's desk.

Esa's phone rang. She waited, but there was no one else to answer it.

"CartoGraphie, puis-je vous aider?" she said, picking it up at Linda's desk.

"Can you come for dinner, Esa?" said Merle's voice. "I'll pick you up. You'll have to hold the fort today, I've got a pile of meetings, but I'll pick you up at five-thirty from the office."

"It won't work, Merle," she said, but she said it gently, because she liked the door.

"What won't work? I'm just inviting you to dinner. All you have to do is say yes. I'm not trying to get you to change your mind about leaving."

"Yes," said Esa. "But you *are* going to try to get me to change my mind, and I need to tell you that it won't work. Do you still want me to come?"

"Yes," said Merle. "Five-thirty."

"Where is everybody?" Esa started to say to the dial tone. She looked at the instrument in her hand for a moment, then fit the receiver back onto the phone.

# Chapter 2

The nightmares returned, slowly, once a week or so at first, only half-remembered upon awakening, disturbing her sleep only long enough for her to glance at the luminous dial of the clock through thick eyelids. Increasing in frequency and intensity over the weeks before she knew she was pregnant, she attributed her tiredness to her nightly attempts to escape from fire and ice. She remembered a game she and her sisters had played in their childhoods, cataloging and ranking ways to die in the same way they listed and recorded their favourite colours or their most hated foods.

"Do you like yellow better or green? Would you rather get hit by a car or fall off a cliff? Would you rather freeze to death or burn?" As a child she had thought only of her own skin freezing or burning, had imagined only the cold blueness or the charred blackness of her arms and legs, had chosen freezing as the more aesthetic option. Now, when she dreamt, she saw and heard the world devoid of her own heartbeat, and it seemed not to matter.

In her nightly fires were the screams of animals, the hiss and crack of moisture leaving the charred trees. Branches fell like bones tossed to howling, flaming dogs. The fire charged across the landscape, racing through fields, suburbs, parking lots, brick-lined city streets and massive office towers, spewing into the gritty, ash-laden sky, a smog that blocked the sun and moon and stars from her dreaming view. The fire ate the hedges full of sparrows, the bicycles parked outside of schools, the stoop-shouldered letter-carriers, the pizza delivery boys standing in doorways waiting for a tip. It roared through spider webs in forest glades and sucked water into steam, leaving hot stones in dry creek beds with no trace of minnows. It melted plastic lawn furniture on the front porches of farm houses, suffocated horses trapped in barns, and drove pond geese frantically into the air in a futile attempt to outrun the spreading darkness. There was a lot of noise. Esa sometimes woke with her palms pressed to her ears so tightly that her arm muscles ached and the fading dream rang like echoes of despair.

The ice, in contrast, was almost soundless, falling steadily across landscapes, effortlessly covering fences and roofs and bridges, enshrouding all in translucent memory, a crystallizing cold. It encased the branches of great oaks and elms as easily as it did the tiny wisps of Queen Anne's lace and the bright petals of ox-eye daisies. It found grouse eggs in their nests and pulled the delicate heat from half-formed chicks. It kissed the scales of grass snakes over and over until, with one last cold wriggle, they froze like twisted, shining branches of green. Out of season, the ice caught the land unaware and unprepared, killing peach blossoms, heaving tender tips of clover from the hard ground, leaving the worn fabric of the earth torn and ragged. The ice glued tires to pavement, felled power lines, froze lakes and rivers and coastal oceans so that the world shone with a piercing light into Esa's eyes. She woke stiff with cold and rigid with fear, her breath hanging close to her mouth in the darkness.

Esa found little of the kind of sleep that brought comfort and rest and renewal. She began to rise at midnight, and again at two or three or five, too hot or too cold, unable to do anything but pace the narrow hallway outside her bedroom door, shaking her head in an effort to send her dreams away.

Esa had thought briefly that she might tell Merle about the pregnancy, to explain her departure so he would not think he had done something wrong. That is, she had thought for a moment of Merle's face with a blanched look, and of him saying, "What? *What*?" and not quite getting it. And then the moment when he did get it all, and his look deepened into constricting concern and over-attentiveness. The pieces would fall into place as he looked at her, reading the hieroglyphs of her closed face. So she hadn't told him any of it; it now seemed much too late to start.

It never occurred to Esa for a moment to tell Serge that she was pregnant.

She read no books on pregnancy. She went for long walks, not with the intention of keeping fit, but merely to wander in her usual distracted fashion through the slick streets along the waterfront, trying to find some meaning in the lines in the pavement or the slapping of the river against the greasy breakwater. She bought no cradle and knitted no baby clothes, no pale ribbed caps and matching sweaters with one useless button. Esa did not drink or smoke, but had she done either she would have continued without a thought. She did not suddenly start making lunches, and Serge no longer brought her sandwiches on freshly-made whole grain bread. Had he done so, she would have finally told him she did not like avocado.

There was an avocado salad at Merle's. The table was already set. Merle, always late, had picked her up close to six at the office, just when she was beginning to wonder if it might be a better idea if she simply went home. When they arrived Daniel was in the kitchen, and came to greet them in the small hallway, wiping his large hands on a worn dish towel that was tucked into his pants pocket. He kissed them both, his wiry red beard brushing Esa's cheek. He had flour on his sweatshirt and left traces of white dust on Esa's sleeve.

"Hello, love," he said to Merle. They exchanged an awkward look, and Esa saw that Merle had told Daniel why he had invited her to supper in the middle of the week. She knew then that she should have refused his invitation. She felt it even more when they passed into the gold-trimmed dining room from the olive hall, the newly-empty door frame warning her to go home. Daniel waved them in, urged Esa to sit.

"We're eating early," he said, "because I have to work tonight." He twisted his lips to one side regretfully, sending his beard off-centre.

The dining room was small, with a worn hardwood floor that creaked as Esa edged her way around the end of the table. At each of the three set places a smaller glass plate nestled on top of a larger one, lovingly arranged with slices of romaine, avocado, and mandarin. Esa sat in her usual chair, her back to the wall, not ready for anything.

Especially for what Merle said as they sat down, Esa taking her napkin from beside her plate and stroking it onto her lap, as if it were a thin cat.

"I invited Serge too," he said.

Esa stared at her plate, inhaled deeply. The edge of her plate reflected the light in a thin crescent.

"But he couldn't come."

Esa exhaled, realizing she need not have panicked. There were, after all, only three places set. Three avocado salads.

"I thought he might help convince you to stay," Merle continued, lifting his cutlery.

Daniel began to eat, slicing the tender lettuce and folding it carefully on the end of his fork. There was the muted squeak of knife on plate, the burr of the pepper mill, a chair creaking as Merle stretched his arm over for the olive oil and balsamic.

"I don't really care for avocado," Esa said into the silence.

The conversation veered away from her proposed departure. While Daniel removed her salad to the kitchen and brought her a fresh arrangement of greens, Esa told Merle about the calls that had come in to the office that day, including the one from Linda's boyfriend to say she had strep throat and would not likely be in all week.

"Not likely," said Merle, and he laughed ruefully. "As soon as she comes back in, I'm going to fire her."

"Don't do that for my sake," said Esa, surprised. "I'm not going to be there."

"Not for your sake, for the sake of the photocopier," Merle explained.

"Redundant receptionist released to reestablish regular reproductions," said Esa.

They talked about some new accounts without actually discussing who would do the required work, and when Daniel went out to the kitchen again and returned with three steaming plates, they talked about what was needed to upgrade the office computers.

Esa ate her pasta with a fork and spoon, twisting the flat noodles around for three or four turns before sliding the wide spoon underneath to lift the mouthful from the plate. Growing up she had learned to cut the tangled, slippery mass into short segments with knife and fork, the way her father did. No one at home knew about spoons.

Esa thought Merle had been born knowing how to use the small fork for the salad, the outside knife for the butter. It seemed as if his instinct always led him to use the correct side plate, without those frantic moments of hesitation that Esa experienced as her eyes would work their way back around the table from the place setting of the person who had taken the first roll and laid it safely down. Merle knew what capers tasted like and what *calamari* was and how much Tabasco sauce went into a perfect Caesar. Despite his often dishevelled appearance and his preoccupied nature, he had an in-grown familiarity, an intuition, that guided him effortlessly through eating and drinking in public. Esa marvelled at it, and when eating alone with him, or with him and Daniel, she always waited for him to take the first bite.

Merle's appetite was alarming to Esa. He ate like every meal was the last supper. She had not yet seen or heard evidence of any food that he didn't like; he found joy on his plate daily. He expressed equal enthusiasm for a fried egg sandwich as for a lobster salad or *crème brûlé*. Esa found it fascinating to watch him eat, but she remained unable to translate his pleasure to her own barely touched meals.

That evening she watched him coil *fettuccine* eagerly around his fork and cast his eyes upwards at the beginning of each bite. He ate like a prayer; there was no need to say grace.

"Mmm, mmm!" he said to Daniel.

And Daniel smiled.

Their small exchange, full of the habit of kindness, stabbed Esa with a deep longing that she could not identify. Even after many years away from her family, she could not get used to kindness.

"It's very good," she said, attempting to make up for the avocado salad.

Merle brought out homemade mango sherbet for dessert. Daniel had to leave for work and said he'd have his for breakfast, to make sure Merle didn't eat it all. Esa watched Daniel putting on his coat in the hall through the empty door frame. She looked at Merle inserting his spoon tenderly into the small glass dish.

"Thank you for the door," she said to them both, "but—"

Daniel leaned his square shoulder against the door jamb and waited. Merle put his spoon down on the table so it made a ring of pale orange on the dark wood.

"Where will you go?" he asked, softly.

"To my grandmother's," she answered, not realizing until that moment that she had, in fact, somewhere to go.

Daniel was gone to the night shift at the shelter. Esa and Merle sat together in the living room, each in a bright yellow over-stuffed chair, separated by a mosaic-topped coffee table. Esa ran her hands over its surface, as she always did when she came there, enjoying the feel of the cool tile. The table was always a surprise, its crazy paving pattern continually yielding a new sensation to her fingertips. That night it was a confusion of colour, a vortex of movement. She felt in danger of falling in.

"You knew," she said to Merle. It was not a question. Her small hand brushed the tile. She did not look at him, but at the movement of her fingers and the play of shadows in the muted light.

"I'm not *stupid*," he said.

The grout between the pieces of tile made a path for Esa's finger to follow, rough and directionless.

"Well, actually, I'm a little bit stupid," he conceded. "It did take me a while. Like, until just before we ate. When I said that thing about asking Serge to come. Now *that* was stupid!"

Esa pressed her palm onto the tabletop and lifted it slowly, the dampness of her hand momentarily changing the hue of the yellow and red tiles underneath. The tile beside her hand was like the mottled green of the cotton sweater Serge had left in her room that night. She had not returned it, and sometimes wore it underneath her jacket when she was going out for a walk and was sure no one would see her in it. Putting that sweater on was the only way she had of keeping him close, her arms through his, her shoulders giving him shape, form, meaning. The scent of him was gone from it, but often still she held its bulk up to her face and drew in air, as if she could breathe hope into her despondence.

"When?" asked Merle, and "when are you going?" he repeated, when she did not seem to understand his question. Esa knew then that he did not know everything, did not know about the acorn baby tumbling in her belly.

"As soon as you can replace me," she said. She knew how much the business meant to him, knew that he and Serge alone could not handle the workload.

"I can't replace you," said Merle. "You're the best *gestionnaire* I've had."

"You'll find another manager," she protested, "and Serge will do well for you."

"Serge is the fur, the fluff. You're the backbone, the brains, the guts. You *understand* about maps," he said vehemently.

"Just trying to find myself," she said mildly, and Merle couldn't help but smile.

Merle drove her home after dinner, as he always did, ever since the day when he had hired her from her thesis advisor's room at the university. He'd taken her to see the office, to show her the computers with the latest GIS software. Every inch of the office walls, floor to ceiling, was papered with test pages from the presses: a kaleidoscope of colour, form, swirl, line, all in different size squares. She'd felt possibility calling her from the contours of the flowing landscapes: crimson, chartreuse, sea green, and orchid. Afterwards they'd gone down to the print shop, where he introduced her to all those inky-handed men. Then, smudged by her new life, they had gone downtown to eat *Sechuan*, Esa unconscious of the comfortable silences that rose between them in her amazement at each new dish as it arrived. Merle was adept with chopsticks, sharing the slippery dumplings between her plate and his.

When they'd climbed into Merle's car again after the meal, Esa had had no sense that the interview was over. He'd turned onto her crowded, treeless street and pulled up outside her house, a large brick triplex with a "Rooms for Rent" sign in the window of every floor. Paint-chipped iron staircases ran up the outside of all the houses on the street, and the steps had been filled with children peeking out at them through the twisted railings.

"See you Monday at nine," he'd said.

She had not asked him how he knew where she lived—which seemed a greater mystery in the moment than the fact that she'd been hired. But these shocks were no less than the one she'd gotten a week later when Merle had come up the office stairs from the print shop and handed a small, weighty box to her across her desk, before rounding the corner to his own office with its window onto the shop floor. When she opened the box she had not immediately known what it contained; the small squares of cut paper packed on end she'd thought might be scraps for telephone messages or perhaps some design aid for uniform lettering. She'd separated one card from the others and read the words: CartoGraphie, Manager, Esa Withrod, Gestionnnaire.

For days she had worried that word *manager* around in her mind, tossing it back and forth in her head like a riddle she couldn't solve. Finally, she could no longer endure the pretence; if she had brought any personal effects into the office she would have packed them up quietly as she resolved to talk to Merle. But she had brought nothing of herself to the office, and in Merle's car again on the way to a meeting she had pulled a card from her pocket and given it back to him while he was stopped at a red light.

"I don't know anything about being a manager," she'd said, and she'd waited for him to say, Oh, I see, and to drive her home.

"I know," he'd said instead, "but you will," and he'd spoken with such a cheerful confidence that there was no argument that Esa could think of to discourage his faith.

They had the same argument this time around that they'd had when they were doing the interviews for Serge's position, Esa claiming to know nothing about hiring, and Merle insisting that she be involved in the process. Merle won again, of course. He simply refused to proceed until she agreed to help, knowing she would not leave him until he had satisfactorily replaced her. He did however, offer a compromise: he would do the first round of interviewing on his own and, once he had a short-list of candidates, Esa would spend some time with them and let Merle know what she thought. He did not ask Serge to participate; there seemed an unspoken agreement not to tell Serge that Esa was leaving. Not yet. They scheduled the interviews to take place during his two-week vacation in Hawaii—he'd shown Esa the two tickets excitedly, like she was supposed to be happy for him.

There began to be a stream of job-seekers through the office, men and women of mediocre talent and counterfeit vigour, their enthusiasm falsely stretched across the muscles in their tight mouths. It was as if Merle wanted to find someone with all of the skills that Esa possessed, but as different in personality and temperament as possible.

"At least you're honest," Merle said to Esa, after two long days of interviewing. "I may not understand you, but I do know you're not playing any games with the world."

"Oh no," Esa said, quickly, "the world is playing games with me."

Merle watched her as she put on her coat, the intensity of his look betraying the fact that he had not stopped trying to understand her enigmatic existence. Esa, however, did not look long in his direction before opening the office door and running down the gritty steps, her footfalls keeping time with the rhythm of the presses below.

On the Friday that Merle hired her replacement—an outgoing Italian with a tendency to chew the skin on the sides of his fingernails—Esa bought a one-way train ticket.

"Every day but Tuesday," the man said, his lips moving behind the Plexiglas screen seemed to Esa unconnected to his voice, like a badly synchronized film. The sounds of withdrawing trains echoed against the high roof of the station, their faint rumbling breath a distant vibration underneath her feet. It was a familiar sensation, like the printing presses at work. Around her, people hurried to their destinations with purpose, encumbered with the paraphernalia of their lives—briefcases, or babies, or baguettes. Esa watched a young woman with three children wind her way through the line of rope, back and forth across the floor like a duck in a pond, ducklings straggling behind. She felt a movement in her belly, unhatched but swimming in the dark. The man behind the wicket cleared his throat, tapped his fingers on the glass to get Esa's attention.

"Wednesday," she said, and she pushed some crumpled bills through the slot.

# Chapter 3

For a few months after Serge came to work at CartoGraphie, Esa's dreams stopped. She fell asleep easily and slept soundly until morning. She didn't dream about the rising ground or the silent wasteland or the airless planet, whirling away distantly until it shrank to a pinpoint in a dark canopy. She didn't dream about hectares of frozen forest with treetops cracked, shredded, peeled like bananas, as if God had come down and hacked at the landscape with a blunt scythe. She didn't dream about stinging smoke and roaring orange woodlands, the deep fierce heat blistering the backs of her hands as she held her palms up to her face. For a few months she slept, as the saying goes, like a baby. It was as if falling in love could save the world.

They took to sitting outside during their lunch hour, on the peeling green bench in the triangle of lawn parched from a long, dry summer. In the three years that she'd worked at CartoGraphie, Esa had never taken a lunch break except when Merle took her out to eat before or after a meeting; but through those early months with Serge she breathed daily at noon the gasoline and cracked pavement scent of autumn in the city. Together, she and Serge watched the thin leaves of the park's one tree—a maturing maple—turn brilliant orange and yellow and burnish in the sunlight. The piercing sun made them squint as they watched the first leaves fall through the windless air, floating down to lie beside their feet like secret messages from another world.

"So there's Zeno of Cittium," said Serge, "standing under the *Stoa Poecile* in Athens, arguing that this great conflagration will be repeated in an endless cycle, and after that, everything will be regenerated exactly the same way it was originally."

They were always alone. The warehouses and offices of the surrounding area were silent as funeral parlours, the few people scurrying the streets kept their eyes on the grey sidewalks. The few trucks delivering paper stock to the print shop, or picking up bound map books or reports or copies of *New Directions*, stopped only long enough to load or unload. Not one driver ever noticed the young man and woman on the island of dingy green, one figure sprawled against the hard back of the bench, the right arm waving mutely, the left hanging comfortably along the bench's shoulder; the other figure seated forward, leaning in toward the action, as a first-time theatre goer would watch a spellbinding play.

"The Stoics thought the world was perfect, and so it couldn't be other than it was, no matter how many times it was re-made."

Esa was listening to him, of course, but also to the sigh of falling leaves and the whisper the sleeve of his jacket made brushing against the back of the bench. At the end of every sentence he paused, exhaled, and nodded, as if he was agreeing with himself.

"So there's a lull, maybe for hundreds or thousands of years, and then fire destroys everything. Well, not destroys everything, but changes it. They thought the world was already all fire, anyway, in one form or another. Fire turned into air and air turned into water and water turned into earth, which eventually turned back into fire. There was an order to everything, a *logos*."

There was a picture of Serge in her mind, a moving picture, lit by a brilliant flaming sun hanging expectantly in the cerulean sky, benevolently poised to return to consume the earth in licking flames. It was like a picture taken just before the moment of death, every detail precisely outlined and each object sharply delineated from all other objects: Serge, like a cat, comfortable in any position; the shape of him, small planes and hollows of dry-leaf colours, flashing in and out of sun and shadow. Once, she caught a skittering leaf in her cupped palm, cradled it there until it felt the heat of her hand, then held it curled against his arm where his sleeves were pushed up below his elbows. He did not notice, and did not stop talking.

The hour passed too quickly for Esa. The sandwiches Serge brought for them bounced on his lap as he talked, the few pigeons—the regulars—pecking around his legs at the seed crumbs scattered by his exuberance. Through avocado and red onion, peanut butter and banana, cream cheese and sun-dried tomatoes, Swiss cheese and alfalfa sprouts, he talked and talked.

"There's this very odd thing about water," Serge said. "It doesn't behave the way any other liquid does when it comes to freezing. Water is heaviest when the temperature is four degrees, so when water freezes, it's lighter than when it's a liquid."

A gust of wind tossed leaves across their feet, and a silent contrail underlined the sun.

"So, in winter, when some of the water in a lake gets below four degrees, it moves up to the surface and eventually freezes. If it didn't do this, lakes would freeze from the bottom up and everything in the lake would die—all the fish and all the plants. They would all just die, in solid blocks of ice. Well, there wouldn't be any fish, or any plants, or any humans, for that matter. We would never have crawled out onto the mud."

For a few weeks Esa simply watched the shine of his dark eyes and the dance of his strong hands against the backdrop of brick and cement, and listened to his mind rambling through history, philosophy, psychology, biology. He infected her like a virus and spread to every cell of her blood, circulating in her body with an endless rhythm of words. The timbre of his voice in the grey air called her from the depths of her nightmares into a world resonant with feeling.

"Seriously," he said. "Seriously. What do you think?" he asked, as he always asked her those first few weeks, his open palm paused outstretched in her direction as though he were waiting for a gift from her. And this day, when he had finally expelled all of her resistance, she put what she thought he was waiting for into his hands.

"What do I think about which part?" she asked him, smiling.

"Just picture it," he said. "All those tiny ships bobbing around out there in the middle of the ocean. All those sailors looking up

31

at the sky, trying to find their way home by gazing at the motion of the moon—the clock of heaven. All those astronomers making endless observations of the movements of the planets. And having absolutely no idea where they were for ten days out of every month, when the moon was hidden. But in the end the answer wasn't in the sky. It was in a *watch*."

"So the answer didn't come from God," said Esa, "and the earth was not the centre of the universe."

"What?" He was momentarily disconcerted, as if she had entirely changed the subject. Perhaps he'd thought she had no idea what he was talking about.

"It's about looking for answers in the wrong places, isn't it?" she said.

Serge exhaled, narrowed his eyes. He put his hand on her cheek, her chin in the centre-point of his palm, his long fingers reaching her neck and the bottom of her ear. She did not read any significance in the fact that his gaze was focussed on a point of ground beyond her shoulder.

"You're gorgeous, Esa," he said. His thumb stroked her cheekbone, softly. Esa did not care that he was the one, after all, who changed the subject.

That evening at home in her rooming-house bathroom, Esa stared and stared at her face in the mirror, looking at the high forehead, the shock of shorn hair, the freckled skin, the grey eyes, the strong nose, rolling the word around in her head like a mantra: *gorgeous*. She couldn't connect the word to what she saw.

She was in the bathroom so long that Mitchell began to bang impatiently on the flimsy door.

"C'mon, Esa! I gotta go!" he said. "I—gotta—hava—crap!" For emphasis he hit the door between words.

"Wait, Mitchell," she said distractedly, her eyes flickering to the vibrations of the door.

"I—gotta—go!" he said. One of the small screws holding the cheap bolt lock began to work itself loose from its socket. Esa sighed, turned from her fruitless examination.

"When are you going to do the dishes?" she asked the vibrating door.

"Jesus, Esa, if you don't let me in I'm going to break this God-damned door down! You've been in there an hour! I don't care if you're *naked*, for God's sake! I'll break the door down!"

"Wait, wait, wait!" She heard one screw drop to the floor and could see another emerging from the wood. She pushed the bath-room door in against Mitchell's fist, unbolted the lock, and pulled the door open so quickly he was surprised to see her suddenly in front of him. He snapped his mouth shut, moved past her into the bathroom, and pushed her out of the doorway by closing the door against her shoulder.

She could hear him fumbling with his belt.

"About those dishes," she said through the door. That she was on the other side of it profoundly diminished her power.

"They're Jean-Pierre's, not mine," he said, and he sat down heavily with relief. Esa heard the broken toilet seat shift sideways, heard Mitchell curse under his breath.

She did the dishes. Not just one evening's worth, but every dish and mug and pot in the dark kitchen was piled on the counter beside the sink, a jumble of stacked plastic, ceramics, and metal. The edges of knives protruded from festering plates. Spaghetti. Macaroni. Mashed potatoes. Scrambled eggs. Chocolate pudding. Esa could review the week's meals for each of her house-mates.

She worked in slow motion. A few knives went into the sink to soak while she sat down beside the chrome table and stared at the crumbs underneath the toe-kick of the counter. She thought about sweeping the floor, but there was no broom. Jean-Pierre had taken it the day Mitchell had seen the rat emerge from the sewer grate in front of the house, and had run frenetically down the street waving it at the departing rodent. The others had all watched him disappear around the corner, had waited impatiently for him to return with an exciting story about having beaten the rat to death with yellow nylon bristles. After ten minutes, though, they had given up and gone back inside; he hadn't returned until two o'clock in the morning, drunk and broom-less and unable to explain where he—or the rat—had gone.

Esa went back to the sink and removed the knives one by one, wiping the blades carefully with the ragged dishcloth. They were all so dull as to be almost useless. The kitchen light flickered dimly.

Esa bought all the light bulbs for the kitchen and the bathroom and the hallway. She bought all the toilet paper and all the dish soap. She'd bought the broom with the yellow bristles.

The dustpan, at least, was still under the sink.

One of the stacked plates slipped from its perch and slid into the steaming water, splashing the front of Esa's cotton shirt and startling her into consciousness. She filled the sink with plates, and waited for the hot water to soften the food glued to their surfaces, sitting in the chair with uneven legs and tipping herself back and forth into a trance-like state. The tapping of the chair legs on the floor kept time with her heart beat. There was an ant making its way across the blue linoleum, holding a toast crumb over its head like a prize.

She sat there for a long time. The water in the sink grew cold, the grease floating patiently among the departing bubbles.

She had no idea what was happening to her.


The interviews had been tedious. Esa knew nothing about asking questions that would draw out the best—and the worst—in people in order to find out who they really were before making even a six-month commitment and putting them on the payroll.

"I don't know anything about interviewing," she said, trying to avoid missing a whole two days from the pile of map-work on her desk. "It doesn't take two people. I can't afford two days away from this," she complained, showing him evidence of the double-duty she'd been responsible for since Sacha, her former co-worker, had done a disappearing act the previous month.

"I need your input," Merle had said. "I need to know you're going to get along with whoever is hired."

"Just don't hire another Lemon, Like Loathsome Linda," she replied, trying to make a joke of it, but that hadn't satisfied him.

"Esa," he said, "it is quite normal for me to ask you to sit in on these interviews. All over the world, people sit in on interviews for co-workers when their bosses ask them. Some people are even honoured to be asked. They understand that it means their opinion is valued." He rubbed the top of his head where his hair was thinning. When he took his hand away a tuft of hair sprang up like a clump of dry grass.

"I don't want to do it," she said flatly.

"You *will* be there," he said then, exasperation seeping out from the spaces between his words. It was the first time he ever used being her boss to get her to do something.

So she'd sat through Gaile, who snorted when she laughed, and Lorraine and Jean-Luc and Walter, who *looked* like a Walter, and Corinne, who *looked* like a Corinne, and Jay, who was so nervous that sweat soaked the armpits of his aquamarine shirt and made them the colour of the ocean on a dark day. At the very end of the second day, as the unattended work piled higher and higher on her desk, there had been Serge.

He was full of confidence, almost cocky. On his way in to Merle's office he had paused for a split second in the doorway, reaching his hand up to hang for a moment on the narrow trim around the empty door frame.

Esa saw first the empty space around him, lit from behind; the artist's ground, cut by his silhouette in the doorway: the shape of his shorn hair, the distance between the top of his head and the door header, in a moment of absolute stillness when nothing moved, and no one spoke, and no one breathed. Then he came one half-step into the room, his hand still on the door frame, almost as if he was holding himself back. The light shifted around this small movement, and Esa could focus on the earth colour of his smooth cheek, and, briefly, glancingly, on his dark brown eyes.

"Well, well," he said, "a place with no doors." He looked openly at Esa and Merle, and at Merle's cluttered desk behind them, and at the empty chair where he was supposed to sit. His height almost filled the doorway, his arm bent backwards above his head like a tree branch, solid and ancient. Linda, squeezing through the opening beside him, introduced him, a blushing cheek half-turned towards his attraction.

"Serge Beroo," Linda said, anglicizing the name, *Surge Bay-roh*. He corrected her pronunciation without looking in her direction. Dismissed, Linda floated from the room back to her desk in the reception area. Throughout the interview, Esa was aware of the distracted presence of Linda's straining ear.

Esa stood up, stretched out her hand towards his long arm. "Esa Withrod," she said. Her palm was damp.

"Withrod, Withrod," he repeated, leaning his head back and narrowing his dark eyes at her. "From withe-rod? Or withy? As in, pliable?" he suggested.

"No, as in resilient," she said.

Merle asked for her recommendation. What she felt in that first meeting with Serge seemed like a curiosity, a fascination. There was something inexplicable about it all. It was so undefined and ephemeral; pieces of him were brought sharply into focus, then receded elusively like moon shadows. All she knew was that she hadn't felt the slightest interest in any of the others.

And he did a great job. His ideas were creative, but his real strength was dealing with people. With clients on the phone he was upbeat and energetic; in person his warmth filled the small meeting room like the air on the spring day when crocuses first appear. He could switch mid-sentence between French and English so easily that no one, French or English or Mandinka, could tell which was his mother tongue. And he could, it seemed, talk to anybody about anything—any subject at all that they cared to mention, he knew something about. His opinions were like gold coins, distributed freely to the masses. Clients were as impressed by him at least as much as they were by the wonders of GIS. Esa saw how people looked at him sideways when he laid their portfolios open on the table in front of them. They were in awe of him; he was something unexpected, like the moon up in the blue sky beside the sun. He made up for her natural reticence a thousand times over.

He brought magic to the office. Even Linda became tolerable.

On his very first day of work he'd brought two avocado and red onion sandwiches for lunch.

"You don't look like the type that brings lunch," he said to Esa, "and you don't look like the type to go out and eat every day." It seemed not to be a reference to her worn, out-of-date clothing, but rather, to how she held her body with a slight air of resignation. Still, her breath caught in her chest, and lay pinned there by the weight of unfamiliar feeling.

"You're right," she said. "I don't eat lunch."

He passed her a sandwich across the distance between their desks, his long arm crossing two-thirds of the way over to hers.

"Forgive the used wax paper," he said. "It's the inside of my cereal box."

Esa looked at the grainy bread in her hands. She didn't tell him she didn't like avocado. She ate the sandwich.

We might as well, he'd said. As if they were deciding to walk home through a pleasant fall afternoon instead of taking the bus. As if they were deciding to stroll into the drive-through on the way to get a milk shake. As if they were deciding to sit on the porch steps for a while, sucking on straws and watching Mrs. Fielding struggle to her back door with the three kids and a week's groceries.

Why had she done it? Esa did ask herself the question. But she had no experience with men. At least, not as far as relationships went. When it came to her own life, she had never thought of the word, *relation*, as anything other than a concept of geography. As in, the relation between a compass needle and a lodestone, or the relation between the earth and the moon. Things were drawn to each other because of magnetism, or gravity, or surface tension, not out of loneliness, or desire, or love.

What was it, this thing that leapt and surged in her like a sickness, so that every particle of her body set like ice or danced like fire? The heat and cold were extreme, and gusted through her body like a tempest.

Having never done it before, she didn't know then that it was possible, even common, to fall in love with the wrong person.

# Chapter 4

*Perhaps it began when she was born, the way everything does, the way everything connects moment to moment in our lives. This moment began when she was born, perhaps conceived, perhaps dreamt of so that her spirit was called down to connect this time and place.*

*There is a pink blanket wrapped around the baby that the nurse holds up to the window. A dark, squalling bundle, complaining of the bright lights and the smell of ether and canned milk and disinfectant. The mother is in a wheelchair because the twenty-two stitches mean she cannot yet stand up. She has already had two other pink bundles held up to hospital nursery windows for her to admire; other years, other cities, other hospitals, other bundles. She wasn't impressed then either.*

*The nurse jiggles the baby up and down, taps on the glass to get its mother's attention. The mother looks, sees nothing that she can recognize in this small shock-haired shape of new person. Contrary to expectation, she does not smile.*

*"That's not my baby," she says to the nurse behind her chair. Her hands on the armrests are white with suppressed rage.*

*"Oh yes, that's her," says the nurse in a cheery nurse-voice. "That's your beautiful girl. Isn't she sweet?"*

*"That is not my baby," the mother says again.*

*"She has a good set of lungs in her, anyway," says the nurse. There are only so many stock phrases to call upon when mothers are seeing their infants for the first time. It is as though the nurse is programmed to respond correctly, but some faulty wiring—or perhaps a power outage—has caused a short circuit in the mother.*

*Later, the doctor comes to her room to have a chat with her* about the baby she refuses to accept as her own. After pulling the bed curtain all the way around them he sits on the edge of her bed like a confidant. He chooses his words carefully and talks softly so that the three other women in the room will not be able to hear what he says. He is a sympathetic man.

"I can assure you, Mrs. Withrod, that I was there when this baby was born, and she is, in fact, yours. It's quite common for women who have been asleep during childbirth to have some question as to whether or not they have been given the correct child—(this, of course, is a lie, but he is trying to bring some normalcy to this inexplicable situation)—but I feel sure that once you hold your baby, you will get over this, this—"

Words fail him. The mother sits propped up by pillows at the end of the bed, her eyes closed tightly. When the doctor says the words "hold your baby," she puts her fingers in her ears.

The following day, he tries another approach.

"I understand you already have two daughters," he says in the curtained cocoon. His patient is still lying in her bed, facing the wall. "Perhaps you were hoping for a son this time?" he suggests gently. "Now, it's very important not to let your disappointment about the sex of your baby get in the way of the love that is every child's birthright." When he says the word "love," the mother pulls the pink-edged hospital blankets up to her ear, and turns her shoulder up.

The unclaimed baby is still unnamed three days later. At 3:00 a.m. on the night the baby is three days old, Nurse Jelena, all alone on night shift, takes the indelible black marker from the nursing station desk drawer, crosses out the word Baby above the last name on the infant's wrist tag and writes ESA in block letters. Nurse Jelena is unmarried, and too old to have children of her own anyway. Esa had been her mother's name, before they took it from her at Birkenau.

On the fourth day, the doctor asks the duty-nurse to find the father of the child. They know there is one, because Nurse Jelena remembers the night Esa was born, a short, noisy hour after her mother was dropped at the maternity floor nursing station by a dark-haired, scorch-faced, heavy-lidded man. He signed all the necessary papers, Burgess Withrod, and left, his scuffed shoes leaving muddy footprints on the newly-polished floor.

"Mrs. Withrod, where can we find your husband? Your husband, Mrs. Withrod?" the duty-nurse asks the mother, who seems content to lie in bed staring at the mottled ceiling, eating compartmentalized meals from plastic trays and using bedpans instead of getting up to go to the toilet.

"We've been calling your home number for days, Mrs. Withrod. There's no answer."

"Burgess doesn't answer the phone," says the mother, her voice horizontal in the evening heat. The fans are blowing air around the ward, stinging the smell of spilt milk into her nostrils.

Finally, the RCMP are summoned to find Burgess Withrod and tell him that his third child has been born, and to suggest to him it was high time he went to the hospital to fetch his wife and baby home. He comes in to the maternity floor smelling of alcohol, without pausing for even a moment at the nursery window. They bring him out the baby anyway, hoping that he will find something familiar in the set of her eyes or the shape of her ears or the particular pointiness of her chin. He looks, however, not at the baby's face, but at the name tag dangling from her tiny wrist.

"Esa?" he questions. "What the hell kind of name is that?"

Burgess Withrod takes the bundled baby from the nurse and tucks it under his arm; the sawdust from his sleeve makes the infant sneeze, the sneeze makes her cry. With the crying baby under his arm he collects his wife from her room, steers her down the hall to the elevator, still in her pyjamas and housecoat. Nurse Jelena runs after them with a shopping bag of the mother's clothes, a few disposable diapers, and seven cans of formula.

"I'll see that she takes care of it," he assures the doctor on his way past the floor desk. The doctor's mouth drops open and closes repeatedly.

"That will never be her child," says Nurse Jelena. The elevator door closes on Esa's tiny cries.

# Chapter 5

This was where Esa slept: A narrow folding bed, its metal frame bent slightly out of square so that it rocked when Esa sat down on its edge; on the bed, worn flannel sheets grey from years of washing, the edges frayed, unravelling; against the wall a precious feather pillow, thin as ghosts, tiny feathers escaping and drifting in the dry air.

In the small room, where Esa could almost stretch her arms across its width and touch the walls, there was a desk, a wooden chair draped with the blanket from the bed, a chest of drawers, a lamp, an electric heater, a white plastic garbage pail. There was no closet, the room having originally served as a back vestibule, but there were two doors on opposite walls, one leading to the gravel yard at the back of the house, the other to the dark hallway behind the kitchen. There was a window, high and curtainless, at the side, through which stubby light eventually made its way into the room. Esa had no view of the narrow lane or the brickwork of the house next door, nor of the veiled moon or the few dull stars that sometimes hung dismally, like lost roofing nails, in the cracked tar-paper sky of the city.

Underneath this window Esa had hung the elegantly framed print of the garden with the golden gate that Merle had given her for her birthday. She had not known what to do with the utterly unexpected package he had handed her that supper, or the cake subsequently brought in by Daniel. She caught the sympathetic look that passed fleetingly between them as she hesitated, felt the panic rise with the blood to her face as she held the brightly wrapped tube away from her on open palms.

"Well, unwrap it then," said Merle, and Daniel said, "Make a wish and blow out the candles." Rescuing her.

But she had left the candles to burn, wax dripping down their sides and congealing on the cold whipped cream, and had slowly unwrapped the tube with trembling hands, opened one end, and slid the rolled paper out onto the table, where it uncoiled like a spring and created a quick gust of wind that extinguished three of the candles on the cake.

The print was of a bright garden, full of both exquisite peace and teeming life. In the foreground was a golden gate, reaching to the very sides of the paper, so that it was necessary to look through the ornate golden bars to see into the multi-coloured world beyond. The distant fields were of a muted green, a summer green, when every living thing is at the peak of its growth and health and energy. The artist had captured the moment just before the edges of leaves turned brown in the heat of shortening days, before the brook stilled to a slow trickle and moss dried on the banks, before a handful of silken petals fell from the peonies with every gust of wind, before the cow vetch ran amok in the hayfield, before the earwigs got into the corn. The air was clear and the colours were bright. Trees and hedgerows were undamaged; there was no rust on the gate. Across distant fields the viewers' eye travelled, washed with recent rain and blessed with a rainbow, the ends of which were hidden by the grape vines, the peach trees, the morning glory, the bleeding heart, the poppies, pansies, roses, iris, foxglove, dandelion, strawberries. Among the climbing, stretching, tangled, growing green flitted every kind of butterfly, flew every kind of bird. The world was filled with partridge flapping, hawk soaring, woodpecker tapping, cardinal singing, sparrow pecking. Bees drank from the pond; snails slid in the fresh grasses.

"The frame wasn't quite ready," said Merle, "but we wanted to give at least part of it to you today."

Esa held the print flat with her left arm and touched the picture tentatively with fingertips of her right hand, here a stone, there a bee skip, here a nest of young robins, there a water lily. Her palm slid across the smooth paper, making a sound like a small wind blowing across open water.

Between Esa and this Eden stood the golden gate.

Then Daniel licked his thumb and index finger and snuffed out the remaining candles. The wish stayed in her belly, unformed.

When she sat at her desk doing work brought home from the office, or sifting through her pile of library books to see which she would read first, she often caught herself gazing for long periods at a blade of grass or a twisted vine in the print. When she sat at the edge of her bed to eat, avoiding the crowded kitchen, she was drawn over and over again into the vivid yellow and crimson and lilac flowers, as if she herself were a bee drawn towards nectar. When she could not sleep, she lay on her bed in the yellow light from the street lamp or paced the short distance from door to door, underneath the window she could not see out of and beside the false window that she could not gain access to. The garden slept serenely in the half-darkness: petals softly folded, colours muted, dew forming. When writing her monthly note to her grandmother, she looked first to the bountiful life woven there in that pathless garden, and was reassured.

*Dear Gam*, she wrote.

*I hope you are well. How is Churchill? I am enclosing a little something extra, this time. My job is still very interesting. I am making quite a bit of money now and there is lots to spare. I am sure you could put it to good use around the house, or perhaps you need new winter tires on your car?*

She didn't think it was lying, exactly, to exaggerate her earnings. She just wanted to make sure Gam accepted the money. She always tucked the new bills in between the folds of the letter, so they would not be visible through the envelope.

Merle almost always had lunch meetings, so he didn't notice when Esa and Serge began to spend every lunch hour together in the park. Neither was he the type that looked for intrigue, so he certainly didn't notice when they stopped. If Linda had said anything about it—which she very well might have done—Merle would have attributed her remarks solely to jealousy, and not paid any attention.

44

Esa and Serge sat in their shared office. There was, of course, no door. Linda was perfectly, gleefully aware of the silence that took hold there, pulsing emptiness, sound waves absent without leave.

The phones rang, and were answered. Clients came, and could be seen waiting in the reception area, beside Linda's desk. Papers moved from one pile to another, and to another, and then, finally, to a dark drawer. Computer screens flickered like darting birds.

Linda eventually got around to taking down the Chanukah and Christmas decorations.

Esa didn't look at Serge. Serge didn't look at Esa, either. But then, he never really had.

Early on, there'd been a red flag, but she had ignored it. It was not that she had *chosen* to ignore it; she had not recognized it for what it was. Instead of a red flag, it appeared in their conversation as a red flannel shirt flapping on a clothesline; a domestic detail, newly exposed to view, and as innocuous when it was clean as it was when curled at the bottom of the laundry basket.

Serge began to drive her home every afternoon. After that day in the park, when he'd put his hand on her cheek, he began to kiss that same cheek before she got out of the car. With the noisy motor running, and the old vinyl smell of his Volkswagen permeating everything, that kiss moved closer and closer to her mouth. Like the view of his ear and neck flashing in the sunlit street, or the grip of his solid hands on the wheel, or the sound of his voice, husky and animated, the feel of that daily kiss on her unversed cheek came back to her at frequent intervals throughout her days, unbidden. The sight and sound and smell and feel of him floated always just below her consciousness, where the slightest movement of that rippled surface caught an edge of somatic memory and cast it to the sky. And always, it made her gasp.

There are only so many days between jaw and cheek and corner of mouth and finally, lips, soft and full, and sweet-tasting. They arrived there late one afternoon after a full day of presentations, together having secured two new clients; their mouths met over the gear shift, and at some point, after what seemed to Esa an eternity, Serge reached up and turned the car motor off, awkwardly, with his left hand, then let that hand move to her collarbone, and her neck, and her cheek.

"Well," Serge said, after a long while, his lips still touching hers, the word a zephyr against her mouth, "Well, I guess there is something I should tell you."

He stopped kissing her and sat back. He had a faint air of amusement about him, but also an uncharacteristic nervousness. Esa also sat back in her seat and waited, unperturbed. She looked at his profile, the bridge of his nose; he looked out the front windshield at the brick-lined street, and at the garbage tossed along the gutter by the autumn wind.

"Well," he said, for the third time, "actually, there's someone in my life who's very important to me."

"What?" said Esa. "Who?" Did he mean her?

"I actually have a girlfriend," he said.

"Girlfriend," repeated Esa. "Where?" And she looked around the car, to see if perhaps suddenly there was another presence there, where she'd seen no one.

"Girlfriend," said Serge, lightly. "She's in New Zealand, going to university. She's studying social work."

"She's in *New Zealand*?" said Esa. There was the faint sound of laundry snapping in the wind. She couldn't imagine why he was telling her this. Esa had a geography degree; she knew very well that New Zealand was just about the farthest place away from the inside of Serge's Volkswagen, parked on her street, outside her house, in the city where they both worked, every day, at the same office, and where their desks were placed only two arm-lengths apart.

Esa laughed, in some confusion, the sound ringing hollowly around the inside of the bell-shaped car.

"Well, that's all right then," said Serge. He seemed to be relieved. He bent over towards Esa, and kissed her again. She leaned into his mouth with no foreboding.

# Chapter 6

*P*erhaps it began in her childhood, place of hazy vision: the dog
on the chain, the woman in the moon, the falling yellow leaves.
This and that become landmarks in an otherwise unremembered
place. What moments make character? What teaches us love or
despair? What oasis or mirage in the desert of childhood can be
called forth and set up for examination?

The three of them are in the bath: Katherine, Jane, and the
youngest, Esa. They are lined up like ducklings; their mother is
washing them with dish detergent on a coarse cloth—between
their toes, under their arms, behind their ears—until they are red
with her efforts. They do not play in the water. They do not splash
each other or wiggle their toes up through mounds of bubbles,
pretending they are worms or sea monsters. There are no bubbles,
only murky, lukewarm water.

"Sit still, Katherine," says the mother.

In the hall downstairs the telephone rings. The mother drops
the cloth into the bath water, pushes her arms against the edge of
the bathtub to lift herself to its call. She knows her husband will
not answer it.

"Stay there," she says to the children. "Don't you move an inch
until I get back!"

They hear her heavy feet on the carpeted stairs, hear her voice
faintly in the distance, "Hello? Oh hello!" In the bathtub the three
children wait quietly. Esa, the water up to her small chin, floats
her arms on its surface and cannot tell where her skin ends and
the water begins.

"...just one of those days ... thought I was going to kill her ...
milk all over the floor ... I know, I know...."

*Katherine pats the water with her hand, punctuating their mother's half-heard words with a quiet rhythm. Jane lifts her hands repeatedly out of the water, counting the drips from each small finger, watching the circles spread outwards over her kneecap.*

*"...get him to understand ... on the couch, drunk again ... well...."*

*The water fades from warm to tepid. The girls examine their wrinkled hands, finding them unrecognizable in the fading light.*

*"... going crazy ... what's playing?... get out of here ... pick you up in five minutes ..."*

*They hear their mother hang up the phone, open the hall closet. They hear the faint twang of the metal hanger as she pulls down her coat. The front door opens and closes. There is a silence. The tap drips.*

*The water fades from tepid to cold. Jane's hands and feet begin to ache. Esa grows tired, her bowed chin touching the water. The light fades from dusk to dark. The taps gleam like the eyes of a cat on the road. The tiles shine like the blue light of a television screen, the programme stuck on pause. Esa slips into sleep and slips into the water, emerges choking and gasping and kicking, her wet hair sending water down her face to mingle with her tears.*

*Katherine cannot get her to stop crying.*

*"I'm going to see," she says finally, and slips from the bath like a slick shadow, drying herself carefully so she will not leave wet marks on the floor, wrapping herself in the towel before making her way down the unlit stairs. From the hallway she can hear her father snoring on the couch in the living room. She bumps her way past the chairs, placing her cold hand on his bristling arm like the chill touch of death. He wakes with a start.*

*"What the bloody hell are you up to?" he yells, halfway from sleep. "Where's your mother?"*

*"She told us to stay in the bath until she got back," said Katherine, and herself begins to howl, the cold and exhaustion coupling with fear.*

*"Well, you bloody well better get back up there and do what she says!" Burgess Withrod pulls a cushion over his ear, turns his face*

*away. Katherine climbs back up the dark stairs, hangs the towel neatly on its hook, places one numb foot and then the other into the water, re-joining her sisters, all now crying uncontrollably, bones aching, mouths wide with pain.*

*When they can cry no longer, Katherine and Jane take Esa on their laps, holding her horizontally and enfolding her with their wet bodies, Katherine hugging her chest, Jane grasping her thin legs. They sit as close together as possible.*

*Esa sleeps like a capacocha baby, frozen in ice.*

# Chapter 7

Getting on the train was like shedding a skin. A thin layer of the past—the recent past—fell away from her cleanly and effortlessly. The steps of the train were steep and to her feet felt more like solid ground than any she had stepped on in months. As from an onion, the dry brown layer fell away from her and slipped softly between the train and the platform. This temporal skin came to rest on the dark track below, filled with steam and diesel and sounds of hissing, and sank heavily through the dirty gravel. She was lighter when she reached the top step, lighter when she turned the handle and went through the carriage door, lighter when she found her seat on the south side of the train. She faced away from the doorway she had just come through, the city she was leaving, and Merle and Daniel, standing on the platform, craning their necks to see her through the dark glass.

She did not look back at them. Merle's last too-tight hug, the water gathering in his eyes, the set of his cheekbones and his lips into lines of graphite, these things had slipped away into the crevice between the train and the land it stood upon, as if there was no connection between them. The train harboured an intent that colluded with her own—to carry her away.

"If you change your mind," he had said, "If you ever change your mind, your job will be waiting for you. If you ever want to come back."

She said nothing, but held herself into his embrace. Merle enfolded her there, kissed the top of her head, held her too long. She did not try to move away from him, but waited, felt his heart beating, his breath on her hair, his unsaid words. Daniel, in his turn, held Merle up without touching him, through a steady understanding.

The conductor on the platform looked at the leave-taking scene before him and imagined it to be the same as many other departures he had witnessed in the past twenty years.

"She'll be back before you know it, buddy," he joked to Merle. "You better get her on the train." And he winked at Daniel, thinking they were sharing a good joke together. Daniel, keeping his own joke to himself, smiled back and nodded.

"Make sure you write," Merle said, letting Esa go.

The train was not full of hope, but of relief.

There wasn't much more to pack this time than there had been six years previously when she'd left home for university, despite the fact that she'd been working for almost three of those six years. A few more books, perhaps. A set of sheets for the bed, a thin pillow, and the sleeping bag she used as a blanket. Her clothes. A few pots, pans, plates, cups. And the print from Merle and Daniel. Everything except the print fit in six boxes and a duffel bag. Six years; six boxes—even with so little, she asked Merle if she could store the boxes and the empty picture frame in the closet of the spare bedroom of his and Daniel's apartment.

Five years in a student rooming house had left Esa with a vicarious taste of family. The young men missed their mothers as they stood in front of the ancient washer and dryer in the small bathroom, peering at the dial options in confusion. The young women missed their mothers when they went to the drug store, finally learning how to buy sanitary supplies for themselves but choosing the brand their mothers had always bought so they would not have to linger too long in the aisle. Their continued reliance on their parents to take care of the small details of their lives was an ongoing fascination for Esa. They did not know how to pay their rent on time, how to buy milk before they ran out, how to wash the dishes before they got hungry, how to replace light bulbs before dark.

The only semi-permanent member of the household, she had

watched students come and go with a predictable regularity. They left always because the house was not enough like their own experiences of home. They thought they could do better; they had been raised to expect more.

Esa knew there was nothing better. The landscape of Thanksgiving dinners, Sunday drives, and home movies shown to tolerant relatives was, for her, alien and inexplicable. In the house's silverfish, dirty pots, and mouldy bathroom she tasted familiarity. And she dealt with it the way she had at home with her mother—by bringing a level of order and cleanliness to her impermanent world: she swept floors, washed sinks and toilets, replaced light bulbs, repaired broken handles. Housework gave her some control.

She cleaned the entire house thoroughly before she left.


The train's lullaby rocked her into sleep. When she woke it was half-dark, so she only half-woke. The train moved her past dreaming grey landscapes, the images that slid by both connected and disconnected in the way that dreams are:

Five deer in a stretch of flatland looked up as the train moved by them. A while back there was a burnt-out cabin, and there were telephone lines hanging slackly, but no one lived in the grey except five deer looking up. Frozen deer, holding in deer-breath, waiting to breathe again, chew again, feel again, waiting for the train to pass. Only their eyes moved, taking it all in, the rest was brown, fur-clothed ice. The grey was deep and full of shadow. Deer tracks followed railroad tracks.

The train shook her, shook the acorn inside her, shook the acorn cells so they divided and divided, without resting. The train wheels turned along the straight path running in the darkness.

Finally, the dark: Car lights, street lights, train lights. Eye lights. She never knew what time of night it was. There was nothing outside but distant candles. Time did not exist, only points of light. Everything was nameless.

The door between the cars opened and closed, and someone walked by.

A wheel squeaked directly under her seat.

Somewhere behind her a drunk old man tried to pick up a schoolteacher.

Finally, the light. Birds washed themselves in the shallow water of the mud flats.

The door between the cars opened and closed, and someone walked by.

The old drunk disembarked; the boys' basketball team disappeared. Behind her a man and a woman talked about the bible. Everyone else listened.

The door between the cars opened and slammed shut.

Esa had packed for university quickly, while her mother was at work. Even though her homeroom teacher had written "Esa needs to participate more in class" on her final report card, she'd won a scholarship to McGill because of her grades. She had had, after all, little else to concentrate on.

She did not show her mother the scholarship letter; Bernadine did not even know Esa had applied.

In the years that she lived as an only child, Esa waited for her disinheritance. She had no boyfriends, so there was no chance of them leading her onto the streets, as Katherine's had. She had no girlfriends, so it is not possible for her to have been taught their addictions, like Jane. Nevertheless, Esa knew it would have been only a matter of time before she did something to confirm that she was not her mother's child.

Esa folded her clothes and laid them on the bed, sweaters in one pile, t-shirts in another, jeans in a third. She removed all the socks and underwear from her dresser drawer and found underneath her secret things: the tiny pieces of worn blue glass in a folded envelope; the stained t-shirt, sized to fit a seven-year-old, that read 'Canada's Ocean Playground'; the photograph of Katherine, Jane, and herself on the front step of some unremembered house, their eyes half-shut, cheeks pushed up, mouths slanting downwards in the glare of the sun.

Apart from her clothes and the treasures hidden in her sock

drawer, there were only a few books, a pair of field glasses, and a map of the world.

Three-quarters of an hour before her mother was due to come home from work, Esa shouldered her backpack and renounced all that was left of her family.

She'd closed the front door, and thought that she was free at last.

And after all there was an end to it. The train rolled with slow deliberation beside the industrial wharf buildings, among the freight cars, along the waterfront. Between the buildings and the abandoned trains and the still-dormant trees, Esa caught glimpses of the bay, steel blue in the April air. Seagulls whirled soundlessly in the sky, muted by the train noise and the excited chatter of people finally arriving after a lengthy journey.

The train stopped at the very end of the steel track. People rose and stretched, pulled overloaded bags down from overhead compartments, shouted instructions to their travelling companions, tucked bags of garbage under seats, pulled on sweaters and spring jackets, looked out the window at the line of waiting faces for some welcome recognition.

Esa took her time. She pushed her feet into her running shoes and tied them carefully, retrieved the worn blue duffle bag and the cardboard tube from under the seat, and watched the backs of all the other passengers retreating down the crowded platform. A waterfall of people splashing off in a multitude of directions. Family and friends to greet, embrace, swim away with. River heaven.

Esa trickled down the platform. By the time she reached the gate, the river had dispersed. The station was a dry riverbed, desolate. Esa left the near-empty building, carrying her bag and the cardboard tube along the waterfront, zigzagging though the unfamiliar streets, the noise of seagulls now sharp in her ears and the taste of sea salt on her lips.

Esa walked until her way was barred by the high chain-link fencing that surrounded the newer docklands, and the naval yard. And then she turned and walked up the hill, not so steep here, the blocks filled with housing projects, the streets filled with people conducting business. She understood this city here, at last.

The air cooled even more as evening descended, and she stopped to take Serge's green sweater out of her bag and put it on under her jacket. In the bus station she went to the washroom, washed her hands and face, and looked at her reflection in the blue cracked mirror. It was only then that she realized how tired she was, and the baby in her belly began to spin.

Esa told the ticket agent where she wanted to go.

"Never heard of it," the woman said. She seemed bored with Esa already. She slapped a laminated map onto the counter in front of her, slipped the edge of it towards Esa, under the bullet-proof glass, and glanced at the clock on the wall behind her.

"These here are the places the bus goes," she said. "Where you want?"

Esa looked at the map, noted the tiny CartoGraphie logo in the corner. The bus lines made a V from where she stood, the ends of the letter stretched and curled both east and west.

"Here," she said, and pointed to a place halfway along the eastern stroke. "It's near there."

The woman raised her eyebrows, rolled her eyes at her co-worker at the next window, even though he was not looking at her. "One way or return?" she asked.

"One way," said Esa.

She touched her computer screen a few times, printed Esa a ticket.

"Forty dollars," she said. *Get lost*, Esa heard.

Esa had not thought ahead. When she arrived at the spot she had pointed to on the ticket agent's map it was almost midnight, and the small convenience store that served as the bus depot was long closed. It did not occur to her to regret, or even to wonder, much less worry about, how or where she would spend the night. There was a phone booth. She had discovered it after the bus had pulled noisily away and left her alone in the blue darkness, but she did not really think to use it. What could she say on the phone in the middle of the night? There were no words that were possible across such a distance, though she believed her destination to be now less than ten or fifteen minutes drive away.

By the safety lights of the storefront, Esa opened her bag and removed a map, worn at the creases where it had been folded and re-folded countless times in the previous month. The road was deserted, all the nearby houses dark. A single streetlight lit the pavement at a nearby intersection. Leaving her bag open in the parking lot, she walked with the map to the corner, traced the last part of her route in the bus, found the crossroads at which she stood. From that point to the red mark of a felt-tipped pen she memorized roads and turns and distances and directions, returned to her bag, put the map away, lifted her belongings, and began to walk away from the lamp light.

When she had gone perhaps a few hundred feet, she stopped.

The sky was filled with points of light. Filled. A dark beach strewn with shining grains of golden and silver sand, the Milky Way like the night's high tide line. And the moon! That night-traveller's compass, crescent-shaped, caught among translucent clouds. The stars were far clearer and brighter than Esa remembered. The wind ran in the cloud-surf overhead, and the heavens pulsed.

Beneath her, Esa could feel the Earth spinning. Inside her, she could feel the acorn baby at rest. Through the star-strung dark she resumed her journey, still looking upwards.

She found the driveway almost three hours later. There was a battered silver mailbox across the road, the letters painted there too worn to read in the starlight and moonlight. A tree-shrouded lane ran up a hill and quickly curved out of sight into complete darkness. She put down her belongings, walked tentatively a little way up the lane, and then returned, nervously. She did not know if there would be a dog to begin barking at the snapping of a twig under her foot, or her tired scent tumbling on the wind.

She remembered Churchill the cat, and started up the drive again. This time she made it farther. As soon as she was under the evergreens, the moon and stars were no longer visible, and the dark was absolute. Esa had never been in complete darkness that had such an open feel; the only dark she knew was interior, or bordered by buildings, and therefore finite, and closed. The immensity of this expansive darkness was like another world.

It was impossible to tell where to safely place her feet, since she could not see them, or the driveway under her. She went forward slowly, keeping the grassy ditch by her right foot through feel: right foot on thawing earth, left foot on gravel, slowly. Soon she could sense the trees overhead pull back, could again see the shield of blue and gold and yellow stars, and the gibbous moon, and made out in front of her a hulking unlit presence, a looming darkness against the sandy heavens.

There were only night sounds: branches tapping, small winds parting around tree trunks. Noises she did not yet recognize: deep things underground that dreamed of breaking the surface, twitching in sleep; the humming of the earth coming into spring. And the watery, roaring rhythm of the sea, the breath of the Earth.

She stood with that dark house shape in front of her for a few minutes, then returned once more down the drive to the road and picked up her bags. She did not know what time it was, did not know what time the sun rose, did not know how long she would have to wait for the light. She jumped over the small ditch and passed beside the trunks of trees, stumbling over fallen branches, brambles tugging her pant legs. She made her way into the woods just far enough to be out of sight from both the road and the driveway, dropped her bag under a tree, and sat down on it, her back against the smooth, cold trunk, to see if morning would come.

# Chapter 8

*T*hese moments are like dripping icicles, still frozen but wearing slowly away, drip-drip-dripping, out of known memory, sharp edges becoming smoother and warmer with time, as if spring always comes. The icicles could be daggers waiting for a ripe heart, or crystal beacons set up to guide us into the future.

There was a dog, once. It ran in the squalid yard on the end of a chain attached to the unused clothesline, baying at passers-by on the sidewalk out front, glimpsed—or perhaps smelled—through the narrow space between the row of houses. Burgess Withrod brought the dog home from the flea market on a drunken whim and carried it into the house by the scruff of its neck, the stretched skin on its face pulling its mouth into a sheepish grin. The dog was thin, and timid, and never grew much beyond a haphazard collection of bones, black and tan spots on dirty white, with eyes like dark stones. Burgess grew disgusted with it, its beagle-like baying the only thing that gave it presence, made it a real dog.

The first time the dog came into heat, calling a collection of neighbourhood mongrels to the muddy yard, Burgess took it to the wide river with an old sack and a few rusty sections of sewer pipe he'd picked up at a demolition site. Esa hardly remembered the nameless dog; its brief sojourn in their yard took place when she was too young to remember anything but a warm moment of small hands buried in a wriggling landscape of fur. But the dog's remnants, the chipped, dry water bowl caked with dirt, half-buried under the back steps, the mouldering red and blue ball that Katherine had found for it in the school yard, split open and shedding flakes of rubber, and most especially the rusty chain on the cracked clothesline—Esa remembers that very well.

*The three of them are playing in the yard with mud and stones. Not smooth multi-coloured stones like those that come washed from a riverbed, or that roll endlessly on the strand, but grey stones from gravel trucks, sharp-edged and dusty. The stones are bricks, or jewels, or coins. The children's hands are always coated in a fine layer of grey dust, ancient and insidious, becoming part of their skin and leaving faint shadow-marks where their small palms rest, however briefly.*

*Jane has a doll that they dress in mud costumes, ornamented with tiny stone sequins. They make villages of stone houses stuck together with mud, with mud roads leading outward to the forest of weeds around their world's perimeter. They make mud birthday cakes with twig candles broken from the bush that pokes desolate branches through their fence.*

*They find a rock, the size of their father's fist, that is almost circular, and Katherine pretends it is the sun and shows them how the little rocks that are the planets go around in their orbits.*

*"The world is flat," Jane argues, and Esa, pushing the chain that dangles in front of her to her back, as she does from habit, looks down at the miniature villages at her feet, and up at the sun scorching a path across the powdery sky, and knows that Jane is right.*

*They play at keeping store, buying twig pens and pencils, leaf plates, dandelion lettuces, cigarettes from Burgess's butts trampled in the weeds. The smallest stones are pennies, the largest quarters. They carry them in the pockets of their shorts, jingling them with satisfaction the way they see the men do on the neighbourhood streets and alleys. They play doctor with mud and leaf compresses, washing carefully at the outside tap before their mother comes home from work, unlocks and unhooks Esa from the dog chain, and lets them all in to the house at last.*

*Unlocks and unhooks Esa. The click of the small padlock, the grating of the chain, the squeak of the worn blue wire—that fleeting moment of freedom before Esa's mother catches her forearm, already blistering red from the sun, and pulls her up the back steps and into the dark kitchen that still smells of yesterday's boiled cabbage.*

# Chapter 9

Esa walked once more up the lane to the house, through the dew-weighted air. Her hands were scratched by brambles, and she was stiff with cold. Her bones were filled with ice instead of marrow. It was not light, but half-light; the clouds had thickened and moved in to obscure the sky, their underbellies tinted orange by the sun that had not yet appeared above the line of rising spruce trees. The sounds grew: her feet still scuffled the gravel, wind moved around bare branches. But there began to be the morning songs of birds: a chorus of tuning strings, random notes played to the growing light, amplifying the dawn. And, from somewhere not too far off, but still invisible, the slide and shift of stones spoke heavily as the sea breathed hugely in and out in a half-waking, half-dreaming state. What did the sea dream of? Broken chair legs, thought Esa. Tangled nets. Bottles begging for rescue.

The morning revealed what had been hidden by the darkness. The woods were not as thick as she had thought, though the undergrowth, in summer, would make traversing them impossible without first cutting a path. There were blackberry canes lying darkly along the ground, where they had been weighted down through the winter by now-melted snows. There were wild roses, their rose hips glinting the colour of small ripe fruits in an otherwise monochrome landscape. Alder trees and scrub willow filled a low-lying slope to her left, where water seemed to seep silently to the surface. There were no greens, only shades of brown, black, ochre.

Esa reached out her hand to pick a rose hip, was surprised by its firmness, its hold on the prickled branch. She pulled hard, and twisted it loose. It was the size of a small cherry. She smelled its pale scent, put it tentatively against her lips, and then her teeth, bit lightly against the skin; it did not surprise her at all that what could look so sweet should taste so bitter.

The drive climbed gradually to a place where it split around a massive oak tree, then turned to the right and rose more steeply to the house, now showing weathered grey clapboard trimmed with white. It was a large house, and appeared to sink into the land around it. In the pin cherry tree beside the house, a goldfinch, still in its winter colours, flew to the highest branch to look at the sun.

She took the one step up onto the porch. The door was painted bright yellow. There was a quartered pane of frosted glass on the top half, and beside the door hung a verdigris brass bell on a rope. The rope shifted slightly in the morning air.

Esa's heart flamed and roared; there was an unfamiliar warmth at her core, despite her morning vigil, and her legs were weak. She moved her feet nervously from side to side, piling the gravel into a small mound underneath her. She knocked three times, and then louder, and the force of her knocking unlatched the unlocked door. There was a click, and the door shifted inward an inch or two, so there was an eye-width gap between the door and the jamb. Esa could smell woodsmoke, could feel the house's heat on her face.

"Come in, come *in*," called a voice, impatiently, as if the words had already been said.

Esa moved closer to the crack in the door, but she could not go in. She could not lift her arm and push. The burning in her chest rose, and stifled her breath.

"There's a draft!" said the voice, getting louder, coming nearer. Esa could sense movement beyond the veiled glass.

"Who's there? Why don't you come *in*?" There was a curious rhythm to the voice, accompanied as it was by a creak, and a shuffle, and another creak, and another shuffle—and the door was pulled open from the inside, and Esa stopped breathing, then, for a full quarter of a minute.

In that timelessness she saw the hunched figure, the walker, the pale crimped fingers, the blue flowered dress, the ribbed cardigan, open at the front, with the sleeves pushed up to the elbows—and then the deeply etched face, the grey braid that lay along the blue collar, and finally, finally, the luminous grey eyes, like her own. She took a quick breath, so her lungs hurt.

"Gam?" said Esa. She recognized nothing in the woman she saw in front of her. Nothing of the woman she'd last seen eighteen years before through a small child's eyes. The cold morning air blew in, and the warm house air blew out; Esa was caught in the crosscurrent, held still by opposing forces.

The old woman tilted her chin.

"Who are you?" she said. Her voice was slow, and she spoke as one would in a dream, on the verge of understanding something profound.

"It's me," said Esa. "Esa." Her voice thawed and cracked, a spring pond stretching the ice wide.

"Esa Withrod," repeated the old woman, and she said it from a long way off, like she was saying "black hole" or "milky way" in a dream about the stars.

There was another silence. The two women looked at each other. Both sets of eyes met and moved away, met and moved away. There was an edge of panic in the old ones; a shuttered, waiting look in the young. The air currents continued to flow past their bodies; the goldfinch at the top of the pin cherry lifted his wings and groomed himself, so that a small olive-yellow feather was dislodged and floated down through the bare branches, and danced in the revolving air above their heads.

The old woman took in Esa's dishevelled state, her raw cheeks, the heavy bag slung across her shoulder, the long tube in her mittened hand. She took a deep breath, as if waking from sleep.

"I forget myself," she said. "Come in, come *in*." And she pulled her walker backwards with one hand, and pulled the door open wider with the other.

Esa stepped across the threshold, and the old woman pushed the door shut behind her. It made a solid noise, a click and a clack and a clearing of the throat.

"Gam—" said Esa.

The old woman shook her head.

"Call me Alice," she said. She seemed about to say something else, but stopped herself.

"Alice?" said Esa. "I never thought about calling you that."

"No," said Alice, "you wouldn't, would you?"

They were sitting at the chrome kitchen table. Esa was sitting on her feet, one at a time, trying to bring some life back into them. The kitchen was very warm—the Kemac stove was going full force in the corner. Somehow, they had gotten Esa's coat hung in the hall closet, the hat and mitts spread on the drying rack, parked her bag at the bottom of the stairs, and had come into the kitchen at the back of the house where Alice had moved the kettle from the rear of the stove to the front burner.

Esa sat facing the back of the house. She could see through the clear glass in the back door to the yard beyond. There were no rips in the bottom of the screen on the storm door. There were no apple trees in sight.

"Did you plan to stay long?" asked Alice as she sat down, moving herself from the stove to the kitchen table with her hands shifting her weight from one surface to the other.

"I thought until the baby is born," said Esa, "if that's okay," and from the corner of her wide eyes she saw the stark alarm in Alice's. Esa looked quickly at the bottom of the table leg, where it looked as though it had been chewed by a dog.

"Baby!" repeated Alice. And she closed her eyes with her hands pressing the edge of the table, thumbs underneath and eight fingers on top, spread like the roots of bonsai, gnarly with pain.

On the Kemac, the kettle rocked and boiled. It was not the welcome Esa would have imagined, if she had allowed herself to think ahead.

Esa went to the front of the house where she'd left her bag at the bottom of the stairs. On her way down the long hall she looked in vain for something familiar in the narrow house, something that would call to her across those eighteen years, something, *anything*, that would welcome her as an adult the way the house had welcomed her as a child. Anything to justify her long memory of buried hope.

The large parlor had been crudely divided in two, to make a main floor bedroom and a small sitting room in the front. The bedroom—Alice's, Esa assumed—was small and dark, with only a small west-facing window with a view of muted light under a giant pine tree. In the morning it was especially dark, as the bright sun climbed the sky on the opposite side of the house. The new wall was thin, and covered in cheap dark panelling on both sides. There was a single iron-bound bed with bent tines on one side of the room, and a battered wooden dresser on the other. The bottom drawer was standing open, and a cat—not the giant Churchill, of course, but a small grey tabby—lay curled among the scarves and cotton handkerchiefs.

Alice had showed Esa where a new little powder room had been cut out of the pantry, just a toilet and sink with no bath or shower.

The rocks and shells and sea amenones and crab legs had all disappeared. The main floor of the house was spotless, with everything precisely in order. The salt dust had been washed away, and banished.

Alice had said she could use any of the bedrooms upstairs that she wanted, since she herself was no longer able to climb the steep steps. Esa shouldered her bag and gripped the handrail, pulling herself upwards, struggling against the current in what seemed a watery, drowned ascent, like floating, heavily, to the surface of things. From downstairs she could hear Gam—*Alice*—run the water in the sink, and then the chuffing of the kettle as it was being heated once again.

At the top of the stairs she dropped her bag again. The bathroom door stood open, and Esa could see the edge of the claw-foot tub, the wire rack for the soap hanging over its edge, the empty towel bar, the french window, now closed, that looked out under the eaves to the yard, and the woods she had waited in all night for this morning to arrive. When she walked in she could see that there were dead flies caught between the glass and the storm window, and a few barely-alive ones crawling despondently across the inside window ledge. In the uncut brown grass at the edge of the yard, Esa made out three tree stumps in a row, cut about a foot from the ground.

There was still a fine layer of salt dust in all the rooms upstairs. Esa walked through the bedrooms—the one nearest the bathroom, and the smaller one off of it, to the back, where Esa had slept as a child. Then the middle bedroom, and the large front bedroom that had been Gam's, with windows on three sides, overlooking the sea in the front and the river to the east. There was not much furniture left; a double bed and dresser and lamp in each room. Esa's sock feet made no noise on the bare pine boards, and she walked from the back to the front of the house, and then back again, and again, several times, before picking up her bag and carrying it into the front bedroom. She laid her bag on the bare mattress and pulled open the top drawer of the dresser. It shot outwards heavily, and the drawer's contents rattled and settled noisily, the front end tipped downwards.

It was filled with beach stones, brittle dried seaweeds, faded starfish, empty seashells.

The cat had come soundlessly up the stairs and sat watching her from the open doorway. Esa sensed its eyes on her and turned, lifting an item from the top of the drawer, and waving it, gently, at the cat.

"Neptune's currency," she said hoarsely, while small grains of grey powder escaped from the sand dollar and fell on the toes of her worn wool socks and the worn floorboards below.

"We might as well," he'd said. It was the week before the holidays, and the streets were decorated for Christmas. He drove one-handed, with the other hand on her knee, lifting it only when he needed to gear down.

And then, afterwards, only afterwards, he told her.

He was lying on his back in her narrow bed, his eyes travelling languidly along the cracks in the plaster ceiling, dark roads in a dark journey.

Before he slept, he had something more to say.

"You know I told you about my girlfriend?" he asked her. "Well, my fiancée? Remember I told you about my fiancée?" His voice tumbled leaf-like across the top of the blankets.

"Fiancée?" said Esa.

"She's coming on Saturday. We're going to be spending Christmas together." Serge's eyes were half-open, unfocused, still journeying the unmarked map above them.

"And then she's just going to be staying," he said.

"Christmas?" said Esa.

"Actually, she's coming here to live with me," said Serge. And he closed his eyes.

Esa lay beside him in the darkness, listening to his breath. She could see, very faintly, the muted print of the garden in its frame, a myriad of creatures breathing there as dreams do, below the surface. Below her surface swam the seeds of despair, darting sight-lessly along a slippery path with an acute sense of direction.

"Yeah, I thought we might as well," Serge said, and he went to sleep squeezing her shoulder.

Esa shut her eyes, thinking she knew everything about what could grow in darkness. She did not move or speak when he stirred himself a few hours later, got up and dressed silently, and let himself out of her house by the back door.

The next day she'd gone, as she had every year since getting the job, to celebrate Chanukah with Merle and Daniel, Daniel singing while lighting the menorah.

"Ba-ruch ata, A-do-nai E-lo-hei-nu, me-lech ha-o-lam…"

There were others there, of course. Merle's sister, and his nephew, and Daniel's father, and several friends from Daniel's work, and a neighbour from down the hall. And, this year, Serge.

"…a-sher ki-de-sha-nu be-mits-vo tov…"

He greeted Esa warmly as he came in the living room door, kiss-ing her cheek in almost the same way he had the month before, when on his way to bigger things. She finally noticed that he did not actually look at her as his face bent towards hers.

"...ve-tsi-va-nu le-had-lik neir shel Chan-nu-kah."

Esa, as she always did at Merle and Daniel's parties, sat on the stool in the kitchen for the hour before dinner, helping Daniel cut onions and stir sauces and open bottles. She had met most of the guests before; no one really expected her to speak. It was just as well: there was a chasm inside her, where a single cell divided in the depths.

# Chapter 10

Esa sat upstairs for a long time, on the edge of the bed. She held the sand dollar in her hand, and listened to the faint noises of Alice in the distant kitchen. After a while, the cat moved from the doorway and jumped up on the mattress, curling behind Esa's back. After another while, she heard a car come up the drive and stop. The driver honked. She shifted slightly so she could see out the east window to where an old sedan was pulled up beside the house. She heard Alice's walker thump along the hallway and out the front door, and saw Alice stop beside the driver's window, where the glass was rolled down. Esa turned the sand dollar over and over in her hand. Every time it turned, a little more sand sprinkled out between her knees.

The driver of the parked car was an old man, with a high weathered forehead fringed by snow-white hair, and a straw fedora pushed back on his head. Esa couldn't hear what was being said, but she could hear the urgent sound of agitated voices—at least, Alice's was agitated, and the old man's was steady and sparse, once or twice sounding like he was debating what she said. Alice gestured frequently towards the front door, lifting one hand from where she leaned on her walker, and they both looked over at the house when she did so. It was clear to Esa that they were talking about her. Neither of them looked up.

Esa lay back on the bed without looking behind her, and the cat yowled and swatted and then moved a few feet away and began calmly washing its face.

The cat grumbled. The mattress dipped in the middle, and held the faint odour of mothballs. The sand dollar held the faint odour of river heaven, vast and uncontained. Esa had a sense of something pulsing towards her on an incoming tide, and she let that water slip over her like the light reflected on the wall. She lay on the bed and her mind swam small circles in the warm brine, like a fish trapped in a tide pool.

The light shifted; her eyes closed. The cat stopped washing itself and moved in beside her armpit, turning itself three times before settling down and joining her in sleep.

Esa dreamed about a charred landscape. The smouldering ground stretched endlessly along valleys cut by dry riverbeds. The fire swept along like a burning tide, sucking up every last ounce of water, leaving steaming rocks brushed with dark river weeds and homeless fish stranded in a foreign country, unable to speak the language of life. Flames ran like ground lightening, rolling destruction on the contours of the hills, flying over stone outcroppings and under barbed wire fences, until it reached the sea shore, and then spread across the waves like a blazing oil slick. And finally, the demon fire reached up and licked the moon from the night sky.

Esa did not ask Alice about the man in the car, but Alice told her anyway. It seemed like she was nervous, and had a need to fill in all the silences. She did not yet realize that Esa swam in the silences as a fish swims in water.

"He lives on the next farm over." Alice waved her hand toward the pantry, and the west.

They were in the kitchen. Esa was having another cup of tea. Alice served up both tea and words whenever she didn't know what else to do. Esa had slept for five hours on the unmade bed and had woken with the sand dollar crushed in her fist, dust and shell fragments covering her heart. She'd gone down the stairs holding tightly to the wooden handrail, the smooth feel of it on her palm guiding her descent into reality.

The radio was on, playing classical music, and Alice was peeling onions: the dry brown outer layer came away, then a golden layer, and finally a thicker layer brushed with green and gold that adhered stubbornly to the bulb. Tears were streaming down

Alice's face. When she looked up and saw Esa in the doorway she quickly took a tissue from her pushed-up sleeve and dabbed her eyes. She rinsed her hands and moved the simmering kettle to the front of the Kemac.

"I guessed you went to sleep, or died up there," she said. Her walker was parked up against the kitchen table, and Esa remembered that she couldn't climb the stairs, had no way of knowing what Esa had been doing noiselessly for half the day.

"Oh," Esa said. "Yes." She thought that going to sleep and going to hell were probably the same thing.

"I've put the kettle on. Sit at this end of the table, the onion is less strong there. Don't need you crying for the onions, too." Alice dabbed at the corner of her eye with the back of her wrist. "I'm making stew for tonight. I hope you like stew? I hope you're not one of those young people who won't eat good meat out of some foolish respect for the cow. Might as well cry for onions!" She didn't really seem to expect an answer, but poured boiling water into the teapot, swirled the pot and poured it into the sink, put tea bags in the pot and then filled it again with water from the still-boiling kettle. She looked over at Esa, narrowed her eyes.

"Actually, you look awful pale. You could do with some meat. Babies, you know, need more feeding when they're on the inside than after they come out. Why when your—" but she stopped short suddenly and took a breath, and pushed over the sugar bowl and the can of evaporated milk. The cup trembled as she handed it across the table.

"Yes," she continued, "babies need feeding, and so do their mamas." And then there was a slight pause and the radio played the little four-note tune that signalled the news.

"Cyril noticed you sleeping in the woods this morning. He was out checking his rabbit snares—you're lucky you didn't step in one yourself. You looked so pale he thought you were a little flaked-off wisp of the moon laying up against a birch tree. He thought you looked harmless enough, but I said you can never judge by appearances." And that was when she said, "He lives on the next farm over." The knife went through the onion keenly, making a sound like the small crackle of fire.

"I'm not sure you can stay here," she said, and Esa knew suddenly that was what she'd been trying to say all along.

Esa got up very early and glided down the stairs like a shadow. There was no sound from Alice's bedroom. She pulled on her jacket and hat and mittens, and opened the door on early spring. She stood for a moment on the wet flagstones, smelling the rising mist, and then walked down along the path beside the river. There was no moon, and the sky was half-lit with the coming morning. The path was narrow and untravelled and the damp brown grasses pulled at her pant legs. The river roiled with snow-melt collected from the hills behind it. Sprays of water were pushed up behind green rocks. The roar of it was like a drowning.

In two minutes she was at the river's mouth, that place where the surging water spread itself on a pyre of stones and ran thinly to join the ocean.

Esa walked down the steep beach to the high tide mark, where the tangled line of seaweeds and shanks of worn wood lay steaming in the apricot dawn. The smell of salt and decomposing kelp hit Esa with surprising force. A few early sand fleas jumped in the bracken.

The sea was pulling out gently, the migration of small stones making a *hush-hush-hush* sound as it travelled backwards into itself. The horizon stretched across Esa's line of vision and was bound on each side by the small bay. The wooden stores and wharves were gone; all that remained were a handful of blackened and gouged poles leaning in the water, like drunken figureheads, about twenty yards out.

Esa walked to the east along the sweep of the bay, picking her way over the larger rocks where the river washed the beach. In the distance she could see something wandering in and out with the waves, tumbling at the water's edge as at the crossing place between waking and sleep. The beach stones shifted beneath her boots; the sun rose higher across the jut of land in front of her, and the sky ran from apricot to coral. She walked closer and closer to the dark object, but it wasn't until she was very close that she saw what it was.

Serge's arm lay in the surf; an elbow-bent piece of salt-tumbled wood.

When Esa came up from the beach Alice was making her way across the drive with her walker. A net bag was slung over one stooped shoulder, an ample cracked leather purse over the other.

"I'm just going to the grocery store," announced Alice.

Esa looked from Alice, to Alice's walker, to the rusty car backed in among the pin cherry trees.

"You can drive?" said Esa.

"Don't *you* start telling me what I can do—I've been driving for forty years," said Alice.

"I just didn't know."

"Somebody's always trying to take a person's licence away," Alice complained. She opened the back door on the driver's side, put in her purse and bag, folded her walker and fit it in front of the seat, and leaned on the car for support while she closed the back door and opened the front one. Esa watched her.

"I'll come with you," she said.

"What?"

"I'll come with you."

"Where?"

"To the grocery store," explained Esa.

Alice was trying to manoeuvre herself in behind the wheel. She looked quickly across at Esa standing at the top of the path, but it was clear that she wasn't paying very much attention.

"Wouldn't it be helpful?" persisted Esa. "I could carry the bags."

"They have carryout," said Alice, and she reached to shut the door.

"I don't have anything else to do," said Esa defensively.

Alice looked again. Esa stood wild-eyed, with her head half-turned away, as if she didn't really care.

"Oh, get *in*," said Alice, and she slammed her door and started the engine.

They drove in silence: down the hill, around the oak tree, down the long sweep of drive bordered by woods, and turned right at the bottom onto the Shore Road. Alice drove one-handed; when she needed to gear up, she pushed down on her left thigh with her elbow to help her foot compress the clutch, and the wheel went momentarily unattended while she lugged at the gear shift.

The ride was smoother once they reached the highway; Alice geared up again and began to talk.

"That's the McKay's house." Alice pointed to a blue bungalow with a broken front step. "John McKay died of a heart attack digging winter potatoes. John's son packed his mother off to an old folks' home as quick as ever you could breathe once. The son, Roger, he doesn't even visit his mother. Nolene can't even make a cup of tea for herself since they don't allow kettles in the rooms. No kettles, hair dryers, floor lamps—not anything you have to plug in. Seems like they think electricity and old people don't mix."

"Electricity and old people," she repeated, shaking her head. "No more zap." And she laughed.

"I worked in that home until Cyril—" Once again she stopped short, drew a sharp breath, and continued in another direction.

"Nolene, she keeps a toaster hidden behind a pile of books in her night table, and when I visit we close the door and make toast."

Alice told Esa about the people that lived in every house they passed, and who from their families had worked at the mine or the fish plant, and who had run off with the neighbour's wife, and who took to drinking after her unmarried daughter got herself pregnant—no offence!—and who left town to go and work in upper Canada—no offence again! She did not tell these tales either gleefully or tragically the way someone telling gossip might. The choices made were neither bad nor good but simply human—and the outcomes were full of spirit.

They took the second exit into town.

"I usually shop there, but I've decided not to shop there any more." Alice said, passing a grocery store. "They always have green bananas. And limp carrots."

They continued driving, past a hospital, and a school. Esa looked out the window at the clapboard houses, most of which needed a fresh coat of paint.

"The bird woman lives there," said Alice, pointing to a small salt box set back from the road on park-like grounds, the chalk and grey and burnt umber tree trunks stark against the brown lawn. From almost every tree and bush hung bird feeders and orange nets of suet. Dark patches of seed hulls dappled the ground. Flocks of birds rose and fell from the feeders like last year's wind-blown leaves.

"Anybody finds any kind of injured bird, they bring it right to her."

Esa trailed around after Alice in the grocery store, pushing the shopping cart. It seemed to take Alice a long time to decide what to buy, but Esa didn't pay too much attention. She didn't even notice what was going into the cart, because while Alice was feeling the tomatoes Esa began to hear a bird singing overhead, and when she looked up she saw a starling perched among the heat ducts in the high ceiling. While she watched it flew back and forth over the produce as if stringing a net, and sang and sang without stopping.

"There's a bird caught in here," Esa said cautiously to the man who was unpacking iceberg lettuces. She wasn't actually sure if it was real.

"Oh yes," the man said, unconcerned. "It's been in here since Christmas."

"What does it eat?" asked Esa, surprised.

The man paused and turned, a lettuce balanced on the tips of his fingers like a bowling ball. He swept his other arm over the rows of romaine, bib, red leaf, gestured to the apples and pears across the aisle.

"A starling's smorgasbord."

Esa wondered if the bird woman shopped there. She watched the dark-starred bird swing through the metal rafters and tried unobtrusively to find holes pecked in the fruit and vegetables, until Alice called her from way over near the lemons to bring the cart.

The drive home seemed to take much longer than getting to town. The road stretched up in front of them like a dark scar on the colourless landscape. The car pulled itself up the hill, its power slowly ebbing as they made the climb. As they neared the overpass, Esa could see a man standing above them, arms folded along the concrete railing. He was in his shirtsleeves despite the cool morning—the kind of shirt you find in old men's closets after they have died: cheap white cotton with pale stripes.

Below the Way Road Bridge Alice honked and waved enthusiastically. As they passed underneath him, Esa could see that the man's long hair was uncombed, his face a mask of smudge and stubble. He lifted his hand from the railing and waved it decisively without raising his arm, a short, sharp movement.

"Who is *that*?" Esa asked.

"I believe he is a MacDonald," said Alice. She shrugged, as if his name was the last thing in the world that mattered.

"But what is he doing there? Why did you honk?"

Alice looked across the four lanes of pavement, the car now slowed to half the speed limit, hazard lights flashing. "He stands on the bridge and waves at people. That's his job," she said, and she began to hum tunelessly, as a bee might in going about its rightful work.

Esa turned her head away, looking out across the shaggy cattle, the marshland, the glint of bay.

"What is the point?" she asked. It seemed an even sadder thing than a starling caught inside a grocery store: the futility of waiting on a bridge, always suspended between two places, caught nowhere.

Alice left off buzzing only momentarily.

"There's a lot worse things a person could do with a life," she said, "than stand on a bridge and wave to people."

# Chapter 11

Esa's pants didn't fit. One day they did, and the next morning, when she got out of bed and tried to put them on again, they didn't. The legs hardly went up over her thighs, and she couldn't get the zipper done up. There was a mirror over the dresser in the front bedroom, and she stood back to watch herself trying to pull them on. She couldn't figure out what was wrong. She dug around in her duffel bag and found two other pairs, but she couldn't get them done up either. She put her pyjamas bottoms back on and went downstairs.

"My pants don't fit." Alice was in the kitchen making squares, and Esa spoke over the noise of the electric mixer.

"Reach that bag down for me, will you?" asked Alice. "No, the sugar—I keep telling Cyril not to put things up so high. Somebody's always putting things just out of a person's reach."

"My pants don't fit," Esa repeated as she put the white bag on the table next to Alice. The old woman transferred the mixer to her left hand, wiped her right palm on the bib of her apron and dipped the measuring cup into the sugar. The beaters clacked against the sides of the ceramic bowl. Esa sat down, put her elbows on the table and covered her ears.

Alice added more sugar and ran the beaters up and down the bowl's sides. She re-read the recipe from the stained cookbook propped open in front of her. One-handed, she broke three eggs into the bowl. She leaned way over to the Kemac like a sapling weighted with snow, and moved the simmering kettle forward so it would boil. The whole time, the sound of the mixer churned Esa's thoughts into dust motes that circled the kitchen like smoke.

Finally, there was an end to it.

"Now, what did you say?" asked Alice. Her voice rang hollowly in the sudden silence. Esa heard her through her still-covered ears as faintly as falling snow.

When the squares came out of the oven, Alice sighed resignedly and drove her to the Sally Ann.

It had been a long walk to the drug store, and that day back in February had been brittle, with a bladed wind that cut through her thin coat. She'd gone there from a working dinner, refusing, for the first time, Merle's offer of a ride home.

She had her wallet ready when she laid the box she'd chosen on the counter. The saleswoman picked it up, looked across at Esa.

"In my day," she said, "you had to wait two hours for the results. You peed in a little tube and then you sat and looked at the bottom of the tube for two hours without moving an inch, and without hardly breathing, and maybe a dark little ring would form at the bottom of the tube, and maybe it wouldn't." She held the box up, peered at the writing on the side, shook her head. "And sometimes the ring looked like a ring and sometimes it looked like a dot, and then you didn't know if you had the donut or the hole." Her fingers punched in the cost, and the tiller drawer slid open. "Longest two hours of my life."

But Esa thought waiting two hours for the result of the test was nothing compared to waiting a lifetime for the result of the life.

The bell rang after her as she left the shop. She took the package home, read the instructions carefully, and unwrapped the test strip. She went in to the bathroom and locked the door behind her. She peed on the end of the strip, then laid it on the edge of the sink, still sitting on the toilet. While she waited she turned a pair of nail scissors back and forth in her hand, and watched the reflection skip up the wall to the ceiling. She made the light be the ticking of a clock, the odd numbered seconds on the wall, the even numbered seconds on the cracked ceiling. The bathroom was a time capsule, and might take her anywhere: Away, away.

In less than two minutes, the end of the strip turned blue.

We could say it begins now, thought Esa.

Alice turned off the radio and opened the back door. An eerie noise flooded through the open doorway, a devil's chorus. The sound of the waves drowned in it; they might have been miles from the ocean. Alice stood looking blindly out through the screen, leaning against the door jamb, breathing in the night.

"What is that noise?" asked Esa in surprise.

"Peepers," said Alice. The mesh of the screen pressed a pattern of tiny squares into the thin blue-white skin of her forehead.

"What kind of thing is a peeper?"

"Spring peepers. Little brown tree frogs. The males are calling to the females."

"Frogs make that noise?" Esa went to the doorway, stood beside Alice, close enough to smell: flour, lavender, honey, old cotton, tender skin. The veins of Alice's arms were dark blue on the inside of her elbows.

"They're down in the wetlands beside the drive."

"Frogs?" said Esa.

"I guess the one with the loudest voice gets the mate."

"Those are *frogs*?"

"Yes," said Alice. "Imagine, never hearing spring peepers!" She shook her head in disbelief.

"There aren't any wetlands where I come from," said Esa defensively.

"When are you going back?" asked Alice.

Esa looked out in bewilderment at the night.

Every third day, in the morning, Alice got groceries. In some ways it seemed Esa was always getting the groceries with Alice, as if those ninety minutes had more sharp edges, more clearly defined boundaries, than any of the other times they spent together. It was as if there was somehow more substance to the hour and a half it took to drive to Sobey's, get seventy-two hours' worth of provisions, and drive home.

It was like this: Fifteen minutes driving down the driveway, along a string of weathered farms on the Shore Road, and along the high-way with its view of marshland, shades of brown and beige and yellow. An hour squeezing the oranges, sorting through the dented tins offered at half price, looking at every *best before* date so they were sure to get the freshest, asking the meat cutter to package a smaller portion, please and thank you—how big do you think families are these days, anyway? An hour spent with attention divided between keeping track of the location of Alice's walker and the movements of the European starling, whose celestial position could be tracked by its exuberant song. And then, fifteen minutes home, driving up the hill where the car almost conked out every time. Esa always imagined them standing by the side of the road with their bag of bargains, hitchhiking home for lunch, leaving the dead car as an offering to the man on the bridge. Perhaps he'd sleep in it, Esa thought. He and the car seemed well matched.

After the Way Road overpass, Esa always dozed a little, as if the tension that had built up on the climb suddenly dissipated, and left her drowsy. Alice kept talking, and the words swirled around in Esa's head without settling anywhere—swirled around like cold tea in the pot, poured out behind the back door among the weeds.

"Isabel Crane lives there, in that white house. She taught piano in her front room for thirty-seven years, and she played the organ at our church every Sunday. Last year she thought she'd teach herself to use her dead husband's table saw, on account of wanting a new countertop in her kitchen. She ran her hands right across the blade. Lost every finger. Now she's learning to play the Irish bodhran—she still has both her thumbs."

Their fourth trip to town together was on a grey day that threatened cold rain; the clouds marched across the sky and the wind tore at last year's brittle bullrushes. The starling hardly showed itself, and sang only sporadically from the duct work. They bought pork hock for soup and a marked-down bag of lentils that had split open and been taped shut again, and they were given twenty pounds of carrots that the manager had been saving for the pig farmer. The lights were very bright in the store, and Esa thought the cans on the shelf were like grains of sand, magnified a thousand times, showing the brilliant and varied colours of quartz. While they waited at the cash, it came upon Esa quite suddenly that she might like to sit down, but she couldn't find anywhere to sit except for the rolling track where the packers put the boxes of groceries for the carryout.

"Watch yourself," said Alice, "or you'll be rolled right into the back of someone's station wagon and be served up for dinner." Alice turned to the cashier, motioned at Esa.

"That one's a bargain, I can tell you! Under-ripe, what?" And they laughed good-naturedly. But Esa slipped over on the silver rail and came to rest with one arm dangling through the bars, her hot forehead cooled by a metal cylinder.

After that, the carryout man did just about carry Esa out to the car, holding her up with one arm across her back and under her armpit, and he brought the groceries in the second load.

"You're just getting paler and paler," said Alice as she folded her walker and stashed it in the back seat, but her voice held a note of worry that stayed in the bottom of the pot like swollen tea leaves. Alice looked over at Esa as she jerked the car out of the parking lot and along the road, but Esa was looking out at the children in the schoolyard. Inside her, something was growing teeth and thinking about eating its way out.

When they reached the Way Road Bridge, Alice honked and waved, lifting her hand from underneath her thigh. "I like to make him feel as if he's doing a fine job," she said. She seemed pleased with herself, a benefactor.

The man looking down at them pulled his hand out of his jeans pocket and traced an arc in the air, like he was drawing the moon from the sky. Esa closed her eyes and waited for the impact of falling body on the windshield. She'd decided he was waiting to jump; perhaps the friendliest car would be the one upon which he would choose to hurl himself down. In her mind his landing made one thudding crash, with no echo. She willed Alice's foot on the accelerator to speed under the overpass and be gone away beyond the hill before he even hit the ground. A mess for somebody else to clean up; she would never need to know about it.

*Dear Merle and Daniel*, she wrote.

*I hope things are fine with you two. Things are fine with me, but I am not sure I am going to stay here after all. I think maybe the house is just too small, and all the grocery stores around here are hopeless and only ever have green bananas. I'm not sure why that is, but Alice says the banana boat stops here first.*

P.S. *I didn't mention it before but I am having a baby on September 12.*

"I'm just going down the road to get the mail," Alice called up the stairs, "and I don't need you to come with me. I hope I can still carry a few letters without anybody's help."

Esa heard the front door shut, and she watched out her bedroom window as Alice slowly triangled down the gravel driveway with her walker. The first blush of green was on the trees and underbrush, and as soon as Alice turned the corner to go down the hill, she was out of sight.

At dusk a woodcock flew right in to the glass of the sitting room window. It made a great crack, like a mottled grey rock mischeviously thrown by a neighbourhood boy—but there were no boys, only old people, stretched up and down the road like a purpose-built retirement village, preserving a dying way of life. Esa ran out and found the plump bird in the crawlspace window well, and she brought it in to show Alice.

It lay in her hands like a fat leaf, its leaf-heart fluttering. Its terrified eyes were like big black buttons, and its long spiked bill hung limply over the edge of Esa's palm.

"Put it in a box," Alice said. "You'll *scare* it to death if you hold on to it like that."

"Box," said Esa, but she didn't move. She was a stone statue feeling a heart beat in her hands for the first time.

"*Box*," Alice repeated impatiently. "In the pantry. Lots of them." From outside they could hear a low whistling sound, like a long, noisy kiss. "That's the male outside, looking for his hen."

But Esa just stood gasping helplessly in the middle of the sitting room floor, so Alice pushed herself up out of her chair resignedly and went slowly down the long hall with her walker. She came even more slowly back, with a large brown bowl, lined with a clean tea towel, tucked precariously under one elbow.

"No empty boxes," Alice said. Esa put the bird in the bowl, and the bowl on the sideboard. The hen struggled briefly, blinked its beady eyes.

"The bird woman," said Esa. The woodcock's feathers trembled under her breath.

"It can stay right there on the sideboard for the night," said Alice firmly. "We'll see how it is in the morning. You find the cat and put it out."

"Tonight," said Esa. She held on to the immediacy of her feeling. Distantly, through the closed window, she could hear the spring peepers begin to sing.

"Tomorrow," said Alice. "First thing in the morning." She looked as if she didn't care if it died. Esa thought she was measuring the woodcock's pain up against her own.

"It'll be dead in the morning." Esa spoke with such conviction that Alice started, and looked wonderingly at the blinking bird. Esa willed her to weigh its fragile heart with her memory. Had she learned anything, in such a long life?

"Oh, go and get the car keys then, hanging by the back door."

They hardly spoke in the car. The injured bird lay in the bread bowl above Esa's belly. The way seemed long.

It was fully dark by the time they got to the edge of town, but at the bird woman's house lights shone from almost every window.

The bird woman was a lot younger than Esa had expected. Esa stood a few steps behind Alice when the front door was opened, and the person who opened it was not even old enough to be Esa's mother, let alone a contemporary of Alice. Esa started.

"I thought you just told me stories about old people," she said to Alice's hunched back. Alice took her left arm from her walker and waved her hand impatiently.

"Don't be smart!" she hissed over her shoulder. She wanted Esa to stay in the background, and to hand her the bird.

"Hello, Alice," the woman said. "I haven't seen you in ages."

"Yes," said Alice stiffly. "Ages." There was an awkwardness between the two women that Esa didn't understand.

The bird woman couldn't see the bowl until Esa stepped out sideways from behind Alice, and the porch light shone directly on the feebly fluttering bird.

"Oh, a woodcock! Come in! Bring it in!" She held out her hands for the bowl, and Esa gave it to her with relief. The bird woman began to live up to her reputation.

"Well, good evening, Mary. This here is Esa—Esa *Withrod*, and this here is a foolish fat bird that just flew right in to my front window."

Mary seemed like she wasn't paying any attention to anything but the bird in the bread bowl. She led them through the house to a back room where, in the moment before she flicked the light switch, Esa could sense the inaudible rhythm of countless tiny hearts. Mis-matched cages lined the walls, and almost every one was occupied by motley and ragged shapes of brown and grey and blue and black. The birds woke as a group and pulled sleepy heads from under warm wings, blinking dazedly in the sudden light. Those that could still fly began to hop noisily from perch to perch, and those that couldn't flapped their wings helplessly.

"Flew right into the window," continued Alice. "I thought the glass was broke. It was the sitting room window. I'd just gotten up to turn the light on, as it was getting too dark to see." She kept stepping in front of Esa as Esa moved down the row of cages, as if they could all agree to forget she was there. "Sure is a full-time occupation you got here. I guess you don't mind the smell? I couldn't get used to it myself."

Mary smiled in a small way, as if she were purposefully holding down the corners of her mouth. She lifted the woodcock from the bowl and gently stretched out each wing. She felt along the short legs, and flexed the backwards knee joints. The bird lay in her hands limply, with half-closed eyes.

"Are you staying long?" Mary asked Esa over Alice's head. She glanced down at Esa's belly, and her words hung suspended in the air, a stillborn question.

"I'll thank you to attend to the bird," said Alice.

Mary turned her head slightly towards Alice, deferring the question—Esa would not have known how to answer, in any case. She shrugged, and put the bird in an airy cage lined with dry leaves and pine needles, and then handed Esa a flashlight and a child's plastic beach pail.

"I'm almost out of worms," she said. "I watered the back lawn this evening. Walk softly and grab fast. You might need to walk on your knees."

Esa went out alone with the pail. It seemed that Alice and the bird woman had things to say to each other.

On the way home Esa dozed in the passenger seat beside Alice, arms still tightly wound around the empty bowl. She heard the car gear down, then felt it slow as it began to climb the long hill.

"Look, look, look!" cried Alice. She was craning her neck at the man on the bridge. "Someone's given him a present!" She honked and waved excitedly.

He was wearing a bright orange vest of the kind that are sold during hunting season. In the indigo light the car headlights picked out the reflective trim along the lines of his neck and armpits. The orange vest was a beacon, a point of light at a dark crossing place. Alice's calm was temporarily restored. Besides, they were on their way home.

"What?" asked Esa, sliding away from sleep. "What?"

"Standing on that bridge in the dark—imagine!"

The old man who'd driven up in the car on the first day of her arrival came back often. He always drove up the hill, stopped by the side of the house, honked once, and waited for Alice to go out. And Alice thumped down the long hallway and went out to stand by the car for a while, one hand on the walker and one pulled tightly across her chest to keep her cardigan closed against the spring wind.

In the end, he almost always eased himself slowly out of his car and came in. When Esa went down the stairs, he was usually installed at the chrome table in the kitchen, with his wooden cane between his knees, drinking tea out of one of Alice's china cups, his big farmer hand holding awkwardly onto the delicate handle. Sometimes, there was an offering on the table: a skinned rabbit, or a half dozen greenish eggs in a chipped bowl.

As she entered the kitchen Esa tasted vicariously something ancient and immutable—a ritual that had been repeated hundreds of times by the same players. Though now, more often than not, it was Esa herself who was the subject of conversation.

"I don't see how a person can survive on what that girl eats, let alone try to feed what's in the belly. She pecks at food like a little bird—little holes left in things on the plate. Doesn't she get paler and paler, Cyril? It's like the life is washing right out of her. Found her outside the other day in the rain, sitting on the new well cover calm as you please, getting drenched—Oh, I noticed there's a few shingles loose beside the pump."

Alice moved in the kitchen like a bee among the clover, and buzzed as she went about her work. Cyril sat like a beetle and dug himself halfway in to the rich earth. Alice talked, and Cyril grunted, or nodded his head, said, "Well now—," but never really seemed to feel much need to follow those two words up with anything else. When Esa joined them, she sat at the table with Cyril, and they both watched as Alice kneaded the bread, peeled the carrots, browned the meat, made the tea. Esa watched as Cyril's stillness rose to meet Alice's bustle.

"Wet right through, she was, and I might as well have been howling at the moon to try to get it to come down from the sky, as to try to get her to come in."

After he'd sat for a half hour or so, Cyril would take the cane from between his knees and push himself upright, then take his empty cup and saucer and lay it the sink.

"Guess I'll see to those shingles," he'd say. He always went out the back door. The screen would spring to behind him, and Alice would shake her head in exasperation.

"Someone's always letting a door go somewhere."

In Esa's dream the ice crept slowly along a dry riverbed and frosted lace onto the tumbled rocks. The ice moved like a white shadow in the moonlight, tatting an openwork pattern onto the granite. Tendrils of ice ate into the smooth stones, deeper and deeper, until the cracks split and jagged charcoal-coloured pieces were birthed from pale river-washed orbs. The sharp reports of countless small explosions grew in an inverse echo until there was nothing in the world but noise. She woke with her hands covering her ears.

Alice was hanging linens out on the line: sheets, pillowcases, handkerchiefs, tea towels. Esa saw her when she came up from the shore with something in her hand.

The linen billowed against Alice's arms and legs, damp white patches of thick fog in an already misty day. Alice hummed tune-lessly and worked with economy. It seemed she was so practised at hanging clothes out that she had no need to look at her hands, or the basket of clothes pegs, or the edge of the sheets. She was looking out through the mist-shrouded trees to the invisible ocean, and hummed over the call of the murky depths.

Esa watched Alice for a while, without speaking, until Alice noticed her leaning like a ghost against the corner of the house, and started.

"Oh!" she said. "You scared me!" She put her fine hand up over her mouth, as if she were keeping something inside.

"I've been on the beach," explained Esa.

"Funny weather for sunbathing," said Alice.

"Look." Esa moved across the yard and held open her hand. "A mermaid's purse."

"What?" said Alice. She looked down at the plump dark rect-angle in Esa's open palm. "That's just an old dogfish egg case."

She went back to the hanging fog.

# Chapter 12

Esa had a dream. In her dream the wind blew a surf of flame across an open field. Cow corn, sunflowers, trembling oats, all of them ripe and ready for harvest; consumed instead by the licking line of fire. Redwing blackbirds were flung to the sky like burning embers, on the ground voles and shrews and deer mice flamed briefly, and lay quivering on the scorched earth. The fire travelled, and the smoke rose in drifts and covered ghostly telephone poles, whole houses and barns.

There was a distant crash—a shout? The smell of smoke? She woke suddenly, and lay in bed, half-dreaming, hot and rigid with fear. The sheets were damp with sweat, the air acrid. Her lungs hurt; she threw off the covers with one arm, shaking her head to loose the nightmare images from her mind. She opened her eyes to a hazy morning light, as though a mist were inside the room. There was a rhythmic beating sound, not her own heart but something bigger, as if the house itself had a heart that pulsed so that the windows shook in their frames, and the floor boards creaked and widened.

There was chaos in the woken world. Alice, yelling from the kitchen. Not words, but sounds, not for anyone to hear, but to express terror, and to call forth the courage to fight—

"*Fire!*" Esa whispered, and she leapt from the bed and ran barefoot down the hall to the top of the steps, where smoke billowed up the stairwell, and stung her eyes. She hesitated a moment, looked back along the hallway to her room where the two front windows opened on to the veranda roof.

And then Alice called her from the conflagration.

"Esa! Esaaaaa!"

She had been called out of the fire, into the fire: Esa slipped and stumbled down the stairs, swung herself around by the newel post, and ran back along the downstairs hall. She paused momentarily in the kitchen doorway, pulled the runner from the hall floor, filled her lungs with smoky breath, and tried to see into the room.

It seemed like everything in the kitchen was on fire: on the electric stove a pot spewing magma like a volcano; above the stove, the wooden shelf in flames, jars popping and throwing glass; on the floor a burning tea towel, a pan of grease, a line of melting fire along the linoleum; on the table wooden bowls and spoons burning, paper curling off cans, cardboard boxes roaring; the daybed under the window smoking like the straw man in the witch's lair.

She had descended into hell. The cat was roasting on a spit. Alice was leaning up against the jack post, as if tied there. The front of her was on fire, her dress caught at the bottom by running flames that quickly ate the fabric all the way up to her neck. Dazedly, she beat the flat of her palms against her hips and her chest, as if she couldn't imagine why she was being persecuted.

"*Esaauuu!*"

"*Gaaam!*"

They were not human sounds, but the cries of trapped animals.

Esa tripped over Alice's up-turned walker, flailed the rug at Alice, beat the flames that curled the paper of the flour bag on the kitchen table beside them, beat the front of Alice where her skin was turning black, over and over with the bunched up rug, the flour dust billowed through the hot air indistinguishable from the smoke. Esa tried to spread the rug over Alice, tried to put the rug between her and Alice, tried to lift Alice forward, tried to tip Alice backwards, tried *everything*. The smoke stuck in her throat and burned her lungs and her sobbing was caught by the fire and burned before the sound could be heard.

The end of Alice's braid caught fire, and a series of sparks danced through the air like fireflies. Alice fell to the floor, finally unconscious, out of Esa's arms.

"*Gaaaaammmm!*" Esa screamed.

And then the top of Cyril's body emerged from the thickening smoke, in his sleeveless spring undershirt, with his shirt wrapped around his face, the sleeves tied in a knot in front, the whole thing dripping wet so he sizzled as he moved. His eyes shone above this mask like fog lights.

Cyril took one end of the rug from Esa, turned Alice into it as deftly as if she were a bale of hay, as if all the years had fallen away and he was a young farmer again. Together they began to drag Alice towards the front of the house along the hallway. Esa battered the front door open with her foot, and they dragged her through, one of them on each side, and down the gravel path to the car, and then they hoisted the carpet-shrouded Alice into the back seat.

"The key!" screamed Esa, and Cyril lurched around the outside of the house to where Alice hung the car keys just inside the back door. By the time Esa had bent Alice's legs up so she could close the car door, Cyril was back, wheezing, with the key, and he handed it to Esa without a word through the damp sleeve across his face. He loped raggedly back into the burning house by the front door as she started the car and drove in a series of panicked starts and stops down the driveway, bare feet pumping the clutch and gas pedal.

The nurse was watching her fill out the form with unsteady hands. Esa was sweating and trembling, fire and ice. Her t-shirt and pyjama bottoms were covered in ashes and flour dust. The hair on her forearms was singed; the hair on her head stood up, and out, in every direction. She leaned heavily on the counter.

First name. *Alice*, she wrote. Her eyes stung, and she squinted at the wavering page.

Family name. *Withr*—

"No," said the nurse, "that's for *her* last name, not yours."

Esa looked up, met the woman's eyes.

"That *is*—" began Esa.

"Norris," said the nurse. "You write Norris there. *Your* name goes down here." And she pointed to the space that said, *Brought in by.*

Esa dropped the pen, picked it up again. She was hiding a crescent-shaped blister that covered her right palm.

"I don't know what you mean," she said.

The nurse took the pen from Esa's hands, and turned the paper around so she could see it right side up. Full of understanding.

"That's all right, dear," she said. "It's awful to have to fill out these forms when something like this has happened, isn't it? Of course you can't think straight."

She began, efficiently, in a neat hand, to complete the form. She crossed out Esa's *Withr* with two inarguable strokes of the pen, and wrote *Norris*, Age 76, Birthdate *January 15, 1927,* Address *16 Shore Road*, Next-of-kin, *none*.

When she got to the bottom of the form, she turned it around again, pushed it slightly toward Esa, and held out the pen.

"You just need to sign here, saying you brought her in. As there's no next of kin."

Esa stared at the paper. Norris. Next of kin: None.

"Do you need to sit down?" asked the nurse.

She'd passed the screaming fire trucks just after she made the right turn coming out of the driveway, but hadn't stopped or even slowed down. She'd met a police car and an ambulance following them, and they'd turned illegal u-turns in the middle of the road, and shadowed her with their lights flashing. She didn't stop then, either. She'd finally got the car into fourth gear and had no intention of stopping for anything. When the cops realized she wasn't going to pull over, the cruiser immediately behind pulled out and escorted her through the red lights, siren calling.

For the whole drive, thirteen eternal minutes, there had been no sound at all from the squeezed-out tube of Alice in the back seat. The car smelled like smoke and charred flesh. Esa could not think at all, but it seemed important to drive fast. She passed under the Way Road overpass without looking up, and drove down the steep hill like a rush of white water.

When she arrived at the emergency doors they were waiting for her. There was a stretcher ready, and three or four attendants rushed to pull open the back door of the car and slide Alice out. She was gone almost before Esa turned the car motor off, took her bare foot off the brake. Esa's hands gripped the wheel; she lay her head between them, feeling the cool rim of plastic press into her forehead. She heard other car doors opening and slamming shut, and when she looked up there was a police officer's chest and arms visible beside her. She rolled down the window, lay her elbow on the ledge, looked up. The cop was a man, grey-whiskered and slightly plump, and he looked at Esa in admiration, and in apology.

"That was some ride," said the cop. "I think you'd better let me help you inside, so they can check you for smoke inhalation."

"I'm all right," Esa said. Her eyes travelled down as far as the name badge: MacGillvray, before sinking to the officer's belt buckle, which shone so brightly that it hurt Esa's eyes. Still, it seemed too much effort to keep looking up.

"Maybe we could just see your driver's licence?" Corporal MacGillvray said, gently.

"I don't have one," said Esa.

Luckily, they gave the car keys back to her. It did not occur to Esa that this might be a deliberate oversight.

Corporal MacGillvray had pried her hands from the wheel and eased her out of the driver's seat. He had a sort of take-charge attitude that was as kind as it was incontestable. There was an ancient wheelchair, which she refused to sit in. There was Corporal MacGillvray's proffered arm, which she refused to take. The sliding glass door of the emergency entrance opened automatically in front of her like the yawn of a whale; inside, the silver door handles and arms of chairs and metal stretchers glinted like whale teeth.

She sat in the waiting room beside a woman whose nose seemed to be broken, while Corporal MacGillvray went to the emergency desk and had a brief conversation with the triage nurse. They moved her quickly to an examination ward and pulled the curtain around the narrow bed. A doctor arrived with a stethoscope, and what looked like a periscope, and an oxygen machine on wheels, and a chart attached to a clipboard, and a concerned smile.

In between the doctor's "Inhale" and "Exhale" a young man's voice said "Knock, knock" from the other side of the stained pink drapery, and when the doctor said "Come in," another police officer stepped into the curtain-room and handed Esa the keys to Alice's car.

"Drive carefully," he said. Esa didn't look at him. Everything was too bright.

"Inhale," said the doctor. The stethoscope was cool on her red skin.

Esa stalled the car three times on the way up the drive. The last time, beside the giant oak, she got out of the car wearily and slammed the door shut behind her. She walked the rest of the way up the hill, placing her blistered feet carefully one in front of the other in the deep ruts made by the fire trucks. At the top, a whole row of young trees was cracked off and bent backwards into the tangled bushes. The drive was littered with broken twigs, and there were odd, snake-like piles of sharp stones where the fire hose had been pulled across the gravel, exposing something red and raw just below the surface.

The front door of the house stood open. From the interior, the smell of anguish seeped into the late afternoon air.

Esa stepped inside the house and the light shifted. She was in a long, dark tunnel, and she walked forward. The hall floor felt cool and smooth, and she ran one hand along the wall underneath the stairway to steady herself.

She hesitated in the kitchen doorway, much longer this time than she had that morning.

Every surface was covered in black blisters. Wires hung raggedly from the ceiling where the light fixtures had exploded. There was a thin black puddle on the floor, and water dripped down between the cracks in the floorboards and from every swollen surface. Piles of sodden ash lay like unwanted remembrance in every corner of the room.

The firefighters had taken an axe to the pantry. Burnt and crushed cans, broken jars, and splintered wainscotting littered the wet floor. She crossed the kitchen carefully, placing her feet between the scorched and the seared.

The back door was gone, and so was the door frame. A gaping hole looked out from the damp charcoal of the kitchen to the tree-bordered yard, lit by a westering sun that gave everything a faint reddish glow, like reflected firelight.

Cryril sat on a low tree stump at the edge of the yard—sat on one of the three sisters—his legs stretched out in front of him and crossed at the ankles. His undershirt was torn, and smudged with soot. His eyes were mostly closed, and he held his face up towards the sky.

Esa looked at him from across the yard, and then stepped out onto the flagstones and sat down in what used to be the doorway.

Cyril heard movement, looked over at the kitchen door with some effort, and tried to focus his eyes.

"Is she alive?" he asked.

"Yes." Esa leaned slowly back against the ragged wall, and wiped her palms on her pyjama pants, examined her right hand where the orange-peel burn had begun to ache. She touched the blister tentatively, and then folded her hand between her knees to contain the pain. She watched the ants trundle around her feet. Moss grew between the flagstones, the ants' small green hills of home.

She knew Cyril was waiting for her to say more, but she couldn't think what. She knew he would eventually ask her whatever it was he wanted to know. And finally, he did.

"Is that a good thing?" He looked up at the sky again when he said it. Just behind him the tree buds were swelling towards spring.

"Is what a good thing?"

"That she's alive."

Esa considered the question. She thought about Alice alive versus Alice dead, but she didn't really think she knew what alive or dead meant in general, let alone what it meant for Alice. The baby in her belly swam through her deliberation. She moved her blistered hand to rest on her lap, felt the small dome there, rubbed gently. The movement was unconscious and she could not have said why she did it. Esa thought about the glimpse of Alice she'd seen through the little square of glass in the door of the intensive care unit, the length of her coming in and out of view behind the great many people who moved urgently about in the room: a white-sheeted hump ravelled in tubing,

"I'm not sure," she said finally. It seemed too difficult to decipher.

"Look," said Cyril in a rush, as if he'd been working himself up to it. "You'll have to come home with me. The house's a bit rough, but I can sleep on the daybed. I do have a daybed. You can have the bed; I'll find some clean sheets. I'll fix us some supper. I've got potatoes, fried boloney..."

But Esa was shaking her head.

"I'm just going to stay here," she said. "I'm not hungry."

"You can't stay here," he said. "You got no power. They cut it at the pole. You got no heat. You got no stove, you got no fridge. You got no god-damned *kitchen*." Already he seemed a little resigned, as if he'd been expecting a protest and knew he would lose. Maybe he just didn't have it in him for a fight. Still, he looked over at her hopefully.

"You got no god-damned *door*," he added after a short pause, as if he'd just noticed.

"I just need you to go now," she said. The sun had dropped below the trees, and the woods' shadow began to fall on Cyril. For the first time, he shivered. Esa suspected he had been sitting there a long time, waiting for her. She leaned hard against the charred wood so that the wall's sharp edge dug into her back, but she didn't feel anything at all.

She had been cauterized by the flames.

"I buried the cat," Cyril said, and he lifted his arm a little way and pointed along the tree line.

# Chapter 13

Cyril was knocking at the front door, bursting with parcels under each arm, and leaning forward on his cane. Esa seeped out of Alice's room like a cold draft, to let him in. She moved stiffly, though she was still trembling, and her heartbeat called to an echo deep inside herself. Cyril's silhouette was visible through the frosted glass, haloed by bright mid-day light. As she opened the unlocked front door she realized he could have just walked in through the wound in the back wall of the house, and he hadn't. And she realized that through all the stories Alice had told her about other people, she had never told her very much of anything about Cyril.

Today he was dressed in a clean white shirt with a maroon cardigan buttoned all the way down over his bulging stomach.

"This here's a camp stove." He shuffled right past her into the house, went into the sitting room, and put the armload of clacking packages and the dark green rectangle down on the sideboard. Esa could see him taking note of the open drawers, the papers and books tumbled on the furniture and the floor, the upturned parlour chair, but he didn't mention the mess. In fact, he swept the back of his arm along the chaos on the wooden surface in front of him, and more books and papers cascaded to the floor without him seeming to take any notice at all of the dust or the noise.

Esa hacked and coughed; Cyril pretended not to notice that either.

The stove looked brand new. He lifted the lid and unfolded the wings at the side. The two burners stared up at them like eyes. What Esa's eyes saw was a melted pot and the blackened stove and the burnt-out kitchen and Alice, rolled in a carpet runner, when all she'd been trying to do was make porridge for breakfast.

Cyril pushed his straw hat even further back on his head, and wiped his forehead with the back of his hand.

"Now, you're not supposed to use these things inside, but I reckon you've got enough air circulation in here at the moment." He tipped his head towards the back of the house and smiled ruefully.

Esa tried to watch carefully while he showed her how to attach the canister and light the gas. He dug a long-nosed lighter out of his sweater pocket, stood back from the small flame when it burst into being. His sleeves were pushed up at the elbows. Esa thought it must be something old people did, push up their sleeves. His skin was bright red and there were no hairs left on his arm to feel the heat. He closed the gas line almost immediately; the blue flame popped once and was gone. They were both glad when the fire was out.

Cyril took a deep breath in through his nose, as if he were smelling the wind in a hayfield to see if the timothy was ripe.

"Smells pretty bad." He walked down the hallway, stiffly, leaning heavily on his cane. "Never get that smell outta here." He looked into Alice's bedroom as he passed the doorway, where the mattress lay at an odd angle to the headboard, the dresser drawers were skewed open and their contents emptied, papers had been pulled out of envelopes and lay like a blanket of spring snow upon the floor—but cleared from a triangle of carpet, as if it had been pulled back from the corner and laid down again. The house looked like it had been burgled, as well as burnt. He continued to the kitchen entrance, where there was a different kind of mess.

"Got yourself a little work to do now, I guess." His voice was matter-of-fact. He already seemed to know better than to offer any assistance.

"You find what you were looking for?" he asked, casually.

When Cyril had gone, Esa went back into the sitting room and looked in the other parcels he had left, kneeling on the floor and spreading the contents around her, among the notebooks and letters disgorged from the sideboard. In the large paper bag there was an aluminum pot, a chipped willow-pattern plate, a white corningware bowl, a knife, fork, spoon, and can opener. In the grocery bags she found a small carton of milk, a box of Shreddies, a half loaf of sliced bread, a package of marble cheese, a jar of marmalade, a bag of Cortland apples, and two cans of cream of mushroom soup.

She sat back on her heels and looked at all he had brought. She looked at the utensils and the food, and at the papers spilling out of the half-open drawer above her head. After a long while she realized she was hungry, despite her raw throat and the lingering taste of smoke. Cross-legged now, she poured herself a bowl of Shreddies and made a cheese sandwich while she was eating the cereal, and while she was eating the cheese sandwich she made herself a marmalade sandwich, and while she was eating that she quartered two apples and cut out the cores with the dull knife.

She was not ready to light the stove.

That afternoon there was a regular procession of cars up and down the driveway. Some people just drove up, and then went right down again without getting out of their vehicles. The community had heard about the fire, and people came to assess the damage personally. No doubt some of them were disappointed that nothing much could be seen from the front of the house except a loose door hinge and a line of broken trees and odd piles of gravel, and they backed down the driveway and turned around awkwardly at the oak tree where Alice's car still half-blocked the way.

Some of them got out and knocked at the front door, and, getting no response, walked around to the back of the house to try their luck there. They always gasped when they rounded the corner and the hole in the back of the house came into view, with the great Vees of black soot on the weathered clapboard of the second story. They gasped again when they finally noticed Esa sitting behind them on a stump at the edge of the yard, her feet crossed at the ankles, and her hands together between her knees, grey and still, as if stone.

Most of them couldn't get the statue to speak, and they went away relatively quickly, in embarrassment. She was Niobe, without the tears.

In the middle of it all, Corporal MacGillvray paid a visit. He came around the corner of the house and saw Esa right away, and went right up to her without any hesitation. He took his cap off and turned it around in his hands while he was talking to her, although Esa knew he wasn't nervous. She watched his cap badge flash arcs on the brown grass.

"Just thought I'd check in on you," he explained, as the hat turned. "I was driving by. Just thought I'd come and make sure your throat didn't hurt. Sometimes it takes a day or two to feel that smoke damage in there—in your windpipe. Sometimes you can get an infection in your lungs after the fact, if you aren't careful with it."

Esa didn't say anything, but she tried to look as if her throat didn't hurt. She needed to cough but was holding it back.

"And I wanted to tell you," MacGillvray continued, "that the doctors think Alice is going to be okay. They've transferred her to the burn unit in the city. The burns aren't as extensive as they thought at first, and not as deep. Only about twenty percent are third degree. Well, except for her hand that is; her right hand is in pretty bad shape. She might have to lose some fi—"

"She's not my grandmother," Esa croaked.

"Well now," said MacGillvray, "I can see how you would look at it like that."

The cap stopped turning, and was placed back on his head. He fished in his pocket under his gun holster, brought out a thin cell phone, opened it up, and listened for a dial tone.

"There," he said, satisfied. "It works up here. The number's written on the side." He handed the phone to Esa, who stared at his outstretched arm. "The wife gave me a new one for my birthday, and I thought you might want to check with the hospital yourself. I've programmed the number right in here." His arm hairs were auburn and gold in the sun, and the line of his tendon flexed like a rescue cable. Where did kindness come from? wondered Esa.

She looked into the dark hole in the back of the house, where she could see right through to the front door with its glimmer of light through the frosted glass.

When the sun began once again to lower itself behind the line of trees, Esa figured she was probably safe from any more visitors.

"That's it then, girls," she said to the three sisters, and she rose stiffly and walked around to the front of the house on the grass that was now showing signs of wear from the day's foot traffic. She didn't want to have to walk through the kitchen.

There was a casserole pot beside the front door. Esa lifted the lid cautiously: macaroni and cheese. Beside the pot, in a canvas library bag that said *Books are Food*, she found a net bag of onions, a tied bunch of carrots with the tops still on, a pale green cabbage, and four oranges. There was a plastic bag just inside the door filled with tins of fish and meat and baked beans, and another with a small carton of milk and sticks of pepperoni and chocolate Pop Tarts.

And, at the bottom, a package of multivitamins with extra iron and folic acid, for pregnant women.


Esa had awakened that first day after the fire with something liquid burning through her. It gathered slowly in the deepest parts of herself—from places unseen, like the far side of the moon. It sliced upwards from her stomach to her chest, where it seized her lungs and then slid along her raw windpipe to her throat. It carved through the bottom of her jaw and split her parched tongue. She leaned over the side of the bed and vomited onto the floorboards. She retched again and again, and what she brought up tasted like black ash and coal tar.

Finally the surging stopped, and she wiped her cracked mouth with the corner of the flannel bed sheet.

Dazed, she rested a little with her head thrown back on the pillows, feeling momentary relief. Then, slowly, she pushed back the covers, swung her feet onto the floor, and rose from her bed. The frost-bound embers behind her breastbone now drove her to creep through the damaged building like a smouldering fire, licking into every crack and corner and crevice of the house.

She started in the room she was in—Gam's room. Her own things were still stacked along the wall: the rolled print from Merle and Daniel, the duffel bag she had not bothered to unpack. She pulled out the remainder of the drawers in the chest, and emptied the stones and shells across the floor. The stones crashed and Esa exhaled, and together they spread their human and mineral pain into every corner of the room.

Esa swept the sea treasures away with her bare feet and pulled open the closet door. The closet was stacked with cardboard boxes and she dragged them out and peeled away the packing tape. She pulled the carefully-folded clothing from between sheets of tissue paper, and mothballs rolled in the room like hailstones. Woollen pea jackets, knitted shawls, ribbed sweaters, mohair camisoles—all tumbled to the floor around her legs. Dust motes swirled through the air in streams of morning light.

In the middle bedroom she emptied the chest of drawers: bright cotton fragments and rolls of batting and half-made quilts, the star-patterned pieces left hanging from the lampshade and the carved headboard of the bed. From the night-stand drawer she swept costume jewellery into an arc like a faded rainbow. Her breath was ragged and every movement tore at her wounded body. From the linen closet in the hall she emptied smoke-stung quilts and sheets and stiff rolled towels. She moved methodically to the next bedroom and felt under the water-logged mattress, emptied the contents of drawers, looked behind smoky furniture and picture frames.

The two rooms over the kitchen at the back of the house—the bathroom and the little bedroom room she'd slept in as a child—had had their windows broken out by the firefighters, and fragments of shattered glass littered the floors. In the bathroom the French window casement hung raggedly out of joint. A damp breeze blew in from across the brown yard. The fire had stolen through from below in a few places, and the walls were black with soot, and drooping with water. The claw-foot tub was tilted with the sagging floor. Esa avoided the centre of the little room where she could see through to the black kitchen underneath her in thin seams of light. She swept the toiletries from the shelf beside the tub, pried open the pipe access door with her toothbrush, examined the names on the sodden prescription labels in the medicine cabinet: Alice Norris, Alice Norris, Alice Norris, Alice Norris.

Esa went down the stairs and into the sitting room that had once been Gam's living room. There were two drawers in the sideboard, and she pulled them open and rifled through the books and papers, piling some on the top surface and letting others drop to the floor. She pulled the cushions from the sofa and the parlour chair, unzipped the covers and stripped the foam, felt in the deep crevasses at the back and sides of the furniture, tipped up the chair and checked the burlap underneath for holes.

She finished in Alice's room. She flipped the mattress up on its side and examined the ticking and the boards underneath it, and then let it drop on the iron frame. She pulled the drawers from the chest, discarding flimsy underwear and socks and handkerchiefs until the drawer was empty. And even then she ran her hand uncertainly along the sides and bottom as if suddenly everything might have a secret compartment filled with bile.

She pulled back the curtain and pulled the shoe boxes and hat boxes from the shelf in the makeshift closet, and turned their contents out on the bed behind her. A few were filled with neat packages of letters. Esa did not read them, but shuffled through the yellowing piles looking at the addresses: to Alice Norris from John Norris; to Alice Norris from Leanne Norris, to Alice Norris from Julia McArthur. Others boxes held bills: to Alice Norris from the Credit Union; the telephone company; the power company; a second-hand car dealer.

Esa's breasts ached. She sat on the edge of the bed with her red, hairless arms crossed in front of her chest, holding tight to the searing pain, rocking herself back and forth. The baby inside her kicked and kicked, but Esa did not feel it. There was such a bitter smell in the damp air.

She dreamt again and again about the fire. There were no more landscapes except Alice: the long lush plains of her thighs, the sparse brushwood between her legs, the rippled sand of her seashore belly, the low, flattened hills of her breasts, the gully beyond her collarbone. Every time Esa slept she watched the fire run along Alice and leave her charred and smoking, the earth burnt from the rock, the flesh burnt from the bone. What was exposed was mineral, sharp and hard.

In her dreams she heard Alice's cry over and over, *Esaauuu!* as if she were a favoured child.

When Esa awoke for the second time on the morning after the fire, her throat was constricted, and every attempt to swallow made her feel as if she would choke. She'd fallen asleep again on Alice's bed, a dead ember, and opened her eyes to the aftermath of skewed drawers, tangled clothes, tumbled papers. She gasped for air, and then she couldn't hold back the coughing any more, and she hacked and spewed, and spat black phlegm into one of Alice's cotton handkerchiefs, and dried her watering eyes with another.

She lay on Alice's bed and thought about Alice, small and low to the ground, unable to climb onto a chair or stool or to lift anything heavy down from high places. She thought about Alice, layers of skin peeled like an onion, and her eyes stung with tears. She thought about Alice, rolled in the carpet runner.

Esa looked at the floor, snowed under with papers. She sat up, reached a trembling hand down to the carpet's red fringe, and pulled up the corner. Underneath lay neat rows of envelopes, all addressed in her own handwriting to Mrs. (Gam) Withrod. Her red arm was a dogwood branch and her fingers were new leaves and the wind shivered through her as she picked up an envelope and opened it where it had been slit neatly along the top edge, as they all had. Inside was a thin, folded page; inside the fold was $400 in hundred dollar bills.

From a great distance, she heard a knocking at the door. It sounded like her heart beating.

# Chapter 14

Esa sat on the middle stump of the three sisters—Jane. She sat there for a number of days, she didn't know how many. Days of cool spring, when the sun drew the smell of desire out from the heavy earth. Days of touching rain, hushed and soft, absorbed as memory swollen from the birthing of buds. The new leaves drank from the sky a double feast of water and light, and sprung into fluttering heart-shaped promises, unplucked. The sound of the wind changed as it blew through bare branches, tiny leaf points, emerald medallions. It caught in the rising green behind her, and though she was aware of it she did not turn her head for long from the place where the fire had chewed clapboard and spat cinders with black teeth.

She sat from early morning until long after the evening stars swam up into the dark sky. She drank water, visited the outhouse, closed her eyes often against the shimmering air. It seemed there was an even deeper anchorage to be speechless from than the one she had always known. People came by in the late afternoons and left food without looking for her, or shambled around to the back of the house and held stilted conversations with the wraith-like young woman with a waxing belly. She sat always at the back of the house, in full view of the hole hacked and burnt in its side, and at certain times of the dying day the shadows moved and the setting sun glinted in her hair and shone on her cheek, and she looked, to those who came at the right moments, like a thin moon reflecting a wan light.

From the centre of all that moved and breathed and grew around her, Esa watched like the eye of a hurricane. She was all retina, measuring and translating sunlight and lamplight and firelight into

103

intaglio impressions. In the dark, the few early fireflies tumbled in the blackness on the periphery of her vision.

She didn't use the cell phone to call the hospital; everyone who came seemed to know all about Alice's condition, and they always fell to talking about that when they ran out of other things to say. They ran out pretty quickly, because Esa didn't say much in response, so she mostly heard about Alice, and how she was still on oxygen, and how they had amputated three of her fingers, and how she impressed the nurses because she didn't cry out when they changed her dressings, but just gritted her teeth and moaned. Later in the week, she heard about how Alice was on antibiotics because she'd developed a lung infection, and about how many bunches of carnations she had in her room, in all colours, even blue, and about how many skin grafts she had on her thighs and stomach, and how some of the skin for the grafts had come from the backs of her legs and some of it from pigs.

What she heard was unfathomable. While people were talking to her, she peeled the bark from tender twigs pulled from the brush behind her, uncovering thin strips of a surprising green.

When it was dark night she rose stiffly from the apple stump and circled the house, gathered the day's neighbourly offerings, wrenched open the off-kilter front door, climbed the stairs. She stepped automatically over broken-spined books, torn receipts, flattened felt hats, worn towels, skewed picture frames. She fell into the damp bed like a stone statue toppling on the dewy grass of a barren and deserted garden.

Early each morning, for an hour or so, Cyril joined her. He rounded the corner of the house stolidly, his cane making small depressions in the newly-green grass. He lowered himself creakily onto the weathered surface of a stump, where the rings of time were still clearly visible: good years and bad. Like Esa, he sat with his legs stretched out in front of him, crossed at the ankles, his mismatched socks showing beyond his pant-legs, and his cane fixed upright between his knees. Sometimes he would grasp the handle and thump at the ground, as if sounding the hollow depths. Other times, like a good farmer, he peered into the thin grass with white-washed eyes at beetles emerging from the soil, and if they were likely, in a few month's time, to be into his corn, or his potatoes, he crushed them firmly with the end of his stick, and he wasn't sorry.

The emerging blackflies began to bite at the backs of their necks and at Esa's bare feet. Together, Cyril and Esa watched the sun climb above the roof of the blackened house like a fireball. They watched the robins come in clusters, bobbing sanguinely on the grass. They watched the wind tickle burnt flakes of wood from the side of the house, and fall into the hearts of dandelions. They watched Alice burning like a human torch. At the end of an hour, just before leaving to see to his chores, Cyril would speak a sentence or two as a way of saying goodbye, and Esa always knew it had taken him that long to think of it.

The second day after the fire, shaking his head, he said, "I *smelled* the smoke before I saw it," as if he couldn't believe the wind would carry him a message that important. He'd been a farmer all his life and knew the damage wind could get up to.

One day when the clouds were dabbed across the firmament like fish scales, he gazed upward for a long time and said simply, "*Mackerel* sky." Esa didn't know if it was an excuse or an explanation.

Another day he surpassed himself with three whole sentences: "Fire's supposed to be good for the land. The seeds of things survive, get lots of sunlight. New trees sprout up like beanstalks in all that burnt earth."

But the next day, reduced again, he said, "Makes one hell of a mess out of a house, though."

Eventually, she stopped sitting. Like a monk rising from a long meditation, she ended her retreat quietly and without ceremony; one morning her quaggy muscles simply guided her in another direction, without her active will. The shock that had immobilized her finally subsided; it was as if the voltage was turned down just enough for her to resume her pedestrian habit. At first she floated on a deep uncharted current, surrounded by a small cloud of blackflies, swirling like bits of biting ash. As she walked, her legs grew steadily firmer and her pace quickened, though she walked without any urgency.

She was drawn to the river. She walked its banks like a lumbering bear, casting about for a place to drown her lost fragment of hope and quench the fire that blistered the backs of her eyes. The water was still high, and ran quickly over the rocks, pulling the river weeds into ribbons of wavering green. She walked upstream, her feet slipping in the mud alongside the steep embankment below the ruined house. Jewelwing damselflies fluttered their iridescent green above the rushing water. The tall trunks of the trees above cast dark shadows over the cut, and Esa walked through the striated world, in and out of sunlight like a moon repeatedly eclipsed.

She walked farther and farther upstream every time she went out. It seemed important to get to the river's source. For countless journeys, on warm days and cool, she passed trout turning in pools and upside-down black beetles waving their legs in the air. This particular day began brightly, and there was a watery sound of bells ringing, and tiny parachute seeds drifted through the air. She ducked under the wooden bridge that took the Shore Road over the river. For a while she was in deep woods, and the poplar and yellow birch drew in close to the banks.

For the first time, she clambered under the larger, concrete bridge that spanned the river over the Rover Road. The land levelled out after that and the banks dropped and the trees thinned, and soon she was walking wet-footed through fields of fresh green that tousled her ankles. The wind picked up and swallows dived and spun over the hay, as if anxious for cover. Dark clouds swept across the blue sky like a wave. In the distance, a piebald dog barked out behind a barn, chasing chickens. Esa tried to pull her jacket collar up around her head.

She was already wet up to her knees when it began to rain. The raindrops hit the river water in a torrent, and even the opposite bank was obscured. With the rain running down her face, she turned back towards home.

She knew then that she couldn't ever get to the beginning of things; there were no more beginnings. Everything was already underway.

Cyril came by. He pulled his car up to the top of the driveway, and honked. It was a dull day, and the ground was wet from rain. Esa looked out of her bedroom window and saw Cyril's thick arm stuck out of the rolled-down driver's window. She went down the stairs slowly, her feet pulsing heavily on the treads like the pendulum of a grandfather clock.

"I'm going to the city," Cyril said when she got out to the car. He was dressed in his best white shirt, with a tie tossed over his shoulder by the wind.

Esa looked at him; Cyril waited. In the space framed by Esa's body and the side of his car, he watched a junco with a grey hood chasing a white-crowned sparrow along a branch.

"What are you going to do there?" she asked finally.

"You *know* what I'm a-going to do in the city." He waited some more. He tipped his new straw fedora back and scratched his forehead with the side of his hand. The sparrow slipped out of sight, and the junco sat alone at the tip of an elderberry branch.

"Well," she said finally, "I have some other things to do."

He pulled his hat forward again, nodded.

*Dear Merle and Daniel*, she wrote.

*We have had a fire, and the kitchen is mostly a black hole with bare wires hanging down and the walls and ceiling sagging in on themselves. You can't even walk in there without getting completely covered in soot. Nobody died in it except the cat, who burnt back to front starting at the tail.*

There began to be all kinds of insects in the house—the quick-flying ones came first, the houseflies and bluebottles, and flung themselves around wildly and cracked their tough insect heads on the windowpanes. The slower ones came after: the lacewings and the ladybugs. Wasps arrived looking for sheltered ceilings, and immediately began building a metropolis of paper nests at the highest point of the second floor landing. Sowbugs and spiders and centipedes crawled across the blackened kitchen floor and found asylum in the dank crevices of the creaky house. Those shy of cool shade, the dragonflies and moths, came in by accident and were caught by the maze of rooms. They fluttered their wings on the glass in the windows upstairs. Grasshoppers and crickets leapt eagerly into all the corners, and played their music with careless abandon. Finally, the snails came to live in the area around the house's gaping wound where the rain kept the wood damp and cracking.

They hatched from larva, or transformed from chrysalids, or woke from hollow trees or the secret places deep in the earth where they'd spent the winter. They were not attracted in by the lights at night, for there were no lights. At night, Esa sat upstairs in the dark and listened to the deep B-flat movements of the stars. But still, the mosquitos and coddling moths and June bugs came through the broken back windows and the crack in the front door, and most of all, through the hole at the back of the house that blurred the distinction between inside and outside for all of them.

Esa viewed this flying, crawling, scuttling immigration with a detached regard. She was not disconcerted to find either a honey bee or a cadelle on her pillow in the mornings. But the thought of some of them stunning themselves against the window glass trying to get out to the light was too much for her to bear. After a few days, she opened all the windows that had not been broken during the fire, and propped the sashes up with picture frames or lamp bases or whatever was at hand on the littered floor. She carefully got a pair of tarnished scissors from the shelf in the ruined bathroom and cut away the screens. She found a hefty rock at the edge of the drive, and used it to prop open the front door.

Esa grew paler and paler, until she was like a piece of driftwood bleached from years in the tossing waves. By the end of the second week, the food left at the front door became slim pickings. To compensate, every day at one o'clock Cyril drove up with a jug of water and half of what he had made for his own noontime dinner, kept warm by a frayed towel wrapped around the pot. The contents didn't vary much: meat or fish and potatoes, onions, carrots. Sometimes there were boiled beet greens or spinach leaves, other times fiddleheads, curled tightly against the world like unborn infants. She ate what he brought because he simply wouldn't leave without his pot, empty, and the fork he'd given her to eat with.

But she waited for him, delayed her restless walking for the afternoons, or returned in late morning with last year's burrs caught in her pant legs and this year's old man's beard trailing across her shoulders. Although she did not recognize it, there was a hunger that was satisfied by his daily visits. Cyril sat on a tree stump while he was waiting for her to finish, or he walked slowly around the yard, pushing his cane distractedly among the white clover and dandelions. She thought he did not quite trust her to eat if his back was completely turned. One day he bent over stiffly and tossed away a pile of burnt boards, one at a time, until long stripes of blanched yellow grass showed underneath. Pink bulbous crowns of rhubarb broke the earth's surface like the burnt fingertips of a giant hand.

"Those sure are tasty," Cyril said, "boiled up with sugar."

In Esa's dreams Alice burned like a torch, and though her mouth was open her screams were frozen in her throat.

Esa woke with ragged breath and sat up in bed. She rose and went downstairs, kicked away the rock holding the front door from swinging wide open. She circled back to the right, along the tree line, looking for the place where Cyril had buried the cat. Once she found the small patch of bare earth she couldn't imagine what she thought she'd find there. Even if the nameless cat wasn't Churchill, it seemed a horrible way to die.

For the first time in almost two weeks, Esa went into the kitchen. The burnt smell was still strong throughout the house, but in this room the acrid odour stung her nostrils and churned her stomach. A startled garter snake slid between the black debris like a length of woven embroidery thread, green and gold flashing over the doorstep and into the grass. It was a cool day, and windy—a throwback to early spring. Through the house's wound Esa could see cumulus speed across the sky, white-topped but pregnant with dark underbellies. The on-shore wind whistled through the house, and the wooden skeleton groaned under damaged skin.

The wind and heat of previous days had dried the boards to charcoal, and fine black dust drifted and swirled on every surface. Wires still dangled, cans and jars with unrecognizable labels still littered the floor, black walls still splayed inwards, heaving splintered cabinets like hollow trees. The gypsum board had fallen from the ceiling and lay in crumbled mounds on top of the fire litter. The cracked lath was exposed, and the floor of the bathroom above sagged so far down that if Esa had reached her arm up she could have touched it with her fingertips. The jack post lingered tentatively like a fragile birch trunk. Blisters clustered on the old table like blackened oyster mushrooms. She lifted one, peeled it away and dropped the chip onto the floor. She heard the sound it made, a sharp crackle.

Layers and layers, thought Esa. She peeled the burning away until her hands were black with it and there was a pile of thin wafers at her feet. She looked at her handiwork: underneath, a shadow of the table's former colour could be seen.

On its cloudy surface there were traces of flour dust and grains of sugar, and the eighteen-year-old apple peelings from three sisters pies.

Esa stepped back and tripped over a dented can, fell backwards onto the hovering jack post, that witch's stake. It shifted sideways, and the floor above her moaned loudly, shuddering as if in pain. Mouse dirt and the shoe dust of ages dribbled down on her, and then there was a great crack, and a heaving sigh, and one leg of the claw-foot bathtub broke through the ceiling like the hock of an enamel giant. Esa flung herself to the back of the house and out into the yard. There was an explosion of sound: wood roaring and bellowing, wood screeching and splintering and shrieking. When her feet were firmly on the flagstones she looked back, heart howling, to see the enormous weight of the tub crash down from above and come to rest in the middle of the kitchen floor in a volley of ash.

When the rumbling had stopped and the dust had settled, Esa could see that a broken-off pipe was poised over the huge hole between the floors like the spout of a fountain, and trickled iron-red water into the tub like blood.

Death broke its dangling chain and ran away like a kicked dog.

# Chapter 15

She'd remembered about the mail. Esa searched for the keys she hadn't thought about since her return from the hospital. She searched the top of the sideboard in the front room downstairs, among the piles of jars and cans and bags—her makeshift pantry—and behind the still-unused Coleman stove. She went up to her room and looked in the empty drawer of the bedside table, and among camphor-scented clothing strewn on the floor, and then she checked the pockets of all of her wrinkled second-hand pants and her scorched pyjama bottoms. There were no keys.

Alice's car still sat where she'd left it the day of the fire, underneath the oak tree at the bend in the drive. Esa pulled the driver's door open and looked in. The key was still in the ignition, others dangling from the leather key ring. Esa took them out, glanced at them briefly, put them in her jeans pocket, and resumed her walk down the gravel driveway. The ruts made by the fire trucks had softened with the weather and the recent traffic. The cumulus and the curious, she thought.

At the bottom she turned left, as she had seen Alice do when she stumped down on her solitary errand. Before the fire. Now, after the fire, Esa measured all that happened in lengths of light and depths of darkness.

The bank of rural mailboxes stood in the wooded triangle formed by the Shore Road, the Rover Road, and the river. Esa shook her head at how stubborn Alice had been, going all that way alone with her walker. Enough gravel had been laid down in front of the boxes so three or four cars could pull off the road at the same time. A few of the compartments had names: Conners, MacDonald,

Davidson, Grant; most had only a number, running from 1 to 15 on each of the three boxes.

There was the ignition key for the car. There was a key for the back door and one for the front door of the house. The was an oddly-shaped silver key, and a thin gold key with a long shank and a string of numbers stamped on the side. She tried each of the two unidentified keys in the locks, working across every row. At the very end of a row, two-thirds of the way down, the silver key turned in the lock and the little metal door opened.

There were three items inside, all addressed to Alice Norris. One from the phone company, clearly a bill. A letter from Judith (Jude) Sullivan, Member of Parliament. A spring sale catalogue from Sears.

On the way back along the road she kicked a rock from the edge of the road into the reedy ditch, and the keychain fell from her hand and hit the wet gravel with a single unforgiving note. Esa looked at the keys splayed between her feet, looked up to a reflected light that hurt her bloodstone eyes.

The sun glinted on the old, unused mailbox that still sat at the bottom of the driveway. It was skewed sideways, and dented. The phone company, Judith (Jude) Sullivan, and Sears slipped unnoticed from under her arm and hit the muddy road. She pushed the box level; the metal shrieked once and was silent. The lettering had faded from black to grey, and was indistinct on the galvanized steel. Esa rubbed the flat of her hands against the metal, dislodging spattered spring dust. In the woods beside her a woodpecker tunnelled into a tree's dark interior. Esa stood at the bottom of the drive, looking at the neatly drawn letters that spelled the name she had been searching for everywhere:

Ellis Withrod.

And underneath, in a less competent hand, in only slightly fresher paint:

Alice Norris.

She pulled unsuccessfully on the front flap of the box, then tried again, one hand balancing the rocking metal so she could get a better grip under the latch. It opened reluctantly, and only after a struggle. There was nothing inside but orange pine needles and road dust and the dried-out shell of a long-legged spider.

"The lung infection's back," he said. "They got a breathing tube down her throat."

He'd let her finish eating first, as always. They were sitting on the apple stumps, as they always did, whatever the weather. They shared a calm disregard for all of the elements—except fire. They felt the sun prickle the new hairs on their forearms; they felt the fog roll over their bodies and leave them goose bumps; they felt the raindrops begin like the ticking of a clock. They felt these things, but had no need for shelter. The weather could not get under their skin.

"It's awful to look at," he continued. "Sometimes looks like the very thing that's saving her life is going to choke her to death."

The pot was resting on her knees, the fork still in her hand. She touched the tines gently to her throat, swallowed tentatively.

"Sometimes I think it would be best to just reach over and yank the god-damned thing right out."

Esa looked down mutely into the empty pot.

"I wouldn't let an *animal* suffer like that," said Cyril, disgusted.

The night the bats arrived, Esa was upstairs in her room, lying on her back with her hand on her belly: a Klimt painting, without the colour. She lay on top of the faded quilt, its tones ebbing further with the thin layer of grey dust that covered everything in the house, as well as from the grime of her naked body. It was dusk, and night mists began to move across the lawn and seep into the waiting house. Day creatures began to prepare for bed; night creatures stirred quietly in their nests, opened their eyes, shook daydreams from their furry heads.

Esa thought her belly was huge; she didn't think it possible that it could get any bigger. Her skin stretched tightly over the dome, and what was inside—now much bigger than an acorn—seemed to be treading water. The dark nipples of her breasts looked even darker in the fading light, and a dark line ran through her navel as if she were two halves of a seed stuck together—or waiting to be split wide open.

A few stars appeared faintly, as if behind the veil of must-coloured sky. A few mice began to chew industriously in the wall behind her head. An owl hooted once from the edge of the woods. The window frames yawned widely, and a dark eddy of swirling shapes flew in through the eastern window and spun around the room like the final *allegro* bars of a symphony. They circled the square of the room's ceiling a dozen times before swooping back out into the night, fully dark now and ripe with insects on the wing. Esa had been looking up, holding her breath, watching the soaring of half-notes and quarter-notes, and she lay awake for a long time after their *ritornello*. In her sleep, finally, they made a dream that was not about terror but about the small currents of air that blew lyrically around her head.

When she woke in the morning, there were twenty-six little brown bats hanging upside-down on the empty wooden clothes rail in the closet, bickering for space and squeaking as if they had come home at last.

Cyril offered her a drive to town, said he thought she might just like to pick out her own vegetables for a change. When she opened the passenger door there was a twenty-dollar bill on the seat, and he waved his hand at it, without looking at her, until she picked it up.

He drove so slowly that Esa realized for the first time that he couldn't see very well, and wondered if he would have been aware of the fire at all if he hadn't smelled it first. He dropped her off at the grocery store and arranged to pick her up again in half an hour, after his appointment.

Esa ran into the bird woman in the dairy aisle, choosing yoghurt.

"It's Esa, isn't it?" asked Mary. Her reach was arrested halfway to the shelf. She didn't seem to be sure if she recognized the dirty, drawn young woman beside her.

"Yes."

"I'm so sorry—I heard about Alice."

"Oh."

"It must have been terrible."

"It was just a pot on the stove." She did not mean to minimize the fire, but to lessen Alice's role in causing it. Without thinking, Esa turned her hands up in explanation, and the blistered place on her palm shone red and raw under the fluorescent lighting.

She quickly put both hands back in her pockets.

"There was a bird in here before," said Esa, not only to change the subject. She thought the bird woman would be interested. "A starling. I don't know what happened to it, but I don't think it starved to death. Because of all the food in here." She swept her undamaged hand across the packaged cheese.

"No, it wouldn't starve," Mary agreed. "I saw it here too. It would have been impossible to catch. Maybe it died from loneliness. Starlings are flock birds, you know."

"Flock birds?"

"Some birds need to belong to a group."

"*Flock* birds," repeated Esa. She studied the tubs of cottage cheese.

"That woodcock you brought me is almost better. Maybe I'll bring it out and release it at your place. Maybe her mate is still around, waiting for her."

"Oh no," said Esa. "He's long gone." And this time, she held out her damaged hand as evidence.

Corporal MacGillvray came again, and brought a social worker with him. Esa heard two cars pull up out front not long after Cyril had gone away with his empty lunch pot, and then she heard two doors slam. She was standing in the rhubarb patch with a blackened knife when they came around the corner. The social worker was very tall and had big bones and mousy hair that hung languidly beside her face. Her bangs were cut straight across her forehead and gave her an innocent look. Her eyes widened when she saw Esa, unwashed and barefoot, and in response Esa's eyes narrowed warily. They were about the same age, but clearly intimacy with dirt was a point of departure.

"This here's Lori-Ann," said MacGillvray. "She's a social worker." It was clear that Lori-Ann knew who Esa was already, had been told long stories of loss.

"Hi," said Lori-Ann. She was staring awkwardly at Esa's feet, which were the grey colour of weathered wood. Esa didn't respond, but looked in turn at Lori-Ann's feet, housed in brand new black leather boots, ankle-length and square-toed, with zippers up the sides. There was fresh mud on the toes from Alice's yard.

"I'll leave you two to get to know each other a bit," said Mac-Gillvray, deliberately obtuse. "Mind if I check out the damage?" He motioned towards the house with his gun hand. Esa shrugged, shook her head slightly, and the Corporal moved off to the periphery of her vision. She could sense him pause at the wound opening, heard his exclamatory whistle as he took in the replanted bathtub and the broken ceiling. He disappeared inside the hole, and she and Lori-Ann stood alone beside the cut rhubarb stalks lying like bloody slashes across the grass.

"Is there anywhere we could sit down?" Lori-Ann asked, and looked around the yard as if she expected to see lawn chairs appear among the weeds.

Esa carefully inserted the blade of the knife into the earth and motioned towards the tree line. Lori-Ann looked where she pointed and didn't see anything, but Esa was already walking over to the three sisters, where she sat down on the stump, looked up at the altostratus brushed across the sky, and waited, knife hand on the top of her round belly, for whatever was coming next.

"So when is your baby due?" Lori-Ann had followed Esa, seated herself tentatively on the middle tree stump after carefully brushing the debris from its surface, and shifted her gaze sideways to Esa's grimy hands. Lori-Ann blinked nervously. She spoke as if they were already in the middle of a conversation, so she would not have to think too much about how to get started.

"September twelfth."

"Have you been to a doctor?"

"There's nothing wrong with me."

"Then how do you know that's your due date?"

"What?" Esa looked briefly at the young woman beside her.

"How do you know when the baby's coming, if you haven't been to a doctor?"

"I counted two hundred and sixty-six days," said Esa. "I read that somewhere."

"From what?"

"What?"

"You counted two hundred and sixty-six days from what?"

"*What?*"

"*Oh*," said Lori-Ann. "You only did it *once*?"

Esa began to count to two hundred and sixty-six in her head, and peeled a piece of bark from the rim of the apple stump. It was thin and blackened like a blister of burnt wallboard.

"I could drive you to your doctor's appointments, if you needed a ride."

There was a long pause while Esa got to the end of her silent counting.

"There's nothing wrong with me," she finally said.

"Maybe you would like to go to prepared childbirth classes at the Y?" Lori-Ann was still trying. "I could drive you there."

"I don't need a drive *anywhere*."

"Or maybe you would like to go and visit Alice?" Lori-Ann's eyelids fluttered over sky-blue irises, as if to push away the cloud cover.

Esa picked the dirt out from underneath her thumbnail: earth, dust, ashes, blood, all the same colour. She heard Corporal Mac-Gillvray come out of the house and cross the yard. Her grimy hands were oracles and she searched there for meaning. When she glanced up she caught Lori-Ann's fierce expression.

MacGillvray cleared his throat and asked after his casserole dish; it was, he confessed, his wife who'd made the macaroni and cheese.

"You can keep the phone as long as you need it, though. I've put more minutes on it."

118

Esa didn't tell him she hadn't used any of his first generous installment.

Esa was walking on the dry verge; Cyril was driving along the road towards her. She had seen the blue sedan turn out of a driveway in the distance, kicking up little dust as it crept eastwards on the loose gravel road.

Cyril pulled the car to the side of the road and parked when he reached her, keeping his motor running. She stopped walking, rubbed her ashy hands together.

"Morning," he said, breathing deeply through his wide nostrils.

"Hi." Esa wondered if he would now always be smelling for burning on the wind.

"Fine day," Cyril said, and looked away from her for a moment, out over the fields of flowering dandelions to the whitecaps running in the bay. He inhaled again, keenly.

"I got a bath at my house," he said, waving back over his shoulder. "Door's always open. I'm a-going to town right now." Esa was surprised to understand immediately how these things were meant to be related. For once, he was not asking her to go with him to see Alice.

But she countered: "I got a bath at my house too," and then, to change the subject, "What's this key for?" She dug the key chain from her jeans pocket, dangled the long gold key in front of him.

His eyes flickered over to the key and away quickly. "You got hot running water?" he questioned, persistent.

"Hot baths are overrated."

"You got no running water *at all*," Cyril snorted.

Esa watched a chipmunk skitter up a maple trunk and shake the new leaves along a thin branch. She let her hand drop, and the keys jangled. Still gazing up, she opened her mouth, took a deep breath.

"Maybe there is something you can do about *that*." She tried not to make it sound like a question.

Cyril rubbed his chin with his calloused hand, nodded his understanding.

"It's a safety deposit box key," he said.

She asked Cyril to show her how to take a door off its frame. He brought a screwdriver and a hammer and banged all the brass pins out of the hinges, moving carefully with his cane from one interior door to the next over and around the debris on the floor. He climbed the stairs very slowly, leaning heavily on the handrail, while Esa carried up his cane and the tools. After the two pins were popped, he told Esa how to lift the door and slide it out of the way. She left them leaning up against the walls beside their empty sockets.

*Dear Merle*, she wrote.

*I am sorry my replacement didn't work out, but I can't come back right now because I have some things to do here.*

What things, she didn't really know. What things could be done anywhere that would make any difference?

*Thank you for the picture. I showed it to Cyril (he's my neighbour). He says your new house sure looks better than mine.*

She peeled away a piece of the wallpaper over her bed, and tucked the bottom edge of the photograph into the hole. Merle and Daniel smiled out at her from the front of a neat brick row house with a small wooden porch. Daniel's hand rested tentatively on the inside of Merle's elbow. The small patch of grass they were standing on wasn't green yet, but Esa knew that for some people it was only a matter of time. She stepped back.

*He also says you should make sure you buy a fire extinguisher, and learn how to use it. The best place to hang it is just inside the kitchen door.*

# Chapter 16

Esa knew that she needed to start getting groceries for herself. And now there was Nimbus, asleep at the end of the bed, needing some kind of formula from the feed store.

She crept quietly out of the room. There was a barn swallow building a nest over the lintel of Alice's door. Its forked tail flashed away through the kitchen as Esa came down the stairs. Above her head she could see a neat brown bulge of straw-stuck mud.

From inside Alice's room, on her hands and knees, Esa swept the paper and envelopes, handkerchiefs and camisoles from the surface of the carpet, piling them on the painted floorboards around the perimeter of the room. It was an Indian carpet worn thin by years of Alice's unforgiving walker. Esa folded it back all along the fringe, and then began to roll it inwards towards the bed. She brushed the trundling ants gently along the pile, through a faded motif of navy, plum, and gold. She was careful not to disturb what was underneath.

Esa sat back on her heels and counted. Four across, nine down: thirty-six. All the envelopes were the same size; she'd bought a box of fifty on sale at the drug store three years previously, and there were still a few of them left, wrinkled and yellowing, upstairs in the bottom of her duffle bag. Esa wiped her damp palms slowly along her pant legs, knees to thighs. Dirt etched her skin as it would a child's who had played all day with gravel in a dusty backyard. Thirty-six letters. She wiped her hands again, took up the letter from the bottom right-hand corner, worked backwards along the row, and then started on the next, making a neat stack in her left hand, with the open tops facing up. From the front, her fingers walked over the top of the letters, pulling open each slit so she could see what was inside.

In her hand she held thirty-six envelopes, thirty-six folded sheets of foolscap, and one hundred and forty-two hundred dollar bills.

Twenty-one thousand four hundred dollars of her own money, sent to lie under a carpet with tapestry moths, feeding on darkness.

Whenever she heard the social worker's car coming up the drive, Esa walked around to the front of the house to meet her. Esa had thought briefly that she might hide in the woods until Lori-Ann went away again, but she knew Lori-Ann would not stay out of the house if she thought Esa wasn't home. Not like Cyril. Or even Corporal MacGillvray, who had at least asked first.

If she got there in time, Esa dislodged the rock that was holding the front door open so Lori-Ann would not see the barn swallows come out insect-hunting to feed their young.

When Lori-Ann got out she shut the car door tenderly, then pushed the remote control to lock all the doors. If her arrival had somehow slipped Esa's notice, Esa became aware of it then, because the horn sounded ridiculously in the country air, and sent an avian kaleidoscope winging to the skies. They always stood in the driveway and talked; Lori-Ann, who clearly favoured sitting down, never stayed very long. When she talked she blinked to the rhythm of her own words and tossed her hair across her cheek bones. It was as if she were trying to stop too much of her inexperience from being visible.

Lori-Ann stood stoop-shouldered in the driveway and looked miserably up at the scudding clouds.

"Maybe today you could show me what preparations you've made for the baby?"

"I don't think that's a good idea," said Esa.

"Why not?"

"I wasn't expecting company."

"Like, do you have a crib and stuff? A stroller?"

"No."

"What about a layette?

"A what?"

"A layette?

"Um, *layette*..." repeated Esa, pretending to think hard.

"You know, baby clothes, crib sheets, baby blankets, towels..."

"Towels," said Esa. "I have towels." She thought of the tangled, smoke-scented piles on the floor of the upper landing where a family of red squirrels had made a nest.

"Baby towels?" said Lori-Ann.

"Baby towels?" said Esa. "*Baby* towels? No, I don't think so."

"You don't even have baby towels?" Lori-Ann blinked and tossed and blinked.

"Hand towels, they're small," Esa said to reassure her.

"Are you planning on *keeping* this baby, Esa?"


Cyril had driven up the driveway on a tractor, an old rust-painted relic with gangly limbs. He had his cane wedged in between the exposed pipes and wires, and he drove one-handed. Tucked under his other arm was a bundled grey sweater, thin sleeves with black cuffs hanging down to the front and back of his elbow.

"Morning!" he called across the yard. He seemed to have more energy than usual. Esa stopped kicking rocks and walked over to the tractor so he would not have to climb down. The back tires were almost taller than she was. Cyril left the tractor running and they shouted at each other above the noise of the motor.

"Hi."

"Brought you something," Cyril said, uncontained.

The grey sweater raised its head and yawned. The black cuffs were tiny cloven hooves, and they swung like puppet-legs below Cyril's arm.

"*Oh!*" she said.

"Astonishing colour, ain't it? Used a black ram this year. Get more money for the wool if it's coloured, and it makes no difference to the meat."

Cyril climbed slowly down from the tractor, one-handed, and wrenched his cane from the tractor's belly. He took one step towards her with its help, then rested the crook over his forearm. He grasped the lamb firmly in his big hands and rubbed it up and down a few times between Esa's shoulder blade and her hip. It bleated minutely in protest.

"Now it'll know who you are." He set the lamb down on its spindly black-toed legs, where it stood underneath Esa's knee like a limp dog. From a wire basket on the tractor's side he took a couple of green glass bottles filled with milk, with large black nipples attached to the tops, and a paper bag with a rolled-over top like a sack of flour.

"Formula," he explained. "Don't feed it cow's milk yet, you'll give it the bellyache."

"I have never even *seen* a real sheep before," she said.

"I called it Nimbus," he stated matter-of-factly. "A nimbus is a—"

"A rain cloud," she said quickly. "Yes, but—"

So he didn't tell her it was the other definition he'd had in mind—nimbus: the radiant light drawn around the head of a saint—but climbed with surprising agility back on to the sieved seat of the tractor and released the hand brake.

"Well, *I* can't look after the god-damned thing, and it's mother *won't*," he said quickly, and he pumped the clutch and nodded, touching the brim of his straw hat as if she had thanked him for doing her a favour.

She could not leave the lamb. There were no doors left to shut it in anywhere, and when she put it down, he followed always just behind her, tripping and falling every few feet. His legs were like the disjointed limbs of marionettes.

She went to get the mail with Nimbus drooping under one arm. His legs swung loosely as she walked, and once in a while with a great effort he lifted his curly charcoal head and protested weakly. He was like a smudged sidewalk drawing that might at any moment be washed away by rain.

At the bottom of the driveway Esa noticed that the flap of the old mailbox was still open. As she crossed the road a killdeer flung itself out of the box onto the gravel, dragging a stretched-out wing along the ground. The lamb started and Esa could feel its heart race in the palm of her hand. The dust rose around the killdeer as it limped along, the two black collars around its neck making a target of its head. Esa thought about the bird woman, saviour of creatures in flight.

Esa took a step towards the bird, and it pulled its broken wing a little farther along the roadway in front of her. She took another step, and it limped a little farther. Esa put Nimbus gently down on the verge like she was setting down a little four-legged stool. The lamb bleated morosely, and the killdeer fell over sideways and then struggled on. Esa crept slowly towards it, and behind her Nimbus shook his long tail and took a few shaky steps. They followed each other along the road: broken-winged bird, crouching woman, wobbling lamb. Esa lunged forward at the bird, and felt the air move under its wings as it leapt into the sky and flew in a low arc around her head and into the grass, calling a high-pitched taunt back over its perfect wings.

Esa felt the gravel dig into her palms. After a while she got up and walked back to the old mailbox, scooping up Nimbus along the way. As soon as she came up to the box, the killdeer rose from the grass and once again threw itself at her feet, feigning injury. Esa looked inside. There was a haphazard collection of twigs, and in the centre nested four eggs like mottled stones. She moved away. Behind her there was silence as the killdeer stopped its display. Her eggs were safe.

The mail car came down the road and pulled up beside Esa. She knew it was the mail car because the driver, a round woman with a face like a postcard from home, rolled down her window and handed Esa a letter in a standard white envelope.

"Morning," the woman said. "Fine day, ain't it?" She drove off again, one hand on the wheel and one eye on the road, sorting the mail on the seat beside her. Esa no longer wondered how people just seemed to know who she was.

The letter in her hand was addressed to her. It was not from Merle, who always wrote everyone using CartoGraphie stationery and stamped it with the office lettermail machine. Esa inserted her thumb into the corner of the gummed flap, tore it raggedly along the top edge, and pulled out a single sheet of paper, folded in thirds and tucked over at the end. The printing was large and irregular, like that of a child who couldn't properly hold a pen.

*Dear Esa.*
*Forgive me, please.*
*Alice Norris.*

It was probably the most concise thing that Alice had ever said.

Forgive me, please. It was the first time that Esa thought of forgiveness as something she could grant, or withhold.

But she didn't think she knew yet what she might forgive Alice for.

When Mary Turner, the bird woman, did come up to the house, she came on foot, pushing a bicycle. Her face was a little red, but she was not out of breath. She had a shoebox in her bicycle basket, which she removed gently and held close to the ground while she untied the rope handle. The box had small pin-holes in all its surfaces.

Esa had been mixing formula and left Nimbus waiting expectantly beside the old well, licking the outside of the newly-filled glass bottle.

"Hi there," Mary said.

"Hi." Esa looked at the bird woman out of the corners of her eyes.

"I know you said its mate was gone, but I thought I'd bring it out and release it here, just in case. You never know. I hope you don't mind?"

Esa imagined what the world would look like from the inside of a shoebox poked though with holes.

"And even if he isn't around any more, it still seems a fine place to spend the summer, doesn't it?"

"Oh," said Esa, "yes." She viewed the ruined house in astonishment, and then looked down at the top of Mary's head, her dark hair streaked with a very few brilliant lines of white. When Mary looked up Esa could see that her forehead was damp with sweat, and the woodcock lay in the open box like a stone.

And then Nimbus, who had tipped his bottle off the well cover without succeeding in getting the nipple in his mouth, galloped awkwardly over and nuzzled Esa's knees, and the frightened bird rose with twittering wings and knocking cry, flapped noisily across the drive, and disappeared into the undergrowth.

"Oh!" said Esa. It seemed too easy.

"Oh!" said Mary. "What a lovely baby!" She reached out and circled Nimbus' charcoal ears with her fists and rubbed his forehead with her thumbs, at the place where the nubs of his horns pressed through his woolly skin. He leaned into her touch, then butted his head spiritedly against her hip so that she almost fell over.

"He's hungry," said Esa. She went and got the dripping bottle, Nimbus dancing behind her. She tipped it up and Nimbus began to suck, crouching down on his front legs and wagging his tail frantically, his whole body shaking in delight.

"Can I feed him?"

"Here," said Esa, passing the bottle to Mary. "Hold tight."

Mary struggled to keep her grip on the tugging bottle, and she laughed, a pure, joyous laugh, as uncalculated as the lamb's wagging tail. Her laugh blew through Esa like a warm wind carrying a storm behind it.

"Aren't babies always beautiful?" asked Mary, but it was not a question. "They're so full of promise." She wasn't gushing. On the contrary, she spoke quite solemnly, as if the sea-gravel at the top of the rise where they stood was a sacred place.

Esa swayed in the driveway like a young oak tree in the wind. Air currents tumbled. The tension rang in her woody ears. Ripe acorns scattered from her branches and fell on the stony ground.

"This is your pot," she said to him.

He reached for it, felt its heft, raised his eyebrows to make a question of its weight. When she didn't say anything he lifted the lid off, put his nose over the rim, breathed in deeply as if he had no more thoughts of smoke.

He smelled the sharp red smell of stewed rhubarb, nodded.

"Guess you got that camp stove lit okay," he said.

# Chapter 17

The rains tapered off and then stopped. The sun grew stronger, rising higher in the sky each day, and lingering later in the evenings. Summer arrived, dry as brittle yellow grasses and heat-bleached bones. Fire season.

In the evenings Esa went down to the river with a bucket and hauled water back to mix with Nimbus's formula. She boiled the water first, and saved it in an old pickle jar for the many small feedings that were necessary throughout each day. She still stood as far back as possible and narrowed her steely eyes when holding the lighter to the burner of the camp stove, and the moment when the propane exhaled into flame always made her jump.

The formula bag was almost empty.

The lamb took the nipple of the up-turned bottle frantically, butting its head against the ghost udder of its rejecting mother, and Esa struggled to hold the bottle. Cyril said lambs did that to stimulate the ewe's let-down reflex, so the milk would flow freely.

"Maybe *I* should have butted a little," she said to him.

At night Nimbus lay at the end of her bed like a curled cat.

There were lamb droppings scattered like dark seeds throughout the house.

Cyril came to install a hand pump on the old dug well. He came up on the tractor, towing a small flatbed trailer laden with lengths of clanking metal.

"Get those arm muscles ready," he said. "Where's my stick?"

Esa dislodged the battered cane from the belly of the tractor and handed it to him. She pushed Nimbus away with the side of her foot, lifted the eight-foot pieces of pipe and pulled them from

129

the trailer so the far end fell to the ground and made dents in the gravel. The long weeds flattened in a wide arc as she dragged them one by one along the yard like firefighter's hoses, as if water was all that was needed. She carried the pump slung across the top of her belly like a second child, long and squalling, all iron arms and legs. Her human child heard it through new-grown ears, and jumped so hard in Esa's belly that she staggered and almost lost her hold on the metal. Her sheep child followed her back and forth like a bundle of iron filings attracted by a magnet.

Cyril got down on his knees beside the old well at the edge of the yard, and slid the concrete well cover to one side. It made a hollow sound like a boulder being rolled away from an empty cave. Small tufts of moss and soil were dislodged as the disc was moved away, and fell a dozen feet down to the surface of the water.

"Scalpel," he said. Esa didn't move at all, so he said: "Wrench."

She went back to the tractor and got his red toolbox from underneath the seat. He clattered around in it and brought out a pipe wrench with a painted blue handle.

"Drop pipe," he said, and Esa swung one end of a length of pipe around where he could reach it.

"Foot valve." He pointed to a cardboard container about the size of a shoe box. When opened the box revealed not sea treasures, but a heavy brass valve like a giant sleigh bell. Cyril attached a cylindrical screen to the valve, then fastened that to the first length of pipe, turning the wrench around with the side of his hand as if describing the motion of the moon around the Earth.

"Rock. Large rock. Maybe a little smaller than your head." She went with her woolly shadow to get the rock from behind the front door. When she brought the rock to Cyril he wrapped wire around it like birthday ribbon and played out several arm-lengths of line before attaching the other end to the bottom of the screen on the foot valve.

"Bleach." Another movement of the hand toward a large white plastic bottle. "You got a *clean* rag?"

Esa and Nimbus went to the back of the house and Esa stepped into the kitchen. Nimbus would not go in, some animal instinct—or perhaps premonition— keeping it from the legacy of the pyre. The charred floor crackled under her feet. When she reached the hall she looked back for just a moment through the darkness, to the tiny lamb's head and shoulders framed by the bright halo of the sun-filled yard. Nimbus called to her anxiously.

Esa brought one of Alice's nightgowns out to Cyril, who looked at it strangely for a moment in his rough hands, then ripped up both side hems and along the belly until he held a good-sized square of cotton. He soaked the rag in bleach and wiped his hands, then quickly scrubbed the surface of the rock before dropping it over the side of the well. As he lowered it down, he wiped the length of wire and the screen and the bottom of the pipe where Esa had dragged it along the ground. The sharp, sweet smell of bleach churned through the air.

He held the whole arrangement over the open well. One-handed, he threaded the second section of pipe to the first with a brass coupling.

"Right," he said. "Let's see about those arm muscles." He handed the line of rock, wire, and pipe over to Esa, who struggled to hold it hovering just above the water.

"Now let it down slowly."

Hand over hand she let the pipe descend into the well. The rock broke the water's surface with a splash and sent small ringed waves against the glistening stone walls. The pull was not so great once some of the pipe was under water. When she reached the end, Cyril slid the concrete well cover three-quarters of the way back over the well, guided the top of the pipe through the pump hole, then pushed the cover until it fit the well surface snugly. He attached another coupling and another length of pipe and Esa stood on the cover and kept lowering. Her arms strained and she braced her elbows on her round belly, leaning backwards to counter its weight.

"Stop when the rock hits the bottom," Cyril said, and just then she felt a slight give in the pull.

"I think I'm there."

"Yep, that's about right." There was about three feet of pipe sticking up through the top of the well cover. He collared it with a clamp and then together they slid the gangly pump over this backbone. He pulled a second concrete plug from the well cover and poured the remainder of the bottle of bleach into the hole.

"Bucket of water," he said, as he replaced the plug, so Esa and the lamb went into the house again by the front door, got the red pail from beside the sideboard, and went down to the river for water. When she got back Cyril was sitting on the well cover wiping the sweat from his forehead with the back of his bleached hand. He got up stiffly and removed the priming cap on the pump, took the pail from Esa and carefully poured the water in, without spilling a drop.

"I'll leave you to it." He put the bucket down empty and found his cane in the grass. He hobbled to the tractor like the tin man, joints cracking.

"Give it a few days before you drink it," he said from the familiar seat. "Give you the bellyache if you drink it now. Pump it out 'til it comes clean."

The tractor motor roared and handfuls of coloured birds scattered up from every bush and tree like thrown confetti.

"A good well keeps filling up," he called over the din. "We'll soon see what you've got there."

After he left she stood on the well cover and pumped muddy water over her feet, working the handle up and down in an exhilarating rhythm. Nimbus bleated and danced a divertissement on the grass. Esa swung like a coryphée on the metal arm, until the water came out clear as ice.

From the top of the bluff overlooking the bay Esa could see the sweep of grey shore stretch away in both directions. She stood in the belly of this arc with Nimbus tucked under her left arm, and watched the ebbing waves whisper in and out like the earth's pulse. Away down along the beach to Esa's left a small bare-headed girl picked up a round white stone and held it in her outstretched hands like an offering. Her thin arms were pale, with bruises like lunar seas on a luminous landscape.

Esa went down to the river and followed its flow. She came quickly to the place where it washed shallow over beach stones. The water murmured as it spread itself into a giant fan and seeped through the break in the wash at the high tide line. The tide was at its farthest turn, and the line between the tangled seaweeds and the waves glistened and steamed in the sun. Esa looked up and down the empty strand.

She put Nimbus down at the water's edge and began to walk eastwards along the ocean's margin. The lamb followed hesitantly, running a few steps after her, then stopping and bleating, running forward again, and vaulting in surprise whenever a wave washed over its tiny black hooves. Esa kept her gaze on the drunken poles that once ran wharf planks from shore to ship's gangway. When she reached the ruined wharf she looked back along the waterline to the house sitting on the rise. From this distance it looked whole and undamaged.

The bottom of the black pole she leaned against was covered in miniature volcanoes waiting to erupt. She shifted her focus to the rocky point and took a few steps further along the beach, but then she turned and walked between the remaining posts straight out towards the sea. The barnacles climbed higher up the posts the further out she went, covering the area that was underwater at high tide. At the middle posts the barnacles reached up to her half-moon belly; they were like the Earth's mountains seen from a great distance in the sky. At the last post they were at eye level, and she examined their tiny voiceless mouths, thousands and thousands of them waiting faithfully for the rising tide.

Salt water on wounds, thought Esa. She looked out at the depths with longing, but there was no answer there for her.

She turned and looked up to the high tide line; there was no sign of Nimbus.

In alarm she ran back, scanning the sweep of beach and the scrubland behind. There was no wobble-legged lamb.

Not behind the broken palate upended in a plane of sand. Not among the bracken that ran alongside the beach's grey shoulder. Not entwined in the snarled netting that stretched down the strand as if to snare the waves themselves.

She ran frantically back and forth along the shoreline. She ran along the gravel between the great stone shelves and came to a place just above the high tide line that was strewn with granite boulders worn smooth by pounding waves.

At her feet an exhausted stone bleated, staggered to its feet, wagged its tail wildly and began to butt her knees with its head.

She knelt down on the gravel, among the boulders. Nimbus butted his warm head into her neck as she circled his wriggling body. His wool was soft against her bare arms. Their noses touched; Esa could feel the lamb's tiny, tender breath. The beach was awash with their delight.

He butted and butted. It seemed so easy, this asking to be fed.

Sand flies swirled upwards in small clouds as she walked back along the line of writhing seaweeds, Nimbus tucked under her elbow. Irish moss, rockweed, dulse, twisted blades of kelp. Ravelled with the sienna browns and olive greens were bright yellow and red buoys on frayed ropes, fragile fish bones, and broken lobster traps, their slats crushed and jagged-ended.

She carried Nimbus past mussel shells, crab claws, congealed jellyfish, driftwood twisting like snakes. The lamb's eyes were bright as black pearls. Esa passed the salt-etched leather handle of a suitcase and broken window frame and a child's sandal and a brown tennis ball lying at her feet. She took note of the seal's bleached rib bone: Rib bone, ribbone, ribbon, she thought.

When she was half way back to the house she caught a glimpse of cobalt among tendrils of bladder wrack, and she stopped so suddenly that Nimbus's hind legs swung on her hip like a secret nudge. It was a tiny piece of blue beach glass. Without thinking, she bent down and picked it up, and Nimbus made a sound like a sigh. The glass fragment was warm, and blazed its vibrant colour.

Every few feet she stopped and bent awkwardly over and the lamb sounded its yearning call. The sun continued its heavenly course and dipped into decline. Esa forgot about food, and a new hunger found her.

Cyril's car was in the drive when she got back up to the house. He was waiting for her in the yard, on the middle apple stump, eyes half-closed. The pot balanced on his knees had completely lost its heat. Esa crossed the yard without speaking, so he did not notice she had returned until she was right in front of him. She held out her fist, her boney knuckles pointing to the sky, then turned her hand over and flattened her palm to reveal a treasure of small tesserae.

Cyril looked closely at the young woman in front of him, raggedly dressed and grey with dirt, the weary lamb slung under one arm like a pampered dog, her outstretched hand filled with blue.

"*Ah*," he said. "Mermaid's tears."

The infant bats complained boisterously about the heat. Nimbus was asleep at the foot of the bed, faint ovine snores sounding on the lamb's tiny out-breath. Esa found the poster of the gold-gated garden in her room underneath her spring jacket and a pile of dirty socks.

The print came easily out of the tube, and she unrolled it carefully. She pinned it to the wall between the two sea-facing, south-seeing windows with sewing pins she found in a rusted tobacco tin in the middle bedroom.

She looked at the print as dusk grew: every kind of butterfly, every kind of bird. When she finally looked back to the room again, she saw the garden's shadow all around her.

*Forgive me*, Alice had written.

Esa thought about Alice lying on a gurney in the hospital corridor, waiting outside the operating theatre for another round of skin grafts. She thought about Alice struggling to hold pen and paper with her patchwork hands; writing that short note with her left hand, as the right one had three fingers missing. What remained of her right hand looked like an unfledged bird, too weak to survive the nest.

Pen and paper were all Alice had now to communicate with. Her voice box had been burned right out of her throat. They were making her a new one out of a plastic valve and a vibrating flap.

Esa knew all this because Cyril told her.

"What is *that*?" Lori-Ann was looking at Nimbus, curled around Esa's neck.

"Just an old sweater," Esa answered. "I thought I might get cold." She was on her way home from the beach when she'd heard the social worker's car come up the long drive. Esa had carried Nimbus up the woods path on her shoulders, two hands securing the lamb's four legs over her collarbone. Her pants pockets bulged with beach stones on each side of her bulging belly. She clacked when she walked: the tide was coming in.

"Is that—*sanitary*?"

Esa considered the question but couldn't imagine how to respond seriously.

"It's a clean sweater," she finally said, and set Nimbus down at her feet, a walking purl stitch.

Lori-Ann was clearly finding it harder and harder to conceal her exasperation.

"Why do you continually insist on misunderstanding me?"

Esa walked past her trailing a ball of grey yarn. She circled through the yard to the right, opened the outhouse door, and stepped inside. She closed the door, but opened it again to lift Nimbus in with her, an ashen rolag ready for the spindle.

From the cracks between the boards of the outhouse door Esa watched Lori-Ann standing in the driveway, tapping her fingers uncertainly on the hood of her locked car.

# Chapter 18

The bats in the closet squeaked incessantly throughout the day, with a crescendo at the approach of dusk. The young hung like clusters of unripe pink fruit and dug their elbows into their infant cousins' hairless sides when stretching their rawboned wings. Their mothers left the house every night as Esa was preparing for bed. When she slept, she did so fitfully, her ethereal limbs casting about restlessly for a place of comfort. She could only lie down on her back, with pillows propped under legs to make her more comfortable—one useful thing she'd learnt from Lori-Ann. Inside her belly something grew fretful and stretched an arm or leg against the inside shell of her, pushing out beyond what was known and safe, blinking in the dark. When Esa dreamt, she saw Alice as a mote of dust would, blowing across a red and blistered landscape.

And she dreamt, still, of ice: etching oak leaves vein by vein, like God's hand drawing in the details with a fine white pen.

She fed Nimbus the last of the formula, shaking the bag out carefully to get the powder from the folded corners. Even then she had to mix more water than usual into the lamb's breakfast and his woolly head kept butting her knees for more once that was finished. It was hopeless to try to ignore his insistence.

From a drawer at the back of the ruined pantry she found a length of twisted blue and red rope, only partially melted. There were rusted fence spikes and roofing nails and halter clips lying loose in the bottom of the drawer. She made a tiny collar for Nimbus by cutting a short length of rope and doubling it through some metal rings, and she made sure the collar fit snugly on the lamb's soft neck.

She attached one end of the remaining rope to the collar and the other to the sagging clothesline on the breezy rise at the back of the house. She walked back and forth along the length of the line a number of times, and Nimbus followed, strung on a loose, dangling leash.

The clip sliding along the cracked clothesline spoke the language of blistered childhood.

After a last turn, Esa kept walking past the pole and continued toward the house. When the lamb got to the end of the rope, it jumped and bleated and strained anxiously, but the collar and the line held.

Esa walked down the driveway with the keys to Alice's car jangling in her hand and two hundred-dollar bills in her pants pocket.

The car was sprinkled with the tiny petals of spent pin cherry flowers. Inside, it smelled like stale fire. Alice's half-burnt shoe still lay on the back seat. It took Esa a long time to start the motor. She let go of the clutch over and over before the gas caught, or she delivered too much gas so the car leapt forward and she braked hard in alarm, while the engine died. At each leap the white blossoms were tossed onto the windshield like flailing snow. Her palms sweat dirt onto the slippery steering wheel; she hunched forward in her seat, still hopeful that, for once, she was really going somewhere.

She didn't stop at the end of the driveway, but rolled the car out into the centre of the gravel road. She didn't slow down or yield as she made the turn onto the highway ramp, didn't dare look up as she passed under the Way Road. She didn't slow down very much at all when she got to town, until she hit a red light and the car stalled again. Someone behind her honked politely, in case she hadn't noticed the light was green.

Every place she went, she parked at the furthest end of the parking lot so she would not have to manoeuvre between other cars.

In the grocery store, she lined the bottom of her squeaking cart with fresh fruit and vegetables, still searching fruitlessly for a sign of the starling. She got a small tub of vanilla ice cream and ate it while standing in the check-out line, peeling back the cardboard and biting off icy mouthfuls. Her lips left faint marks like small kisses. She lay the flattened container on the conveyor belt like a pressed flower.

"You ripped the bar code," the cashier complained, without even looking up.

In the Sally Ann, the beady-eyed woman behind the cash watched Esa gather elastic-fronted pants and billowing shirts from the maternity section until she had a whole new wardrobe slung over her arm.

"Don't even think about trying those things on," the woman said. "We spend a lot of time washing the clothes before we put them on the rack!"

Esa paid for them with the forty-five dollars left over from the groceries, and the woman pushed some plastic bags across the counter at her. Esa packed her purchases herself.

The teller at the first bank she stopped at told her with visible relief that the key she showed him was not one of theirs. With one hand he pointed at another bank across the street while his other hand hovered on the security button underneath the counter.

Esa went across to the other bank and stood in line. People moved away from her in small, tactful steps. When she got to the teller she held up the gold key.

"I think this opens something here," she said. "A safety deposit box?"

The teller was a dark-haired woman with an open, placid face. Her nametag, attached haphazardly to her ribbed cardigan, read *Bobbie-Jean, (B-J)*. Bobbie-Jean (B-J) seemed excited by the sight of Esa rather than alarmed by her. With great effort she transferred her eyes from Esa's dirty face to Esa's grimy fist.

"Yes, that is one of ours. What is the box number?"

"What?" said Esa.

"You don't know the box number? What is your name?"

"Esa Withrod."

The teller turned slightly to face her computer screen.

"Did you say Withrod? Did you say Esa?"

Esa nodded.

"We only have an Ellis Withrod in our files, but all the accounts are closed and she is entered as deceased."

*Dead*, thought Esa.

"That's it," she said.

"But that's not you. You're not deceased."

"No," admitted Esa. "I'm not."

*Dead*, she thought.

"There's no record of a safety deposit box under that name, anyway. Let me see the key." She typed the number into the keyboard. There was a pause. B-J seemed to be struggling between duty and curiosity.

"There are two names attached to this box," she said, "but neither of them is you."

"I know that," said Esa.

"But you can't just get in to someone else's safety deposit box. They have to sign to get in. Is this a *lost* key that you found somewhere?"

"I found it in a house," she said, "on a keychain. Is Alice Norris one of the names? It's her house. Her keychain."

The woman hesitated. "I've probably told you too much already—Yes, Alice Norris."

*Dead.*

Esa turned away. And then turned back.

"And what is the other name?" she asked.

In the feed store parking lot Esa left the car where it stalled—sprawled across three parking spaces—and went in to the store. As soon as she pushed the tinkling door open the smells threatened to drown her: grass seed, horse feed, fertilizer, weed killer, saddle leather, iron. And the noise: there were crates of day-old chicks stacked at the ends of all the aisles.

She walked slowly up and down the cluttered rows of dusty shelves and the air was alternately sweet, sharp, sour, dull. The soprano peeping followed her everywhere.

So did the eyes of the two men behind the cash. They did not ask her what she was looking for.

Esa found the formula section—there was a different kind for every animal. She dragged a twenty-pound pail of Sav-a-Lamb Milk Replacer from the bottom shelf, then dragged it along the floor to the cash counter. Neither of them offered to help.

She took a perfect hundred-dollar bill from her pocket and laid it down in front of them. The men looked at each other, and the younger one spoke.

"Where did you get this money?"

"It's mine," she said.

"But where did you get it?" He was belligerent; perhaps it had been a boring day.

"It's mine," she repeated.

"I'm sure nobody dropped a hundred in your hat when you were sitting on a street corner," he laughed. The older man disappeared through a door behind the cash into a grimy glass-walled office, and picked up the phone.

"I don't wear a hat," Esa said, and she put her hand back on top of the money.

"But you do sit on a street corner—clearly!"

"I would just like to buy this formula," she said. She took the bill off the counter and clutched it in her closed fist.

"For the baby, is it now?" He motioned to her belly, laughed again.

Esa dropped the pail's metal handle and it made a sharp crack as it hit the side of the plastic bucket. The chicks called frenetically. Esa felt the money in her hand, all edges and corners. She stood beside the pail in the feed store waiting for something to happen. She couldn't tell what would come next. The man behind the counter continued to talk, and Esa saw his lips moving, and heard his voice, but the meaning of his words was lost among the peeping.

And then the older man came out of the back room, and Corporal MacGillvray walked in the front door. He stopped abruptly as soon as he saw Esa, one arm holding the door part way open. There was a jangling sound that cut across the clamour of the chicks.

"*This* is why you called me?" he questioned the older man from where he stood, disbelieving.

"You take this woman's good money, Earl," he said firmly, in response to the man's sheepish nod. "A little dirt doesn't spoil it."

Esa exhaled and put the hundred dollars back on the counter. The younger man rang in the amount, and laid her change down in front of her. MacGillvray marched across the floor and picked up the pail. He walked her out to the parking lot carrying the formula, and he put it carefully in the trunk for her when she opened it, among the other bags and parcels.

"Sorry about that misunderstanding, but you know, you do look—" he began, but he stumbled over his words. He watched as she eased her belly in behind the wheel and shut the car door. Then he leaned up against the rusted body and rapped gently on the window, and she rolled it down.

"You do anything about that learner's permit, like I told you?" he asked apologetically.

"Oh," she said. "Um, no." She looked at a button on the front of his shirt, the clean fold of beige fabric.

"I told you that you couldn't be driving this car without one, didn't I?"

"Oh. You did."

"And I told you that even when you had your learner's permit, you'd need to have somebody in the passenger seat who had a valid driver's licence, until you passed your driving test."

"Yes, you did, you did."

He blew sadly out through his nose and the skin sagged under his cheekbones.

"Well now, you really leave me no choice but to impound this car," he said. "I can't really let you drive it one more inch. Not legally. I do have to uphold the law."

She bobbed her head rhythmically, ran her tongue over the inside of her front teeth.

"So I'll have to ask you to get in the police car with Corporal Dean there, and he'll drive you home, and I'll drive this car—well,

I tell you what, I'll just take the car and the keys and park it in the lot at the station, and when you can show me a learner's permit, and some automobile insurance in your name, and a driving teacher, I'll just give you the keys right back."

His shirt buttons were translucent white with a deep white swirl, like something cut from an abalone shell or a pearl.

"And don't be showing up with old Cyril MacDonald, because he's got no driver's licence either. Now get out of there. We'll move these bags over for you."

When she got in the passenger seat of the cruiser Corporal Dean put the back of his hand quickly over his mouth and then rolled his window all the way down, even though it was a cool day, flecked grey with rain.

When they got to the Way Road overpass Dean put his arm out of the open window and made a high-five sign at the man on the bridge. The man was dressed in a mechanic's orange coverall and he put both hands up in the air in a mock surrender, and smiled.

# Chapter 19

She found the flecked cotton sweater that Serge had left in her tenement room; the sweater he'd left behind the night she'd slept with him; the night he'd crept out before it was light. She found it under her bed in Gam's old room, bundled with dust.

In the apricot light of early morning she held it to her face, and inhaled deeply. It smelled like dust, like ash, like history. She pushed it back underneath the bed and gathered Nimbus from the tangle of blankets at the end of the mattress. The curled lamb stirred briefly, then snorkelled back into sleep.

Pressed against her collarbone, this living sweater smelled like earth, like warmth, like tomorrow.

"They wouldn't let me look in the safety deposit box," Esa told him.

Cyril put an over-large fork-full of fish stew into his mouth.

"It's not enough to just have the key," she continued. "You have to have the key *and* have your name on a little card that they keep at the bank."

"God-damned bank," Cyril said without conviction. The fork trembled a little on the way to his mouth this time.

They were sitting on the apple stumps—Jane and Katherine—eating lunch off plates, for a change, instead of out of the pot. The grass in the yard came all the way up Esa's bare legs and tickled her kneecaps. She was wearing a pair of maternity shorts she'd bought for three dollars. The elastic waistband had already broken but she'd found a safety pin lodged between the floorboards of the middle bedroom.

"There are two people who can sign to get into that box," she continued. "Alice is one of them, of course."

Cyril closed his eyes, held his breath.

"And the other is you."

Birds flitted and sang from the tree limbs. Chipmunks ran bossily up and down the trunks. Cyril exhaled.

"Well now—" he began, but he didn't finish. Esa had learned it was what he said when he didn't know what to say next.

At their feet Nimbus played at eating, nibbling the tips of red clover flowers with tiny white teeth.

"The RCMP took Alice's car away." She changed the subject; she knew all about not speaking. "You probably already noticed it wasn't in the driveway."

Cyril nodded so the brim of his hat shook up and down, and he wiped his mouth with the back of his hand.

"I have to get someone to teach me to drive before I can get it back. And it can't be you."

"God-damned Mounties," he said.

They ate in silence for a while: potatoes, carrots, new peas, cod. Their forks dinted the enamel plates in 2/4 time.

Then Cyril said, "I'm a-going to town after dinner tomorrow. And I'm a-going to the city on Saturday."

Esa looked at him. His white hair was sticking out from one side of his head like a burst milkweed pod.

"Okay," she said finally. "Alright."

They were dancing a tango: step, step, step, step, pause.

Step, step, step, step, close.


*Dear Merle*, she wrote.

*Cyril (he's my neighbour) came and put a new pump on the old well so I don't have to go down to the river for water any more. Yesterday I found a dogfish egg case on the beach—around here they'd call it a mermaid's purse. Every day there is something new washed up by the tide.*

*P.S. I do not know how people survive in the country without a decent public transportation system.*


The tide was going out. Esa and Nimbus lay on the beach in the mid-morning sun like chameleons, listening to the sound of seagull wings on the wind. There was a long-legged sandpiper strutting down the shore, poking the strand with its darning needle beak in search of lunch, running seaward after each retreating wave and chuckling at the periwinkles.

From her stony bed Esa could feel the vast ocean stretch and contract in a rhythm that matched that of her belly. She ran her fingers through the pebbles, gathering hot handfuls in the sweep of her arm and trilling them from her fist. She looked up at the house; this morning the darkness behind the open windows and doorway seemed cool and welcoming. There was a white-haired woman rocking in the shade of the porch; in her lap lay an open book, from her hand a pair of reading glasses dangled. Her face was hidden by the leaves of the rose bush that climbed along the length of the porch roof. As she rocked the chair travelled slowly across the wooden boards.

The sandpiper ran by gleefully with a sea snail in its beak.

Back up at the house, Esa laid a sand dollar and a fingernail-sized veined rock on the windowsill in the sitting room, and she looked back out through the open frame down to the shore. She could see the place where they'd been lying; a small mound of pink and grey stones rose just above the high tide line like a memorial.

Cyril made an eight-point turn at the top of the driveway. She got in the car and slammed the door.

"Might not let you in without shoes," Cyril said, without looking at her.

Esa got back out of the car and went up the stairs to her room and rummaged around until she found a sneaker under a worn quilt and found the other one in the closet, spattered with bat droppings. She didn't put them on right away but carried one in each hand, slapping the heels together as she ran down the stairs, and dropped them carelessly on the floor of Cyril's car after she got in and slammed the door shut once again.

Cyril did not speed up much once he got on the highway. They did not speak at all on the way in to town. This time, Esa was able to look out the window at the landscape transformed by shapes of green: a sweep of malachite, a triangle of jade, a low cloud of chartreuse, a slash of beryl. Everything was fresh and bright and singing: a green chorus. As they went under the Way Road Bridge Cyril looked up and lifted his index finger in greeting to the man standing above them.

He raised his index finger at many of the cars that passed them. He seemed to know who all these people were without taking his eyes from the road and really looking. He recognized them and knew what they needed: the tiniest of waves communicated volumes.

In slow motion they passed the houses of Nelly McKay who'd lost her son, John Davidson who'd lost his livelihood, Isobel Crane who lost her music, the Bird Woman who'd found her wings. They did a number of errands: pale striped shirts picked up from the laundry, neatly folded and packaged in cellophane; a quick trim at the barbershop, so Cyril's hair settled on to his head like thin snow; a stop at the liquor store with the box of dirty beer bottles that he had gathered from the shoulder of the road and the riverbank. Esa sat in the car the whole afternoon, and Cyril hauled himself out from behind the wheel, and pried himself back in again without either of them worrying about the time at all. At the end of it, Cyril edged into the bank parking lot and parked the car in the handicapped spot and looked over at Esa, and asked the question without opening his mouth.

"I'll wait here," she answered, and she looked down at her tumbled shoes.

So he went into the bank, and after ten minutes, or maybe twenty, he came out again with a fat brown envelope and laid it on the bench seat between the two of them—an unspoken promise.

She told him to let her off at the bottom of the drive, so he wouldn't have to turn around at the top. He didn't argue. She swung the envelope in one hand and her unworn shoes in the other as she walked up the hill. There was a blue jay in the oak tree, crying like a squeaky clothesline.

Lori-Ann's car was parked beside the house. Lori-Ann herself was just coming out of the open front door, stepping carefully over the cluttered sill, shielding her eyes from the barn swallow that spun in the air around her. As soon as she saw Esa, she began to shake her head.

"You can't be serious," she said, and then repeated herself with increased volume: "You *can't* be serious?" It was still a question, as if all that she had just seen was not to be believed, like a dream fragment in a woken world. Esa kept walking up the drive, passed right by her, said nothing. Her eyes were fixed on a point of ground by the side of the house where a chickadee was teaching its black-bibbed young to peck insect eggs and summer seeds.

"You can't have a child in this mess!" She spoke to Esa in retreat.

"I've recommended that the baby be apprehended as soon as it is born!"

Esa said nothing. The chickadee family flew into the cedar tree to clean their beaks on their breasts.

"I've been *trying* to help you Esa, but you aren't doing anything at all to help yourself here! You think I'm having *fun* coming out to see you every week?"

Nothing. No.

"You think you're the only one who's ever had bad things happen to you?" Lori-Ann's voice rose and fell like rough waves, breaking on the jetty of Esa's back. "I went through *five* foster homes before I was eighteen. Do you think I *want* to consign anybody else's child to *that*?"

No. No.

"At least have the decency to answer!"

Oh. Nothing.

"Stop treating me like *dirt*, Esa!"

Esa stopped suddenly and turned, slowly, to face the social worker; the breakwater shuddered. Lori-Ann slapped her hand over her own mouth, as if to stop more words from diving out.

Esa opened her mouth to speak, but her voice died for lack of air.

Into this pithy silence there came an urgent call. Both women inclined their heads, tilted their chins to the sky. A bevy of birds swept up from their various nests as if a sudden, violent gust of wind had shaken them loose and tossed them toward the clouds.

The call came again, faintly; almost a human voice, it filtered through the trembling leaves like sunlight.

The women looked at each other across the expanse of crushed stone.

Again, the voice, small and helpless. A zephyr. A feather. A falling leaf. A tuft of grey wool caught on a barbed-wire fence.

"Nimbus!" Esa cried, and the shoes and envelope fell from her hands and papers scattered languidly along the dusty gravel. A terrible dread clenched her core and radiated through her body in an endless instant; it was as if her heart boiled over and filled her hands and feet with churning sap. She turned and circled the outside corner of the house, running awkwardly through the long grass, holding her hands underneath her belly to steady what was inside her. At the edge of the yard she did not stop, but her eyes registered the torn grey lamb, the dangling blue and red rope, the long-legged piebald dog, the blood.

"No! No! No! Get! *Get away*!" She crossed the yard and began to kick at the dog's flank with bone-breaking feet. Its jaw was covered in red froth and it turned on her and snarled and snapped its yellow teeth.

"*No!*" She kicked tawny ribs and haunch and elbow.

"*Nooo!*" She kicked shoulder and neck and jaw.

"*Nooooo!*" The dog began to ebb away from her screaming fury, ears bent back, growling. She kicked and yelled and kicked, and her voice was hot as searing flame. And finally, finally, the dog gave up its prey and bolted away through the lank grass and into the shadowed woods.

Nimbus lay at her feet. His shoulder and neck were torn open. He lifted his charcoal head slightly and his eyes rolled. There was nothing in them but suffering, and a mute appeal that it should be ended. He butted his head once in an infant appetite for death.

"*Cyril!*" Esa stood in the lush yard and the radiant light swirled around the creature at her feet like a Catherine wheel.

"*Cyril!*" She looked around wildly as if Cyril would once again appear miraculously through the smoke, but all she saw was the sun glinting on the glass in the upper half of the bathroom window.

Sun gleaming on the burnished silver pot left on the apple stump since breakfast.

Sun glittering on the underside of tempest waves in the long view to the west.

Sun flashing on the knife handle, blade still buried, shaft sticking up from the ground where she had left it when she was cutting rhubarb.

And she went and pulled the cool knife from the ground.

And she went back to Nimbus and knelt down as if to pray.

And she lifted the knife in both hands and brought it down with the full force of her weight into the lamb's heart. Fleece and flesh and bone gave no resistance. The lamb twitched, and his eyes dulled, and he shuddered, and the flame went right out.

She took the dusky sweater in her arms and pressed it over her collarbone, and she wailed. The birds high in the trees were pregnant with fear. The lamb's soft, warm blood ran down her hands and over her belly like a baptism.

And the witness, Lori-Ann, leaned in shock against the corner of the burnt house, her new dress, and her heart, weighted with ash.

# Chapter 20

Esa knelt in the garden holding Nimbus until his blood congealed and the sticky fleece began to attract flies. He drooped over her arm; his gashed neck was a deep purple streaked thinly with yellow, the colour of johnny-jump-ups running through the garden.

Lori-Ann found an old spade leaning up against the side of the house, and a trowel in the lime bucket in the outhouse, and she dug a deep hole at the edge of the garden next to the unnamed cat. It took all afternoon. Lori-Ann's spike-heeled shoes were quickly cracked by pushing down on the edge of the spade; after only a few shovel-fulls of sod and topsoil she tossed them aside and pulled on a pair of black rubber boots that she found outside the kitchen doorway. Lori-Ann's soft hands were quickly broken by the smooth, heavy handle of the spade, and the blisters cut into her palms like knives. Esa sat awkwardly near the hole and scraped one-handed at the edge of the dry earth with the trowel. She would not let go of Nimbus' body to dig, and wore the grey sweater across her chest until the tops of Lori-Ann's boots were well below the earth line.

Lori-Ann went into the house and gathered an armful of towels from the floor of the upstairs landing. She was careful not to disturb the squirrels. She came out and held a bright yellow hand towel under the spout as she pulled the squeaky arm up and down. When it was soaked with gushing water she stopped and wrung it out, and went and wiped Esa's smeared face and uncurled her hands from the blood-stained wool and washed the red from her fingers. Esa would not let go of Nimbus; she cradled his lifeless body in her arms. She took the wet towel from Lori-Ann and stroked his woolly face with it until it was clean.

After a while Lori-Ann gently pried the lamb from Esa's stiff fingers, trying to shield herself from the sight of his wounds as she did so. The social worker buried Esa's sheep child wrapped in a pale blue terrycloth shroud. While she pushed the earth clumsily over the bundle at the bottom of the small grave, Esa lay curled on the brittle grass and keened her lament.

Lori-Ann sat on the apple stump and watched Esa, and Esa sat Shiva by the fresh-dug earth, and the sun began to set over the ocean like a slice of pink melon. The mosquitos came whining out and bit at Lori-Ann's legs through the tears in her stockings, and bit her sunburnt arms, and her furrowed forehead. She slapped at them with stinging palms, looked at her watch and wondered aloud, without really seeming to care, how many appointments she'd missed that afternoon.

"Esa," she called. "Esa, you *have to* get up." Lori-Ann rose and placed her hand under Esa's grey elbow, tugged at first tentatively, then more assertively when she felt Esa respond with movement.

"Here. Come on. Come on. Come on." She was like a child with an aging, stroke-injured mother, and she encouraged every feeble step that Esa took away from the grave: past the house's wound, around the corner, over the scattered papers and photographs, towards Lori-Ann's car. When they got there Lori-Ann leaned Esa up against the wheel well, got her plaid car blanket from the trunk, and spread it over the passenger seat before guiding Esa in. From her place in the driver's seat she reached over and buckled Esa's seatbelt carefully underneath her swollen belly. And Esa let her.

Lori-Ann drove down to the end of the driveway and idled the car while she looked up and down the road in the dusk, waiting for a sign.

Directly in front of her the killdeer flung itself out of the open mailbox and limped along the road to the left, dragging its wing. So she turned left out along the gravel road and drove down past the banked mailboxes and the Rover Road. She slowed and looked at the name on the old mailbox beside a driveway on her right:

–ril Mac–ona–d, it read; the missing letters long gone in road dust and weeds.

The house was set back from the road: a tiny, tilted, clap-boarded structure rose lowly from the fields, like a frost-heaved rock, dwarfed by nearby barns and drive sheds. A soft light shone through the small front window and the screen door.

Lori-Ann parked beside the house and by the time she'd turned the engine off, Cyril had appeared in the doorway in a sleeveless undershirt, his suspenders drooped loosely over his shoulders, cane in hand.

"Esa—the lamb—" Lori-Ann called to him over the roof of the car, half out of her seat. Cyril pushed open the screen door and let it slam behind him, and he came down the three steps and across the drive before Lori-Ann could think of what to say next. He opened Esa's door and leaned hard on his cane to pull Esa out, and she, sweat-stained and blood-soaked, folded herself into his bristly arms.

"I didn't know what to do," said Lori-Ann apologetically. "I didn't know where to take her. I couldn't leave her there, but I didn't know what to do."

"You did right," said Cyril. "You did fine." But he wasn't look-ing at Lori-Ann. The side of his cheek hovered over the top of Esa's head.

"Can she stay here tonight? I could bring her home with me—" But as she spoke it seemed she didn't really know if this was true.

"She'll stay here," he answered, and he turned Esa toward the house.

Lori-Ann watched them while they walked up the porch steps. The screen door banged shut again behind them. Esa turned back and saw how she stood for a moment underneath the evening's first stars, leaning on the car roof, looking like she had nowhere to go.

Cyril had heard the whole story. He'd made her tea, and had brought a multi-coloured crocheted blanket to cover her scratched and bruised legs where she sat on his daybed, and he'd found her a large clean cotton handkerchief and lay it folded on her knee. Then he'd busied himself in the kitchenette beside her, putting the dishes away out of the drying rack, and setting the small chrome table with napkins and spoons. He took a pot out from underneath the counter, filled it with frothing milk from a glass jar, and set it on the stove.

"I tied him up," she said. There was a heaviness in her words that sank them quickly to the ground and buried them underneath the pine floorboards in a grave of their own.

Cyril took another glass jar down from a shelf and threw handfuls of rolled oats into the pot of hot milk.

"Comfort food," he said, stirring the pot.

"What?" said Esa. She was a long way away.

"My father always made my mother oatmeal when she'd delivered a baby," explained Cyril. "Or lost one. Didn't matter what time of the day or night it was."

"It's night." Esa looked out through the shutterless window into blackness, as if she had just recognized the dark.

"She never wanted more than two or three children, but there were nine of us."

"Oh," she said. A thin branch tapped against the glass. There was a long silence of words, and Esa heard the wooden spoon in the pot and the wooden branch on the glass, and the filling of Cyril's lungs with summer air, and the creak of the springs in the settee as she shifted her weight around to find a resting place for her one remaining child.

"Nine?" Esa asked, as if what he had said had just registered. "*Nine* children?"

"We're all tied up one way or another," Cyril said, and he put a jug of cream and two bowls of steaming porridge on the table. "Now come and eat."

"Eat?" Esa rose slowly from the daybed, looked down at the steam, and saw fire.

"Alice was making porridge," she said. She picked up the silver spoon.

After supper she fell into an exhausted sleep on the daybed and Cyril lit a small fire in the Kemac so she wouldn't get cold during the night. She woke early in the morning stiff and raw, and slipped quietly out of the house, closing the screen door gently behind her so as not to wake Cyril in the little back bedroom. As she walked home along the misty road she noticed she could no longer see her feet below her rounded belly. At the top of the rise beside Alice's house there was no sign of the spilled envelope from the safety deposit box. She searched half-heartedly underneath the cedar trees, and at the mouth of the path to the river. All the while the barn swallows flew in and out of the open front door of the house like a fleet of wartime carrier pigeons carrying secret messages.

Esa was sitting down on the beach, rusty with dried blood. Cyril made his way carefully across the strand towards her, his cane shifting small holes in the fine stones as he leaned on it. When he got close to her, it seemed as if she had been waiting for him.

She got up and dragged a tree root down from the high tide line, and he eased himself onto its knobbly side. He uncovered the basket he was carrying and took out a teacup full of wild strawberries and handed them across to her.

"Neighbour brought these to me this morning. I don't care for them much." He motioned for her to eat. Esa looked at the fresh grass stains on the knees of his work pants and ate the tiny berries one by one, pressing each against the roof of her mouth with her tongue. The tide washed in slowly, the foam on the water's surface making a white net to try to catch them both.

"Where are they all, those nine children?"

"Eight of them, gone," he said. "There's just me left."

"Gone?"

"Dead."

"Oh," she said. "Dead."

"I was the youngest," he said, as if that explained it.

"I was the youngest, too. But there were only three of us."

"I know."

She didn't ask him how he knew, assuming Alice had told him. She didn't hear the waiting in his voice, didn't notice how he held his breath, as he often did with her.

"I don't know where my sisters are. They could be dead," she said, doubtfully. She looked at the inside of the empty cup, stained red with berry juice. "There was so much blood."

"I can see that."

Esa looked down at her maternity blouse like the shroud of Turin, stained with the shape of Nimbus' body.

"We came down here every day, walking. He was getting much stronger. He could walk all the way to the point and back without needing to be carried."

"You were taking good care of him," agreed Cyril.

"But I tied him up." Finally, when she said it, it was not a question to herself, but a simple recognition of the tragic result of an ill-conceived action.

"Yes," he said.

"You never come down to the beach," she said.

"No." Again he held his breath, but there was nothing more.

They looked out over the ocean. The sky was wide, and long, hook-ended cirrus clouds stretched across the sky from east to west.

"Mares' tails," said Cyril.

"Lambs' tails," corrected Esa.

In the early afternoon, dark clouds moved in and threatened rain. Lori-Ann drove up the driveway and got out of her car. She had a new pair of red shoes on; wine red, not blood red.

She handed Esa the brown envelope, apologetically, the bulging contents in disarray.

"I came back last night after—I came back and picked all this up." She wouldn't look Esa in the eye. "I just gathered it all up and put it back in the envelope."

"Oh," said Esa. The package smelled of old fear and dampness. There was a black and white photograph half sticking out; a woman's legs were visible striding along the beach stones, in flat old-fashioned pumps, the picture taken from the side.

"Are you okay, Esa?"

"Oh, I'm okay."

"That was awful. I'm so sorry."

"I'm the one who tied him up," said Esa.

"I mean, I'm so sorry that happened—to Nimbus—and to you."

"Oh."

"Do you need anything?"

"No."

"I read everything in there," Lori-Ann said, pointing to the envelope. "I'm sorry, but I read it all."

"Oh," said Esa. She was not surprised.

"Do you want me to stay for a while?"

"No."

"You might be upset. I could stay—"

Esa shook her head.

"Do you need *anything*?"

But Esa did not move or speak.

"Well, if you're sure—" Lori-Ann hesitated, then turned to her car. She seemed surprised to realize she'd left the driver's door wide open.

"I need someone to teach me to drive," said Esa quickly. She tried not to make it sound like a question. The words froze on Lori-Ann's shoulder blade and the social worker turned her long neck back. They looked at each other, looked past the eyes.

"Esa, you look really awful," said Lori-Ann gratefully. "And you really smell."

Esa got the bucket and filled it at the pump until it overflowed, carried it in through the back door to the tub, laid it down on the charred kitchen floor in a space she cleared with the side of her shoe.

Upstairs in the bathroom she crawled carefully along the perimeter of the hole and found a bar of yellow ash-covered soap, and she collected the straw broom from the linen closet, and an armload of towels from the floor—leaving the one the squirrels had claimed. As she passed Alice's doorway the swallows dived from their nest and darted around her head in the hallway.

It was impossible to sweep the floor clean; melted metal and plastic objects were fused to the sheet flooring. Esa pushed the larger objects and the broken glass away from the tub's perimeter. She reached into the half-full bath and pulled the rubber plug from the drain so the rust-coloured stagnant water from the leaky roof poured out on to the floor and bathed her bare feet. There were a series of concentric red stains around the tub's perimeter where the water level had steadily evaporated since the storm, and she lifted the bucket and swirled the water along the enamel sides to rinse the tub. Then she replaced the plug and went out to the well with the bucket and pumped it over-full so that bright water washed blood and rust from her toes.

Esa hauled buckets of water until the scar on her hand had reddened, and re-blistered, and finally the tub was full.

She laid a towel carefully along the floor beside the bath, peeled off her ragged, blood-crusted clothes, stepped into the cold water. After scrubbing so hard with the yellow soap that her skin looked as if she had once again come too close to the fire, there was as yet no hint of resurrection. But she was clean, and smelled like Sunlight.

# Chapter 21

"Gear up," instructed Lori-Ann. "Can't you hear the engine whining?"

Esa shifted into fourth gear and from underneath their feet came a grinding cry.

"Clutch, clutch!" cried Lori-Ann. She held on to the door handle as they went around the curve.

They had gone together in the social worker's car to the police station. Lori-Ann no longer felt she needed to use the car blanket from the trunk to protect her passenger seat. Esa had showed Corporal MacGillveray the insurance papers and her new Learner's Permit, and he had given Lori-Ann the keys to Alice's car.

"You are the keeper of the keys," he'd said to Lori-Ann. "Promise?"

They'd both nodded.

"And make sure she wears shoes." He'd looked down appreciatively at Esa's clean bare feet.

They had been driving the back roads for almost two hours. Lori-Ann had showed Esa where she recorded it in her log book as a Home Visit to a Child in Danger of Apprehension. She said she tried not to think of that as lying. She thought perhaps Esa could be the child, for even though Esa was not much younger Lori-Ann believed that Esa was surely in danger of being arrested if she kept driving Cyril's farm truck to town without a licence.

Esa was ready when Cyril pulled up at the bottom of the driveway on Saturday. He rolled down his window in the soft rain and stared, not caring at all that his sleeve was getting wet. He was all dressed up in a white shirt with silver cufflinks and a yellow bow tie, and his tweed jacket was draped over the back seat.

"Weeeell, now," he said, and he whistled through his false teeth. He pushed his straw fedora away from his forehead so he would have a clearer view of Esa, newly washed and dressed in clean clothes, with a pair of rough leather shoes dangling from her hand by their laces. She stood waiting at the edge of the drive as if caught innocently in a state of inaction, having forgotten, herself, about the rain. She was wet through in all the exposed places: the top of her head, her shoulders, her bulging belly.

"I guess you're still coming," Cyril said.

"We made a deal," said Esa, as if that explained it.

"Yes, we did."

"And you did your part."

"Yes, I did."

"I didn't read any of it yet," said Esa. And she got in the car and threw her shoes on the floor in front of the passenger seat while Cyril once again exhaled his waiting breath.

"You look like you're going to church," she said.

"Oh, church," he said. "There's better things to get dressed up for."


The open envelope was on the sideboard, propped up against the wall. The black and white legs of the unknown woman on the beach hung upside down: a suspended letter 'V'.

Esa had looked at the envelope when she made her dinner, and again the following morning when she made her breakfast, and then after that she hardly noticed it. It blended into the disarray of the sideboard, the sitting room, the house, her life. Nimbus's death had changed the camera lens. The photographic legs kicked out in vain.


The fog rolled in from the Atlantic as Cyril drove. The wind picked up and lashed the rain in buffets against the side of the car, but the car was too heavy to be knocked about. Esa didn't resent it. She knew that Cyril would not have driven any faster—would not have seen any better—had the road been perfectly clear. On the contrary, the weather made the vehicle into a time capsule, and they fledged aimlessly though a cloud-filled universe. Esa could pretend they were going nowhere in particular, running before the wind.

For Esa, there were three kinds of nowhere. The first was close-up, and shifted as they drove along the road, what was familiar and everyday appearing and receding as if viewed with failing eyesight: scraggy fir trees, rural mail boxes, one-dimensional houses. The second nowhere loomed in the middle ground, a lurking presence of something only very slightly darker than white, like all the parts of herself she could only take for granted. The third, a fog-bound, white-filled, thick-walled nowhere, stretched beyond that in all directions as far as time itself.

They went nowhere in particular for almost two hours, and then the city emerged from the fog, gradually, like something surprising revealed on the lawn after the snow slowly melted—something looked for distractedly all winter, without any idea that it lay beyond reach until spring.

The burn unit was on the fourth floor, beside plastic surgery. When they got out of the wide elevator, Cyril sat down in a chair by the nursing station, his cane under his folded hands.

"How are you today, Mr. MacDonald?" said a nurse, as Cyril tipped his hat. She was wearing a uniform that looked like pyjamas; Esa had been looking for her scars.

"Just down the hall," Cyril said to Esa, firmly. When Esa didn't move he pointed down the long hallway. "There on the left."

She stepped alone towards the door of the left-hand room. She had arrived somewhere in particular after all, despite her belief that time had been on her side.

"Fine, fine," said Cyril complacently to the nurse, receding behind Esa. "Quite a bit of weather we're having."

There was a door, and it was open. The room number was written on both the inside and the outside of the door. There were two beds in the room, both of which were occupied. A large rain-teared window gave a view of the parking lot shrouded in fog.

161

There were wires and tubes running everywhere. The room smelled like stale fire and raw wounds. A television was on across the hall: the volume was very loud; the words were indecipherable.

As soon as Esa appeared in the doorway, the television was turned off. For a moment all that could be heard were machine noises: intermittent beepings, a soft whistling like sleeping breath, a metallic humming, a distant telephone.

"Visitor, visitor!" sang a voice from the room behind her. When Esa looked over her shoulder she could see a raw, hairless woman propped in her bed, beckoning with umber arms.

She looked forward at the two prone figures. There was no movement, no turning of heads. Esa did not know if she would recognize Alice. She did not know how far up Alice the fire had climbed before she had been wrapped in the carpet runner. She thought about that carpet runner as she looked around the room, how being wrapped in a carpet runner could somehow lead to this. How beating the spilled rolled oats, aflame on the burner, with a clean tea towel could somehow lead to being wrapped in a carpet runner. How being alive was an unbearable risk.

"Come in, come in, visitor!" There was a cheerful quality to the voice from across the hall that was entirely false; even Esa could detect it.

She took one small step away from the voice, into Alice's room. The figures had faces. The one in the nearest bed had thickly-bandaged eyes. In the far corner, beside the window that overlooked the parking lot, Alice lay propped in her metal-framed bed, fast asleep. Her head was turned on her pillow; she drooled out of the side of her mouth. A single white sheet was pulled up to her neck and carefully folded over at the top edge. The skin grafts were visible just underneath Alice's protruding chin.

Esa took another half-step toward Alice.

"The visitor is for Alice," called the voice. The disappointment was real. "Wake up, Alice! You have a visitor." Esa put her hand out behind her to shush the voice.

Even with half-steps one eventually arrives. Esa made the journey across the room with one pair of eyes watching her from across the hall. At one point, the eye-blind man in the bed next to Alice spoke to Esa out of the side of his mouth. He couldn't seem to move his head.

"Don't be afraid," he said, tenderly. Esa could see that the sheet flattened at his knees, where his legs should have been. She thought about his legs, his puckered skin, his lost bones.

She sat in the chair next to the window, beside Alice's bed. She watched Alice sleep.

After a short while the television was turned back on in the room across the hall.

Esa slept and Alice slept. Out in the hallway, beside the nursing station, Cyril had his afternoon nap. His fedora fell from his hands and rolled down the hall like a tumbleweed, and the nurse in pyjamas picked it up and laid it on the counter beside a potted geranium, fire engine red.

In Alice's hospital room, Esa had a dream. She dreamed of icebergs floating down the reach and into the little cove where the ruined house sat on the bluff. The icebergs washed right in on the tide, grinding their massive haunches on the sea floor, kicking up fine grey sand and lanky seaweeds, and scattering bottom-feeders to the currents. The frozen mountains crumbled, and the growlers tumbled silently to the shore. Everywhere the ice landed, frost gathered and spread, like white ink on green blotting paper. It ran up past the high tide line, and the beach grass turned to cut crystal. It ran up the rise and turned the house into a frosted relic, a rotting wedding cake forty years old.

When Esa woke, Alice's eyes were wide open. They looked at each other. Esa looked at the triangular patch of skin underneath Alice's chin, and wondered if it had really come from pigs. Alice looked at Esa's very large belly, the top of which was at the height of her head on the bed. Neither of them spoke at all. Neither of them could speak. Alice could not speak because she had no voice box; Esa, because she had no voice.

A nurse came in; her cheerfulness more honest than that of the raw woman across the hall, but less tested.

"Someone has sent you a fruit basket, Frank," she said. She carried a tall, cellophane-wrapped bundle in two hands.

"A fruit basket!" said the man in the next bed. Tender Frank. "What's in it? Who is it from?"

"I don't know. Do you want me to open it? Shall I read you the card?"

"Yes, please."

"Well, here's the card. It says 'To Frank with love from everyone at Windy Motors.' And let's see—there's apples, all colours, and tangerines, and kiwis, and grapes—"

"Grapes," said the voice across the hall. "Are there green ones?"

"Pass it around," said Frank. "Can you please pass it around? Make sure everyone gets something. Make sure Alice's visitor gets something, too."

The nurse offered fruit to Esa, but Esa shook her head, so she took the basket down the hall, taking out a kiwi or a fat pink grapefruit or a bunch of green grapes for each patient and laying it on each bedside table. They were all pretending she did this to be kind, and not because they all had useless, bandaged hands. Perhaps later, other visitors might come who would have time to cut the fruit into bite-sized pieces and place it, morsel by morsel, into waiting mouths.

The nurse brought the still over-flowing basket back, left it beside Frank's bed and disappeared once again into the hallway.

"Hello, Alice's visitor," said Frank. "You needn't be shy. I'll never eat all this myself."

"Esa," Esa croaked. She lifted her eyes from Alice's neck.

"Esa," Frank repeated. "I thought it might be you. I've heard Cyril speak of you."

"Yes."

"The gang at work sends me something every week," he chuckled. "Last week it was a singing clown with balloons. You'll be glad you missed that one!"

Esa looked down the length of Frank's bandaged body to the stubs of his legs.

"Car accident," Tender Frank said, even though he couldn't see where she was looking. "Company car. Windy Motors. The gas tank exploded. Luckily, the people in the other car weren't hurt at all. Not a scratch on them." And he smiled.

After that, Esa looked Alice in the eye, seeking a kind of permission, then carefully lifted up the edge of the sheet and peered down into the fog-white nowhere. When she looked back at Alice's face, they were both crying.

After a thick fog, it is always easier to see things more clearly. Blades of grass, tiny pebbles, the edge of tree trunks, the distant rocks erupting along the shore, the horizon line—all stood out in such painful sharpness that it was difficult for Esa to recall how they were ever safely obscure or indistinct. The tiniest details could be discerned at great distances. And the colours: the delicate blue of the sky, woven through with fine white feathers; the startling blue of the bluejay's wing against the robust late-summer green of the spruce branches; the fireweed sweeping the lower fields with dusty violet blankets. Their clarity shone keenly in the sunlight, and when she turned her head, the dew shimmered silver and gold and red over every surface.

The early morning just after a fog lifted was the most surprising, the details stinging her eyes, as if the light itself was caustic.

When Esa looked up, Cyril was in the doorway, leaning on his cane with both hands, his hat brim folded between his thumbs. He appeared like a saviour, as he always did, and Esa sagged visibly in her seat at the sight of him, knowing that, soon, he would take her home.

"Afternoon, Frank," called Cyril. The television was abruptly switched off. "Afternoon, Linden," he called over his shoulder, in acknowledgement of the relative silence. "Afternoon, Florence." There was a small chorus of replies. He made his way across the room until he was opposite Esa on the other side of Alice's bed.

Alice turned her head up to greet him, smiling.

"Afternoon, Alice." He leaned stiffly over the bed and lightly kissed Alice's forehead.

Tenderness, everywhere. Esa blinked, looked down at her hands where the crescent-shaped scar shone pink and iridescent under the ward-room lights, like a giant fingernail cut into her palm—as if Death's hand had pointed, but she had not gone.

"I've been talking to the nurses," Cyril said to Alice. "They were telling me how much trouble you've been giving them, hollering for this and that and everything else, all hours of the night and day." They smiled fondly at each other, but Cyril's eye caught a piece of dust and he turned away for a moment and took his handkerchief out of his breast pocket.

"Never mind," he said, speaking slowly. "One day you will, sure enough. Won't she now, Frank? You'll be after me: 'Cyril, there's a loose shingle; Cyril, there's a leaky tap; Cyril, there's a colony of mice, Cyril—'"

He looked up at Esa's stricken face. Esa saw a shadow of the frozen house, lingering from her dream.

"Well now," he said. "Well now."

There was a silence.

"Can I offer you some fruit, Cyril?" asked Frank. "Apple? Tangerine? Grapes?"

"Well, thank you very much, Frank. That's very kind of you. Let's see if there's a Cortland apple in that big basket. Ah, yes! The best!" He bit into it as if he were biting into life itself.

Cyril said only one thing about Alice on the way home from the hospital. He told Esa the doctors had abandoned any thought of transplanting a new voice box into Alice's throat. Instead, they were teaching her to talk from a different place lower down in her windpipe.

"She wanted to surprise me," he said. "But they said she'll be quite difficult to understand for a long time."

Esa thought that Alice's reedy voice had always come from the depths.

They had only two other short conversations during the whole drive. When they were halfway home, and the land beyond the middle ground had turned ash-coloured in the dusk, he said:

"I need your help with the haying."

Esa was surprised into the near nowhere, where the trees stood darkly by, waiting to hear her answer as the car crawled slowly past them.

"I don't mean throwing bales," Cyril clarified, motioning to her belly. It was the first time he had directly acknowledged her pregnancy. "I want you to drive the truck. Basil's come down with the bellyache, so I'm left short."

"Basil?"

"Too much rhubarb, likely."

"Short?" she said.

Much later, at the bottom of Alice's driveway, when all of nowhere was an inky black shadow, he said:

"Same time next Saturday for the hospital."

And then:

"It'll be the second fine day in a row for the hay."

He did not leave her any room to say no, so she found herself unable to say it. On both counts.

"Esa!" cried Lori-Ann. She put one hand out against the dash, and grabbed the shoulder strap of her seat belt with the other. "Brake!"

"Oh!" gasped Esa. A deer leapt out of the ditch and crossed the road in front of the car, its white tail blowing behind it like a handkerchief come loose from the laundry line. She kicked the brake, the car stalled, and they were bounced backwards into their seats. Dust rose up from the wheels and was blown forward by the sultry wind. Esa's belly was wedged underneath the steering wheel.

"Breathe!" said Lori-Ann.

They sat in the stalled car in the middle of the deserted road and inhaled the dust deeply. A small herd of deer emerged from the wood beyond the ditch and promenaded nonchalantly in front of them. They looked at the car with great distain, lifting their feet like princesses at a ball.

"Well, la-de-da!" said Lori-Ann, and they laughed.

# Chapter 22

Cyril's farm was a maze of open fields bordered by evergreen woods, with occasional birch trees stark against the deep green, hung with pale green tufts of old man's beard. Some of the fields held sheep grazing lazily in the distance like black and grey and white stones; some held heavy mustard-coloured cattle, with great curving horns, who stamped their feet impatiently at the intruders, and snorted wetly through their wide nostrils. Other fields held cut hay fluffed up in rows of golden green, steaming in the hot morning sun, or baled hay stacked upended in triangular pyramids, dry as kindling.

Esa could not imagine how Cyril kept track of it all. She could never tell where one field would exit into the next, always thinking that they had finally come to a dead end, only to see, at the last minute, a gate in the fence around an unexpected turn. She drove the truck slowly on the disconcerting slopes, and stalled it often. No one seemed to mind.

Of course, Cyril drove the tractor. He exhausted himself doing it, since haying days stretched from early morning to dusk. But it seemed to be a rule that it was his job to sit high on the rust-red metal seat and pull the hay rake and the baler through the rolling fields. His cane was always in his hand and he thumped the metal engine casing in front of him whenever he wanted to attract someone's attention.

Two wiry men, Tom and Ralph, followed behind the truck and tossed bales lightly into the hay wagon, where a woman named Robbie built them neatly into a solid tower of green. There was also a team of black Percheron horses, Bud and Jake, on stand-by for pulling the hay wagon up and down the steepest parts of

Cyril's back fields.

There was a steady on-shore wind, but Cyril said that was good for drying the hay out after the day of rain and fog.

"No need to buy salt blocks for the animals," he said. "Sea wind puts the salt right into the timothy."

Regularly, Robbie would climb to the top of the tower as it jostled behind the truck, and beat her chest and yell like Tarzan. And Tom, who was her husband, would turn cartwheels in the field, and his cigarettes would fall out of his shirt pocket every time. And then gap-toothed Ralph would start to yell:

"No smoking on my property! No smoking near the hay!" in a fine imitation of Cyril, and they would all lie down and kick their heels into the ground in delight.

When the hay wagon was full, Esa would drive back to the barn with all three of them perched on the tottering hay, singing "Amazing Grace" and "The Teddy Bear's Picnic" so loudly that the sheep bolted in the fields.

Esa had never seen people work so hard and have so much fun at the same time.

At lunchtime they sat in the warm stubble in the shade of the hay tower, and picked the heads of purple clover and tossed them at each other, and ate thick baloney sandwiches, and drank gallons of fresh lemonade.

They were all so odd that no one thought anything was particularly strange about the very pregnant, silent woman who drove the truck instead of Basil.

When they were done haying for the day Cyril nodded them all goodbye, when all had gone but Esa, he pushed his hat back on his damp forehead and wiped his brow with a red bandana.

"You might as well drive yourself home in that there truck," he said to her. "But *duck right down* if you see any god-damned Mounties." And he winked, and staggered stiffly up the two steps to his side door.

*

"Keys," said Lori-Ann, at the end of each lesson.

Esa handed them over without argument.

*Dear Merle*, she wrote.
*I have been helping Cyril (he's my neighbour) get his hay in. I
am also learning how to drive.*
*Lori-Ann (she's my friend) tells me I am getting bigger by the
minute, but I do not think that can be true.*

Esa had hesitated over the word "friend" for over half an hour.
It was not a concept she had much experience with. She wrote
the word, in the end, simply because she could think of no other
that would do.

Cyril and Esa were drinking lemonade in the field. Cyril was
sitting on the tractor seat, and Esa was sitting on the top of the
right rear tire. It had been quite a feat to climb up there; she kicked
her heels against the wheel bolts with a sense of achievement. Far
down the long slope to the barns, they could see Tom and Ralph
step-dancing in the field, and they could hear, faintly, Robbie clap-
ping the rhythm while carrying the empty picnic basket balanced
on her head.

"You went to college, didn't you?" said Cyril.

"University, yes."

"Geography, wasn't it?"

"Yes," she said.

"You know the capitals of all the countries in the world?" he
asked.

"Most of them."

"You know all about plate tectonics and soil erosion and volcanoes, things like that?"

"Quite a bit." She looked at him swirling lemon peel around in
the bottom of his tin cup.

"And all about those fool satellites up there, keeping track of
us all."

"Yes," she said. "GPS." Esa remembered Serge on the apple-green
park bench, waving his hands among the falling leaves.

Cyrus took one last gulp, tossed the peel out onto the mown hayfield, and waved his empty cup skyward.

She looked at the curled lemon peel, a fingernail moon on a stubbly sky, and thought about the real moon, the clock of heaven, and all those lost sailors looking for answers in the wrong places.

"Could you figure out our exact location right now, using this GPS?"

Esa looked up at the blue ceiling, deep and cloudless, and saw there the silvery web being woven by twenty-four invisible sky-spiders. "If I had a special computer, I could," she admitted.

"So you could tell exactly where you are," Cyril nodded, pursed his lips, and kept looking up at the summer sky, "with the help of the right kind of computer." He just kept nodding away, and Esa watched the white hairs on the side of his head lift like feathers in the wind.

Feathers, faith hers, faith lures, she thought. Satellites and stars. A leaf in the palm of her hand, cradled against his arm.

"I can tell you exactly where you are, and I don't need no god-damned computer," Cyril finally said. "You're *home*." And he turned the key and the engine roared, and Esa climbed down as quickly as possible onto the tractor step, and rode down the bumping hill standing by Cyril's right side.

"Do you want this baby, Esa? Have you thought *at all* about moving into a different house? Maybe you'd like to get an apartment in town? Have you made any plans to get a job? Do you know how you'll support yourself and the baby, after it comes? You can't just live on other people's charity forever, you know."

The rain had drawn fat toads onto the surface of the road, and Esa was doing her best to avoid running over them. They both knew that Lori-Ann's questions would elicit no verbal response; even so, she felt duty-bound to ask them. She'd told Esa she still needed to do her job.

"You can apply for social assistance, but you have to have a plan for the future. Maybe you'd like to go back and get your high school diploma?"

Esa manoeuvred around the amphibian obstacle course like a precision driver.

"Or you could maybe go to hairdressing school, or take a computer course?"

Esa put her foot abruptly on the brake, depressing the clutch at the same time, and shifted easily down into first. It was sometimes difficult to tell the difference between toads and skittering leaves.

Lori-Ann head's knocked gently against the headrest.

"Cut it out, Esa! You're making me carsick!"

On a bright, piercing morning soon after their visit to Alice, Esa pulled the black and white legs from the manila envelope on the sideboard, and turned them right-side-up. Attached to the legs was a sturdy, middle-aged body, strong arms, a careless head with a serious, vulnerable face, half obscured by curling strands of hair, like fine, dark seafronds, blown by the wind. The woman was caught striding along the beach, a broken eel basket under one arm, but she had turned slightly—perhaps in annoyance—to face the photographer. Her other hand was flung outward from her body as if to shoo the camera away. In that hand she held a large round piece of quartz, its grey-veined shine still detectible through the faded picture. The effect was rather as if she were Amphitrite offering the moon to the viewer.

It was Gam.

Esa sat cross-legged and poured Corn Flakes into a bowl and poured the entire contents of the envelope onto the floor. There were a few more photographs, some letters and cards, legal documents, newspaper clippings, a Death Certificate. And a short, neat, handwritten note on a pure white page.

Esa watched a carpenter ant drag a dead moth over the empty, discarded envelope. It arrived at the edge, over and over, and always turned back.

\*

Alice's car was parked on the shoulder. Esa's window was rolled down, although it was beginning to rain. The sky was covered, end to end, with low hanging cloud, making a flat grey roof on the world.

In the field beside the car, across a barbed wire fence, a newborn calf lay slick on the wet grass, the afterbirth still trailing from the standing mother cow in a glutinous and bloody rope.

"Ew," said Lori-Ann.

The cow began to lick mucus from the calf's nose, and the infant trembled at her touch. Esa felt each rough lick on her face, tasted the blood.

"Ew," said Lori-Ann again. "Esa, can you drive on?"

"What?" said Esa.

"Drive on, James!"

"Huh?"

"We've been sitting here looking at this icky sight for half an hour."

"I guess it takes a while," said Esa.

"I guess it does." Lori-Ann, exasperated, looked the other way, and rolled her window down a few inches. "At least we're not sitting here waiting for you to have your baby!"

"Why?"

"It takes a lot longer for humans," Lori-Ann said.

"It does?"

"Esa, where have you *been* all your life? Under a rock?"

"No," said Esa, "under an illusion."

On one side of them a blinking calf with legs like wooden spindles struggled to stand.

"So how long does it take?" asked Esa.

"Hours and hours. Sometimes a whole day. Sometimes a whole day *and* a night."

"No," said Esa.

"Oh, yes, indeedy."

"*Oh.*"

"Esa—" The calf took one shaky step forward. "I have to tell you that there's a court order to apprehend your baby. The Children's Aid will come and get it at the hospital, as soon as it's born."

Another step from the calf, and another.

"I have to tell you that they don't think that house is a suitable place to have a baby. And there is some question as to whether *you*—well, whether you can *manage* with a baby. If you want to keep this child, I'd advise you to get out of the county before it is born. Better yet, get out of the province. Maybe you could go back where you came from? This is all strictly off the record, of course. Do you know what that means, Esa? That means if you tell anybody I told you to skedaddle, I'll lose my job."

"Where I came from?" said Esa. She thought of the rope on the laundry line.

Lori-Ann sat in the passenger seat of Alice's car and just shook her head. The rain fell like pins and needles on the windshield.

"Who's 'they'?" asked Esa.

"What?"

"You said *'they'*, but the only social worker who's been out to see me is you."

The calf found its mother's fresh pink udder and began to suck.

*Withrod, Ellis Isabel (MacDonald)*—accidentally, near her home, on December 21, 1999. She was the youngest daughter of the late Cyrus and Emily (Harrison). She was a member of Stone Harbour Anglican Church and was active in the Ladies Guild. Ellis was a teacher at the Shore Road Elementary School until her retirement, and the school's closure, in 1980. Predeceased by husband James, brothers George, Joseph, William, Edward, Douglas, and sisters Lillian and Eileen. Survived by brother Cyril, son Burgess (Bernadine), and granddaughters Katherine, Jane, and Esa. In her younger years, she was a frequent sight along the area beaches. She will be sadly missed by everyone along the Shore Road. Cremation has taken place. A memorial service will be held at 11 a.m. April 26, at the Shore Road Community Hall (the old schoolhouse), Stone Harbour, with Rev. Gilles Trimbel officiating and Pipe Major Han MacGillveray lending a musical tribute. Interment will be in the family cemetery. In lieu of flowers, donations may be made to any children's charity.

"I want a baby some day, and I'm going to *keep* it!" she said fiercely to the passing landscape: wind-torn spruce trees, rocky fields, mackerel sky.

"Why?" said Esa. "*Why* do you want a baby?" She was trying to understand.

Lori-Ann was taken aback by the question, and cast about for an explanation.

"Well, I don't know," she said doubtfully. "I guess I want something that's mine—somebody to take care of. Somebody to be related to. I guess I want to be part of a family."

"You were in five foster homes before you were eighteen," Esa remembered. "You told me that."

"Oh, yes, I told you that." Lori-Ann was embarrassed. She looked down at her hands: the perfectly filed fingernails, and the chewed, raw skin at their sides. "Most of them were just for the weekends. I was in what's called 'voluntary care.'"

"Voluntary care?"

"It means the parent has a bit more control, and they can get their child back when they're ready. And the Agency has to take their wishes into account."

"Like what?"

"Like where they want the kid to live, what school they go to, stuff like that. They can visit regularly. The whole point is that it's supposed to be temporary, while the parents deal with some crisis or other. But it can be abused, just like anything else. My mother signed me over every weekend from the time I was eleven. She said she needed the time to get herself together, but she just wanted to party."

"Well, now," said Esa, gearing down smoothly.

"It wasn't like having a home and a family," said Lori-Ann sadly.

Esa turned the car into Alice's driveway. The trees were so thick there was no view of the house from the road. They might have been driving right over the rise and into the frothing ocean.

"I guess we're all homeless one way or another," suggested Esa. She applied the gas going around the curve.

There was a pile of sympathy cards tied together with a short length of baler twine. Esa slipped the twine off the end of the package.

*Sincerely.*
*Such a tragic loss.*
*Most Sincerely.*
*So sorry to hear.*
*Do let us know if there's anything we can do.*
*Such sad news.*
*Such sad news.*
*A tragedy.*

There was a rocking chair in Cyril's front room that lay low to the floor like a crouching animal, so when she sat in it her feet were firmly planted on the ground. Its woven seat had been repaired with netting; the wooden arms were worn at the ends and felt like the softest human skin. The rockers themselves were mismatched—one side bowed out slightly, so that when the chair was rocked it crept stealthily across the floor. Esa sat in it and felt the front bar of the seat press behind her knees. As she rocked, she felt the sun on her bare legs, intensified by the glass, and watched the bright day distorted by the imperfect pane in the quartered window. A brisk wind charged the light outside with a fine translucence. The gusts trailed bark ribbons from the bending birch trees. The squeak of the draft baffle in the stovepipe was like a bird claiming territory, insistent and unremitting; it brought her back to her feet, the chair, the room, the house.

"This house is big enough for one person," she said.

"Oh, plenty," Cyril agreed. He was sewing a button back onto his best shirt, squinting fiercely and holding the needle awkwardly.

"Alice will be able to come home eventually," she said.

"Yes."

"She can't live in that old house up there."

"Oh no," he said. "No, that's right, she can't."

"How do you build a house?"

Cyril looked up at Esa. She was watching the uneven rhythm of his stitching.

"Well, you pour the foundation, frame the walls, run the wires and the pipes. Then there's roof trusses, sheathing, floor boards, shingles—"

"Is it hard?"

"Hard?" he said, considering. "Not what you'd call hard, no. Lot of lifting and hammering, that kind of hard."

"How much would it cost to build a house for one person?"

"Well, I don't know now, today's prices—"

"Just for the foundation, then, how much would it cost?"

"A slab now, you could lay a small slab for a few thousand dollars."

"Slab?"

"Flat," he explained. "No basement."

"I have that much," said Esa.

The needle faltered. Esa was rocking hard. Cyril resumed his painstaking task, bit his lip in concentration.

"Got to dig a hole first."

This time, the needle went right into the eye of the button.

"All right," she said. Without even noticing it, she had rocked herself right across the room. The rising wind caught the front door and blew it wide open. There was a ruffled rooster on the front step, pecking beetles. It looked at Esa in indignation, as if she were responsible for the meteorological disturbance.

# Chapter 23

Surname and given name: Withrod (MacDonald), Ellis
Sex: female
Date of death: on or around December 21, 1999
Place of death: Rover Wharf, Shore Road, Stone Harbour
Date of birth: December 15, 1928
Age: 71
Place of birth: 16 Shore Road, Stone Harbour
Residence: 16 Shore Road, Stone Harbour
Occupation: schoolteacher (retired)
Marital status: widow
Name of spouse: Withrod, James
Name of father: MacDonald, Cyrus
Name of mother: MacDonald (Harrison), Emily
Name of attending physician: Dr. William Nieforth
Name of funeral director: Earl Grant, Grant & Sons Funeral Home
Disposition: Cremation
Place of disposition: MacDonald Family Cemetery, 67 Shore Road, Stone Harbour
Name of informant: MacDonald, Cyril
Address of informant: 67 Shore Road, Stone Harbour
Relationship to deceased: Brother
Date of registration: March 1, 2000
Registration number: 2000-261-1-45
Date of issue: April 27, 2000
$30 PAID

They began to play a sort of game, though neither one of them could have said exactly how it started. Esa drove and drove, taking right turns and left turns at random, without either of them looking at the map. If a place began to look familiar, she always chose the route she did not recognize. Lori-Ann would time them, and after precisely twenty minutes she would yell "Stop!" and Esa would pull over to the shoulder, avoiding the potholes.

"I think we are near Glendean," Lori-Ann might say.

"No, we're west of there, nearer the old mill."

"No, I think maybe near Sander's Cove. I went out with a guy who lived there—once," she clarified. "I only went out with him once."

"No, we're near that farm where they leave their scarecrows out all year round, and the tourists come and take pictures."

And then they would get out the road map with the creases worn through in places, and, holding the pages together, they would snake their fingers along the roads in an effort to find themselves.

Neither of them was ever right.

One day, while finding their way home, Lori-Ann said: "I'm sorry Esa."

"Sorry?" Esa looked across the split seats, and the clouds shifted in the sky. They were passing a field of marsh grasses, through which ran a curling glinting brook.

"I set something in motion, and now I can't seem to take it back."

"What?"

"I'm talking about the baby, Esa." Lori-Ann blinked repeatedly, trying to clear the watery view.

The distant ocean was blue like heaven, and seemed a long way off.

Esa drove and drove, but nothing looked familiar for a long time.

"That's okay. I'll take it back. *I'll* take it back." Esa looked out to the left, and Lori-Ann looked out to the right, but even so, they both seemed to see each other.

After a while, left turns and right turns, they found the highway. When they passed under the Way Road, Esa looked up.

The man on the bridge was silhouetted against the sky. The tawny light revealed a crop of greying hair sticking straight up on his head, a torn place in his jacket sleeve. He was walking away from his accustomed spot, perhaps calling it quits from a long hard day at work, perhaps just going home for his dinner before resuming his duty.

Esa honked, lifted her hand and waved.

Without turning towards her or pausing in his departure, the man lifted his hand slightly in acknowledgment of her greeting. He wagged his hand once, sharply, coyly. In her rear-view mirror Esa saw him reach the end of the bridge, then disappear into the grey glare of the sun on concrete.

Nimbus ran in the corners of her eyes like a woolly shadow. He unravelled her like a skein of yarn, turning and turning on the spindle. She looked for grey everywhere, but could only see in black and white.

The unsigned black and white note said:

*Whatever we can imagine, worse is true.*

The envelope from the safety deposit box was finally empty.

On the last day of haying, Cyril ran over a wayward whip-poor-will nest with the baler. The air was damp with coming rain, so they were baling and bringing in the last field on the same day. Still, he stopped the tractor at the outer edge of the hayfield, un-hooked his cane, and climbed laboriously down. He walked back to the corner of the field where last year's dead leaves pushed up against the hay bristle, and poked at a cracked white egg with the toe of his boot.

He leaned on his cane and picked up the second egg, still intact. It was cool, and covered in fine grey lines, like thin veins on the palest skin.

His farmhands, Robbie, Tom, Ralph, and the recovered Basil, watched in silence as he limped over to the truck and handed Esa the egg through her open window. High above them the dark undersides of cumulonimbus began to fleck their cheeks with rain.

Ralph did not even think of making fun of him.

That evening when she went into town to get groceries, Esa took the rattling egg to Mary Turner.

"Cyril found it in the field," she explained. She held the egg in the palm of her scarred hand, like a small white stone in a chipped bowl. "I think the nest had been abandoned, but I thought you could put it in your incubator—"

It seemed suddenly ridiculous that she was there, offering the bird woman an egg with a dried-up chick inside it. Her hand began to close, but Mary said:

"Esa, come in. It's good to see you." And she squinted at the egg in the dusk like it was treasure, and held it up against the hall light. A still dark shape appeared against the translucent oval.

"You never know," she said. She got Esa to come in and together they walked through the house to the aviary in the back.

"How's Nimbus?" she asked.

Esa stopped beside a caged woodpecker, asleep with its head under its wing, its red cap barely visible.

"Nimbus?" she said. The woodpecker woke, shook its downy head, and stared at her with white-ringed eyes.

"*Pik*," it said.

"Nimbus went back where he came from," she said.


"So where is the family cemetery?" asked Esa. They were sitting on the lawn swing behind Cyril's tiny house, picking the hay dust from the inside of their elbows, sticky with sweat.

In that moment, after such a long time anticipating her possible questions, Cyril hadn't even thought to hold his breath. And it seemed, after all the unnecessary expectancy, a question that was easy to answer. He simply lifted his hand and pointed across the field.

Between the trees of the old orchard, Esa could see a small section of white picket fence.

She pushed herself up and waded through the green. In the white fence was a small wrought-iron gate, painted gold. The gate was closed, but the latch lifted easily. There were about two dozen leaning headstones of white marble, in two rows. Esa walked along reading the inscriptions, trailing her hand on the tops of the weathered stones. They felt like sandpaper, and most were stained with draped shrouds of grey lichens. The grass had been carefully cut, and the white and grey of the stones and the olive of the end-of-summer grasses were bright against the muted sky.

IN LOVING REMEMBRANCE
Edward MacDonald...

Lillian Conrod
Baby Conrod
AT REST...

Born August 30, 1915 Died August 1, 1942
LIFE'S WORK WELL DONE...

Cyrus and Emily, Together Forever...

MOTHER...

Their SON, Joseph
EVER LOVED...

The newest grave was in the farthest corner. The stone was small and smooth, but still, small eyes of orange lichen had begun to grow in the chiselled words. What she read was this:

ELLIS
1928-1999
GONE BUT NOT FORGIVEN

The words and dates slipped their moorings and tumbled to-gether in the milky air.

The edges of leaves dried out and curled; rivers ran thinly over grey stones; brooks dried to damp patches in the fields. Flower petals shook and dried and fell like coloured rain onto the cracking earth. Cow vetch clamoured in the hay fields. Earwigs chewed in the corn.

It was the day in late summer when the weather turns and suddenly there are endings everywhere, despite the bright sunlight. There was a fierce wind that blew all day, dragging the snapping sheets from the laundry lines all the way up and down the Shore Road. The rusty-hinged cries of swinging gates rose on the swirling wind like departing birds. On Esa's line the blue and red rope dangled and danced; she watched it from the open window of the little back bedroom where she'd slept for three months as a child.

Esa went and lay on Gam's bed and stared at the ceiling. She watched the reflection of the light in the leaves play on the old paint. She was flickering, lost in the waving branches.

Her skin was stretched so tightly it alarmed her.

After a while, she fell asleep and dreamt that the racing clouds froze on the surface of the sky and spread like frost on a pane of glass.

Esa emptied the old clothes out of her duffle bag. She went through the house and gathered up all the treasures she had collected from the beach: the purple lobster claw, the nest of tiny mussels, the red plastic toy boat, the worn alabaster ear bones, the brittle white seaweed trailing from the giant snail shell like Cyril's unruly hair, the sand dollar—Neptune's currency—that still dusted grey sand on her palm when she turned it over.

The seaweed root anchored to a briny rock like a length of rope. Even this.

She filled the bag so full she couldn't get the zipper closed. She lugged it out to Cyril's farm truck in the drive, and she drove over to the family cemetery in Cyril's side field and parked in the hay outside the little golden gate.

When she had finished arranging this salvaged seascape on the shorn grass, she looked up to see Cyril leaning on the outside rail of the fence, his cane hooked up between the pickets.

"That looks real fine," he said, approvingly. "But she's not really in there. I threw her ashes on the beach."

Robbie's brother's brother-in-law Ray lived way up the Shore Road and drove a backhoe. He came up to give his advice.

Esa had picked a spot for Alice's new house just to the west of the old one, on the far side of the well and the stumps of the three sisters and the two animal graves beside the wood.

"Sure, sure," Ray said, and he kicked his heel into the tall grass until he'd dug a little hole. He looked up at the heat shimmering in the breeze by the ruined house and wiped the back of his hand across his face.

"I can push that old thing down while we're at it," Ray volunteered.

"No," said Esa.

"I won't charge you nothing extra for it," he said, surprised.

"No."

"Be much safer for ya. We could just burn the—"

"No."

"Well, suit yourself."

The next evening he drove a squalling yellow-ochre machine up the drive and manoeuvred it carefully between the old house and the trees, as Esa had instructed. He ripped a shallow hole through the land's yellow-green surface, exposing dark, rocky earth. Esa made herself watch. When he was done she paid him cash, in hundred-dollar bills.

"You going to be reporting this?" he asked, his fist closing tightly over the money.

"Reporting what?" said Esa, blankly.

He took that as a no.

"What do I do now?"

"Well, if a person had an idea of what they wanted, they'd draw a plan or get some kind of blueprint, and then they'd order a pile of lumber and get started."

"All right," she said.

They were standing on the rectangular concrete slab, dark and hard under their feet. Esa was placing her bare foot in and out of the footprint she'd left there, at Cyril's urging, a few days before when Tom's uncle's former boss had come with a churning concrete mixer and a handful of lean men. They'd hammered up forms for the outside of the footings, and had leapt like rubber-booted deer from one corner to another, pushing long-handled shovels and trowels, up to their ankles in heavy grey slush.

The footprint was hard and cool and comfortable. A familiar home for her calloused foot.

Cyril walked across the wooden gangway—the forms still had to be taken away, and the foundation back-filled—and waded through the long grass to the old house, where he pulled on a piece of burnt clapboard until it splintered in his hand. He brought the wood back to Esa and handed it to her, a giant pencil.

"Draw the rooms," he said. "Draw the windows and the doors."

"What?" said Esa. The wood was hot in her hands, the blackened end resting on the top of her foot, making a black mark and an indent in her skin.

"Where's the front door?"

"Well, here."

"Where?"

"*Here*."

"Make a mark." He waved his hand at the length of wood. "Three feet long."

Esa dragged the charcoal over the edge of the concrete, leaving a dark line the width of a door.

"Here now, look at the views. Here's Alice coming home making ginger cake—what does she want to see out her kitchen window?"

Esa stood on the slab and looked east, south, west, north. She turned like a compass needle without a lodestone. To the north and west the house was contained by woodland dropping from the bluff. To the south the land rose a little, blocking the beach below from view, the grassy knoll like the end of the world, and beyond the vast ocean stretched to meet the sky. To the east, the old, wounded house sat tilting, and a red squirrel ran up the spout of the gutter, and a swift flew down the chimney.

"I don't know," she said, but Cyril pretended he didn't hear, and Esa still turned and turned, and shook her head, until the baby in her belly began to feel dizzy, and squirmed in complaint. When she stopped, surface tension broke the distant waves.

"If the house was for me, I think I would like to look out over the water," she said, "but I don't know about Alice. I've never seen Alice look out at the ocean—not once. Maybe the kitchen should face the road, so she can see who's coming." She looked doubtfully eastwards, where the old house blocked the view of the long driveway, weighing one disaster against another. Cyril followed her gaze.

"I think she'd rather look at the ocean," Esa said, looking over at the charred walls, smelling fire.

Esa drew windows and walls and doorways with her burnt stick.

Cyril did a lot of math in a little notebook he'd pulled from his back pocket, muttering about board feet and roof pitch. They drove together to the mill, and stood in the lumberyard while a toothless man scribbled down their order. Sawdust had settled in the creases of his clothes like crumbling yellow lichen on rock.

Esa paid for the order in cash: nine thousand, three hundred, and twenty-seven dollars. The toothless man didn't charge her any tax.

# Chapter 24

*P*erhaps *it ends without her knowing it. She could look back-*
*wards into the past, and speculate, like a mining baron, as to*
*what is buried there beneath the looming landscape. But perhaps*
*the moment that matters is this one, before the surveys have been*
*completed, before the site has been mapped, before the shovel*
*has been lifted, ceremoniously, by soft hands. Before the blade*
*deals the frozen ground a glancing blow, ice sparks startled from*
*winter sleep.*

*It ends with the alcohol in his belly, absorbed drop by drop,*
*drop by drop into his veins. Ends with the coursing of this alien*
*substance, pumping through his restless body, touching the inside*
*of his rough fingertips, the crusted slash on his forearm, the bleary*
*backs of his eyelids. It ends with an obsessive love affair between*
*the house of his mind and the key to the deadbolt on its front door.*
*It ends with the 12-pack out behind the gym, or the flask in his*
*hip pocket while he worked in the dwarfing dockyards. Perhaps*
*it ends with this particular bottle, like liquid fire running down*
*his raw throat. This particular bottle, Listerine, that marks the*
*boundary line, the border, between what he'd like to have and*
*what he must have in order to survive.*

*Burgess Withrod is a blighted kernel, ill-sprouted in illicit 180-*
*proof. He is known to the police by a different, less resilient name.*
*They find his body cooling by the river, sitting upright in a stolen*
*truck, the floor in front of the bench seat littered with empty*
*bottles of the finest mouthwash. This is the improvident result*
*of the life brought forth by Ellis Withrod, nee MacDonald. This*
*is the terrible news that sends her down to the beach in despair,*
*feeling that her whole life has been eaten away inside her, the way*

*the receding tide pulls at the sand.*

  *Burgess' ex-wife Bernadine reluctantly identifies the body. The police make a desultory effort, at the request of the dead man's mother, but they cannot locate any of his three lost daughters. It is as if they have all three been cut down and burnt for firewood, and there is no trace whatever of the ash.*

# Chapter 25

"**V**isitors!" cried Linden. "Visitors for Alice!" She muted her television.

"Morning Linden, morning Florence, morning Frank," said Cyril from the doorway.

"Morning Alice," he said, when he got to her bedside. His lips brushed her forehead, and she smiled crookedly, her face unbalanced by pain. Her arms lay over the top of the white sheet, an overexposed picture of driftwood on the beach.

"I'll be back. I've got an errand to do," Cyril told her. "But I've brought Esa, keep you company in the meantime."

Esa had followed Cyril into the room but had been invisible behind his large frame. When he turned to go she was exposed like the moon at the end of an eclipse, her light uncertain, her orbit askew. But it seemed that the very sun shone out from Alice's eyes, and blinded her.

She circled the bed, and sat once more in the farthest corner beside Alice, her back to the parking lot.

"Hi," she said to Alice's fire-ravaged arm. The bandaged hand lifted in greeting, an inch off the bed. After that, there seemed nothing more that Esa and the arm could discuss.

There was a long period of silence. Esa looked at the floor, the cracks in the white tiles. Her eyes began to adjust to the shine of everything, but still, she couldn't look up.

"Now, Esa," said blind Frank, believing he had waited long enough. "Look what they sent me this time. Come and see."

She rose as bidden, and circled once more around the two beds and looked down at Tender Frank's weekly booty from Windy Motors. It was a stack of thin crossword puzzle books, a set of sharpened pencils, and a long eraser with "misteaks" written on the side.

"Visitor! Visitor!" cried Linden, and her voice was a slice of pink hope, juicy with longing.

"Perhaps," Frank said tentatively, "you wouldn't mind—?"

"Oh, God!" called Florence. "Please! Save us from ourselves, and this deadly boredom!"

Esa looked resolutely at the cover of the top book where the rows and columns of black and white squares tumbled.

"Just read us out the clues," said Frank encouragingly. "It helps if we know what we're looking for—how many letters in the word, or if any of the letters have been filled in by solving other words."

She lifted the book, pencil, eraser. She pulled a chair over to the doorway and sat down. From her bed, Alice's hand spoke again, a cryptic message, but Esa hadn't yet read the clue. She didn't even know the language the clue was written in. Esa opened the cover of the crossword book, and turned slowly past the first few already-completed puzzles, all in different handwriting. She looked for a moment, without being able to help herself, at the end of Frank's bed, and the end of Frank's legs.

Esa took a long breath.

"Parentless Child. One two three four five six letters." Her voice was husky and carried well to the room across the hall.

When Cyril came back an hour later, with a long cardboard tube under one elbow, and six chocolate milkshakes in a paper bag, they were all trying unsuccessfully to think of a six-letter word for "drink of life.'

"Elixir," he said immediately. And he went around the two rooms and carefully placed a straw in each reclining mouth.


"Let's stop and get ice cream," said Lori-Ann.

Esa's belly was abutting the steering wheel. She thought she could probably drive with no hands, just by leaning from side to side.

"Ice cream. I want an ice cream," Lori-Ann repeated. "It's *hot.*"

"Where?"

"Turn here. Just turn here."

Esa pulled up in front of the ice cream bar, and Lori-Ann got out and slammed the rusty door. Esa sat in the car in the heat and waited, with the windows all rolled down. There was not a cloud in the sky to shade her from the sun's glare.

When Lori-Ann came back out she held a garish ice cream cone in each hand.

"C'mon, get out of the car. There's picnic tables over there." She didn't wait for Esa to answer, and after a minute Esa couldn't see the point in sitting any longer in the hot car, so she struggled out and went and joined Lori-Ann in the shade.

"Mine is called Bubblegum," Lori-Ann said. "It's got bits of bubblegum in it, see. Makes the whole experience last longer. Yours is called Rocky Road. I thought you'd like that." And she smiled, and handed the melting ice to Esa with her long, boney arm.

A little later, as they were passing the Sally Ann, Lori-Ann said, casually, "You've got ice cream stains on your shirt, Esa. Don't you just want to stop for a minute and get yourself another one?" Once they were inside, she suddenly remembered that one of her co-workers was looking for a scarlet camisole, and she sorted carefully through every bin to try to find one, just in case someone had been in before them and mixed things up.

"I need to go home, Lori-Ann. We've been out all day."

"Just one more stop, Esa, I promise. I just have to get one more thing."

"You can get it in your own car, after we get back."

"The stores will be closed by then. *Really*, just one more thing."

So Esa stopped at the strip mall in town, and half-dozed in the car while Lori-Ann went slowly up the sidewalk, and slowly in and out of every store: the drug store, the dollar store, the post office, the video store, the bank. She came back empty-handed.

"I thought you just needed one more thing," questioned Esa.

"Oh, couldn't find it," said Lori-Ann airily, and she turned away and hung out the open window to catch the sultry air as it moved by them.

So it was that Esa arrived back to her burnt-out life-filled home on the Shore Road almost seven hours after Lori-Ann had come on her day off to take her out driving, when Esa hadn't even wanted to go in the first place. Coming home, finally, Esa was so tired that at first she did not notice the cars parked along the road past the little bridge. But when she turned into the drive she could see more cars and pickup trucks at the turn under the oak tree, and more still as she reached the top of the lane.

There was a great noise of hammering and lifting, of sawing and spitting and cursing. As a backdrop, a motor ran somewhere that sounded frenzied in the heat. Esa and Lori-Ann got out of the car—Esa was looking back and forth from the noise to Lori-Ann's bursting countenance.

On top of the new slab, an anthill had sprung up in clouds of sawdust, and the industrious human ants were raising walls and framing windows and cutting stair risers and laying out roof trusses on the flattened grass. In the middle of the half-framed house, Cyril stood whacking his cane against an upright two-by-six, but as he opened his mouth Ralph's voice cut in over him.

"No spitting on my building site! No spitting in the grass!"

Tom turned a perfect cartwheel on the lawn.

He noticed Esa on his upward journey.

"She's here! She's here!" he cried, and then there was a cacophony of human voices as he righted himself and tucked in his shirt-tails to a flurry of shushing. Someone went and turned the generator off, and then there was dead quiet. The only thing that moved was the bindweed that crept unseen a little further into the front doorway of the old house behind her.

Esa's feet were in the ground like something planted there. It was as if the shock of so much unaccountable activity had rooted her at the precise mid-point between an old burnt-out farmhouse that felt more like home than any place she'd ever lived, and a new one sprouting up from spruce lumber, galvanized nails, and neighbourly feeling. She was facing a momentarily silent chorus of eleven men and two women wearing baseball caps and carpenter's aprons, all watching her and waiting to see what she might do.

She took one half-step forward, swayed in the breeze.

The air smelled like dry leaves, salt, and sweat.

Cyril came to meet her, stepping carefully through the open framing of what would soon be a door. Everyone knew better than to try to help him down.

Cyril, Esa's philosopher's stone. He stood in front of her and looked fiercely into her face.

"Afternoon, Esa," he said. "Afternoon, Lori-Ann. Fine job you did." Praise, after all, where praise was due. He and the social worker exchanged a look of conspiracy over Esa's shoulder, but there was something more. Not exactly forgiveness, but perhaps truce.

"About time you got here," he said, smiling. "There's work to be done."

"I've spent pretty much all the money," Esa said. "I probably can't afford to pay all these people."

"Oh, never mind these hooligans," he said. "Don't imagine they got much better to do on a Sunday. We're certainly not keeping them from church—Are we boys?" he called out over the rising clamour.

It seemed Cyril had been busy organizing for quite some time. He'd found eight solid windows stacked unnoticed at an auction, and bid fifty dollars for them after it started to rain and most people had gone home. He'd asked the Rotary Club for money for the ramp, and the special bathtub, and the door handles that could be opened without any need for fingers. He called in favours from the electrician he'd given free gravel to, and from the plumber who was indebted on account of the services of an ancient Percheron stallion. Esa walked through the house's skeleton and marvelled.

"Those are *stairs*." She had been watching two men attach wide lengths of pine with a rounded edge onto a pair of boards that zig-zagged up the side of one wall.

"Yep," said one of the men. He held a nail in his mouth while he searched for his hammer. "Stairs." He nodded slowly, as if what she'd said was profound.

Esa found Cyril overseeing the opening for the kitchen window that looked out over the ocean, one hand on a roll of pale blue papers that he'd pulled out of a long cardboard tube.

"They're making stairs, Cyril, but there aren't supposed to be any stairs. Where are the stairs going *to*?"

"The second story," said Cyril, and he turned away, breathing deeply, before she could ask any more.

*Dear Merle*, she wrote.

*We are building Alice a new house. The doctors say she will probably be ready to come home next month. Practically the whole neighbourhood is working on the house, so maybe it will be ready for her by the time she is ready for it.*

*Thank you for letting me know that Serge has left to take another position, and also for your job offer, again. I think that must be the seventh time…*

*But I think I belong back where I came from.*

Esa drove all the way into the city in Cyril's farm truck, and she did not get lost. It was a miracle she wasn't stopped, for there were no licence plates on the truck except one that said "Knowles Farm Feeds," the left rear brake light was out, and the passenger door was tied shut with baler twine. She spoke to the nurse in pyjamas about a wheelchair, and she waited in the hall by the fire engine geranium until Alice was wheeled out in her pressure suit, looking like a modern-day mummy.

They didn't go very far: up and down the halls and up and down the elevators. Alice gurgled almost constantly and drew hieroglyphics in the air with her better hand, but the only part of it all that Esa understood was that Alice was overjoyed to see her.

It was not a little thing to know.

When Cyril sat in the rocking chair his knees rose to his chest.

"That chair doesn't fit you, Cyril." Esa said it without thinking.

"It was Ellis's chair," he said bluntly.

Suddenly in the small room the only sound was bent wood on floorboards, a rhythm like a heartbeat, magnified by pain.

They were both taken by surprise. As always, Cyril tried to make the best of it.

"She loved the sea," he continued, and Esa knew immediately how it was that that truth was connected to the chair. She saw Gam rocking along the porch of her house, overlooking the ocean, rising periodically to drag the chair back to its starting position, her needlework or her newspaper clutched to her belly.

"She always said the seashore was the only place where she could think bigger than her own life, but I surely don't know how her life ever got to seem so small."

From the porch Gam looked down the shore, and the child Esa walked on the beach, in full sight of her, picking up Neptune's currency, seahorses' bridles, and mermaid's tears as if her life depended on it.

"*Why* did it ever seem so small?" Cyril asked, sadly.

Esa looked at her great uncle rocking in her grandmother's chair. His wispy hair was in its usual dishevelled state, but his face wore openly an expression that up to then she had only seen veiled, and had not clearly understood: his own fear.

"She thought she wasn't any good at giving; those last years, everything she touched seem to fail. We tried so hard to find you. She thought there was nobody left that needed her. After Burgess died, all her life's work didn't seem to count for nothing. It was like she judged herself entirely on how he turned out."

"We tried so hard to find you," he repeated, and looked around his tiny house like a boy lost in the woods. There was a long pause before he continued.

"Alice moved in to take care of her, because she wasn't taking care of herself. Oh, we made it seem like Alice needed a place to live, that it was more for her benefit. Your grandmother was so fiercely independent. She wouldn't have accepted help from any-one, if she knew help was what was being offered."

The pace of the wooden heartbeat quickened, and the volume was turned up slightly.

"And then the accident—Oh, accident, accident!" he said. "She had a rock the size of her head tied around her waist!"

The room tipped and spun around them.

"Good knot, too," he added angrily. He rocked that chair like a child on a rocking horse, as if he could get away.

"She never gave one thought to what we would do without her." His calloused hand slapped the worn wood as he galloped furiously across the floor.

She'd taken Alice's car, because the timing belt in Cyril's truck had broken, and the entire muffler had fallen off. She asked Lori-Ann first.

"There's something important I have to do, Lori-Ann," she'd said. "And I need the car."

Lori-Ann hadn't even asked what that important thing was.

"Please don't get caught," she'd said anxiously, and she'd handed over the keys. "I know this is how people lose their jobs, even if you don't."

"Maybe there are things more important than rules," protested Esa.

"Of course there are," Lori-Ann said.

Esa drove to the city on the quiet back roads, avoiding the potholes. She was tired when she arrived and only nodded at the pyjama nurse before going right into Alice's room.

"What is it," she demanded, "that *I* am to forgive *you* for?" Esa stood at the end of Alice's bed and gripped the metal railing at the bed's foot.

Alice gurgled.

Esa looked at her: the stubbed fingers, the pressure suit stretched over her arms and torso, the newly regrown eyebrows. The pleading eyes.

"Frank—" said Esa, desperately.

"Hello, Esa," said Frank.

But Frank had been blinded, and could not see what she wanted.

Alice gurgled again.

"I don't know what she's saying, Frank."

"She said she lied to you," said Frank gently, "and she stole some of your money."

More gurgling.

"Two hundred dollars," said Frank.

"What did she lie to me about?" asked Esa. She didn't take her eyes from Alice's face. She didn't stop trying to make sense of the noises Alice made for words.

"She didn't tell you she wasn't your grandmother."

Alice looked at Esa expectantly, but Esa took her time answering.

"You didn't steal any two hundred dollars," she said finally. "I sent that money to you."

On the way back, Esa drove right over as many potholes as she could stand. Lori-Ann had told her that was the way women started their labours when they were fed up with waiting.

"I caught the belly-ache, Cyril," she told him, calmly. It might have been the best joke that she had ever made. Her brow was drenched with sweat that ran down into her eyes and blinded her. There were craters underneath her eyes.

He had finally found her out back of the old house, sitting on the last old apple stump, clutching her stomach. Her maternity pants were soaked down the inside of her thighs.

"Did your water break?" he asked.

"What?"

"Did your water break?"

"It's like a rock, Cyril, my belly is like a *rock*!"

"How long you been sitting here?"

"What?"

"Here, now, we got to get you moved. Can't have a baby on a tree stump." He started to pull her up, but she stood of her own accord as soon as she felt his touch, leaning lightly on his free arm. "You want me to take you to the hospital?"

"What? Why? *What*?"

"Just asking," he said.

Halfway across the yard her fingers began to tighten on his wrist, and he hurried her to the corner of the house so she could lean there while the next contraction took her. In another few minutes she was able to walk again, and Cyril guided her through the burnt-out back door, through the blackened kitchen into Alice's little bedroom. He tore the blankets from the mattress and satisfied himself that the sheets underneath were reasonably clean. Esa sat silently on the edge of the bed and kept her eyes fixed on the maze-like pattern of the Indian carpet.

"Where's that phone?" he asked.

"What?"

"That cell phone. MacGillivray's cell phone."

"Oh," she said. "The phone." But he could not get anything more out of her.

Cyril left her there. Before he searched the front room, he lit the camp stove and put a pot of water on to boil. He checked on Esa every few minutes. She did not cry out, but sat moaning lightly, rocking slightly, as the rough tide came in over her and crashed forcefully against her supple frame.

As Cyril went in and out of the room the barn swallows, who were feeding their second nest of young, chattered liquidly in complaint.

He found the phone under a pile of purple mussel shells underneath the sitting room window, but he couldn't get it to work.

"God-damned satellites," he said, and in disgust he threw the beeping phone behind the up-turned parlour chair.

Once, she looked up and saw him standing at the end of the iron bed, his two hands grasping the crossbars of the foot-rails, and it seemed he had been there forever.

"Are you still here?" she asked. "Aren't you going home?"

Cyril looked around the room: the crooked walls, the smoke-stained panelling, the worn carpet, the disorder. He looked at the iron bed frame in the dark makeshift room that was almost directly underneath the bright, three-windowed room where he'd been born seventy-two years earlier.

"You're having a baby, Esa," he said gruffly. "I wouldn't leave a *sheep* to give birth alone."

# Chapter 26

*P*erhaps it ends now, the way that icicles thaw and drip down the rock face, warmed by the returning sun. The way the icy drip descends through dormant moss and dead leaves and dark earth, skirts stones deep down, and down, and further down, until it reaches a place where it joins a cool, mineral trickle. It makes a tinkling sound deep in the cracks and fissures of rock, wears away at them gently as it meanders to join other unseen trebles. It ends when this dark waterway widens and quickens and its growing force pushes it upwards again to the surface, where it emerges into the day: a liquid miracle. Or when the spring becomes a brook becomes a creek becomes a river that courses down hillocks and through towns and fields—becomes the river that spreads over the beach rocks like a fan and empties into the ocean, that river heaven, just below the old house waiting on the rise, empty of human promise.

It ends when the ice in the bay cracks and heaves and lets loose a captive form, bleached by cold and bloated by water. It ends when the grinding ice wears through the length of red and blue rope anchoring the body to a moon-coloured rock on the sea floor.

It does not end without Esa knowing the truth of it after all, even though everything has been done to prevent her from having to find her way in this bleak, pitted landscape.

Mary Turner is walking along the beach, looking for snails to feed an injured sandpiper, when she sees in the distance something that looks like a human figure washed up along the high tide line. She runs and runs over the uneven rocks. What has been held frozen under the surface reappears like a cry caught

*on the relentless wind. And blows away, away.*
*Whatever we can imagine, worse is true.*

# Chapter 27

There was part of her body that was luminous quartz. Periodically, the rock softened. She surfaced with no sense of waiting at all, no effort to get to the end. There was no end. Time was always only now. Esa sank, and she surfaced, and when she began to sink again, she was not surprised. The room was filled with a muted tree-green light that hurt her eyes. The tone was of thick water. When she breathed out, air bubbles rose languidly around her face.

Cyril spoke to her constantly.

"There now, there now. Strong legs, strong legs. Strong belly. There now. Strong baby. Strong Esa." It was what he said to his animals, a kind of praying.

His words held no meaning for her, but the sounds entered. Distantly, she understood at last how such sounds could be used.

Once, she called out to Cyril from that remote, underwater place.

"*Why didn't you tell me?*" she cried, but he didn't know which pain she was unprepared for.

She took all of her clothes off and lay back on the bed.

"It's all right," he said, as much to reassure himself. "I've been seeing babies born in barns all my life."

And after all, there was an end to it. Her thin skin stretched and pulled and split apart like over-ripe fruit. The pain ran like a line of searing fire across the dome of her belly and between her legs. The dark head of another erupted into the world, and gasped. The baby's first breath was of air filled with the odour of old fire.

Cyril moved forward then, reached out his abiding farmer hands to make a calloused cradle.

The baby was a slippery, moss-covered stone. The baby was the inside of a seed bursting with sun and rain: warm and damp, and sprouting.

There was no cry.

Cyril laid the baby on Esa's soft belly; the tiny head nuzzled her breast. The umbilical cord, a twisted blue and red rope, still tied them together.

Esa lay sleeping on Alice's bed; the baby lay sleeping on Esa's belly. Cyril had pulled the sheet up and covered them both lightly. He sat in the hard-backed chair he'd dragged in from the sitting room.

When Esa opened her eyes, he was drying his forehead with one of Alice's handkerchiefs. In the evening light, through the spruce-shrouded window, his hair shone like pale green lichen.

"Where's the porridge, then?" she asked him.

"Astonishing colour," said Cyril, looking at the brown, black-haired baby in Esa's arms.

"Makes no difference to the meat," said Esa, smiling. Her second best joke.

"No, that it doesn't," said Cyril. "It's just that you didn't tell me."

"I didn't tell you anything," said Esa.

"Nor I, you," he said.

When he'd gotten them back to his house, Cyril pulled out a blue plastic Sears bag from under the bed, and handed it to Esa. From it she took receiving blankets, clothes and diapers, size newborn. She spread everything out on the daybed.

"Where did all this come from?"

"Oh, it was just laying around," said Cyril, embarrassed.

"A layette!" she said, incredulous, and she held a tiny sleeper up against the wriggling infant.

"Alice said white was the right thing," he explained. "Do for either kind of baby." She unwrapped the blood-stained hand towel from the squirming body. Cyril took the towel from her and threw it in the Kemac and put a match to it, and then he handed her a bowl of warm water. While he took down the rolled oats from the shelf and set a pot of milk to heat, Esa washed the blood from her human child, and dried her brown body with a white towel from the brand new layette.

Cyril was watching her, leaning up against the stove.

"I didn't know anything about all that money," he said gruffly into the gentle air. "Why did you keep sending it when no one answered your letters?"

"If I had stopped..." She faltered.

The baby yawned and bleated.

"If I had *stopped*— Do you know how these things go on?" she asked him, holding up a diaper.

Esa slept and woke and nursed the baby and changed her diaper, and slept again. She dreamed that the slope down to the ocean below the old house was lined with icy stalactites, the sharp teeth of the land. Melting water dripped from the ends of the icicles in a steady rhythm, like the beating of a small heart—a lamb's perhaps.

She woke and nursed the baby without remembering that she had dreamed at all.

The car they had been expecting drove into Cyril's driveway and parked beside the house. Cyril went out onto the little porch to meet it, unshaven and in his undershirt, on purpose, to emphasize how early in the morning it was. He held the screen of the side door from slamming shut behind him, so as not to wake the baby.

A woman got out from behind the driver's seat of the car. She was big boned and large-chested, her face was plump, and her hair was beautifully greyed. She looked like the universal mother, and like she thought of herself that way too.

"Come on, now," she said firmly, and somewhat impatiently, to her companion. Lori-Ann climbed reluctantly out of the passenger seat, closed the car door carefully behind her. She walked as though she held a very great weight in the soles of her feet, and dragged them through the beach gravel of the driveway until she was standing only slightly behind the driver.

"You ladies lost?" Cyril held back from telling them where to go.

"I'm Nancy Mosher from Community Services. Is Esa Withrod in there?" Mother Mosher looked pointedly at Lori-Ann. This is how it is done, the look said.

"Who?" said Cyril.

"We have come to get the baby, Cyril MacDonald. We have a court order."

"Baby?"

Nancy narrowed her eyes and sighed.

"Mr. MacDonald, please don't make this any more difficult for Esa than it already is."

"I don't imagine it is Esa you are thinking of when you want it to be easy," he snorted. He thumped his cane against the step. "Do you think I am going to let you in here?"

"We have a court order to apprehend the baby. I can show it to you." She motioned to Lori-Ann, who turned back to the car with relief.

"You have no evidence that the person you seek is here. And this is my house, and I am not letting you in," said Cyril. Thump-*thump*-thump-*thump*.

The universal mother seemed to be considering her situation.

"Fine," she said, wearily. "Fine. We'll get the police." She took out her cell phone and dialled.

"Hello? Hello? Hello—I—" But all she was getting was static.

"We'll be back shortly," she said, and she got in the car and tossed the phone to Lori-Ann. "Tell me as soon as we get a strong enough signal."

"See you later, then," said Cyril, blithely. "I have revised my opinion of satellites." He nodded once at the turning vehicle and pulled up the straps of his suspenders.

Esa saw it all through the mesh curtain of the small window over the bathroom sink. She heard it all through the screen door.

Lori-Ann had not spoken one single word.

Cyril watched the car pull out of the driveway.

"All right," he called through the screen door. "We've got about twenty minutes, maybe." And he went in to put on his best shirt that was waiting over the back of the kitchen chair. Esa carried the baby and Cyril carried her bag out to his car. He had trouble with it knocking against his good leg; it contained the baby's entire layette.

They got in the car, Esa in the back beside the baby in the special seat Cyril had borrowed from Robbie and Tom.

The drive into the city had become intermittently familiar. Esa could pick out a house here or there, or a road sign, or a sweep of distant bay that she remembered. It was as if she held a piecemeal map of the landscape in her mind, fragmented through time.

In Cyril's car they moved slowly across that map. Every once in a while Esa looked behind them, as if half-expecting to be followed. Cyril, catching her in the rear-view mirror, said simply: "Naaaaah. They wouldn't bother."

Esa wasn't sure, but she stopped looking back.

"We're here," Cyril announced. He touched her arm lightly. She awoke to a parking lot world, untangled the baby from the borrowed car seat.

They limped together from Cyril's car to the burn unit on the fourth floor.

There was no chorus as they passed down the hall. Both Linden's and Florence's beds were empty. The television was no longer on.

"Morning Frank. We're a day early this week," Cyril explained to Alice as he delivered her kiss. "We've brought Esa's baby to show you. She's a fresh one—born day before yesterday at sunset."

Cyril pulled over the chair for Esa to sit in.

Alice made a low gurgling noise. It seemed to come from deep in her belly.

"She wants to know if it's a boy or a girl." Frank was still the official interpreter.

"Girl. She's a girl."

"She wants to know what the baby's name is."

"Eden," said Esa.

"*Eden*?" exclaimed Cyril. He hadn't asked.

"She wants to know if Eden has a second name," said Frank.

Alice inched her arm across the bed so there was a hollow place near her armpit. Cyril took Eden and lay her down in this fire-warmed place, and the baby, already familiar with the scent of burning, turned her downy apple head to Alice's heart, and nuzzled for milk.

"She's hungry," said Cyril. Esa looked at Cyril's white head, at the furrows of the plough across his damp forehead. She saw Ellis on the beach, frozen and full, a drowned Selene. She looked at the bandaged stumps of Alice's burnt fingers, heard the voice that was lost forever calling her into the fire.

"Eden Alice Withrod," she said.

Alice gurgled.

"Did you say Ellis or Alice?" asked Cyril. He was getting the hang of it.

"I said Alice," said Esa, and she lay her head down on the clean white bed beside Eden's feet and Alice's thigh.

"Are you ready?" he asked.

"Yes."

"Are you sure?"

"Yes."

"Well, now," he said.

Instead of taking the exit that would take them back to the Shore Road, Cyril continued along until they came to the one for town. Esa looked up as they went under the Way Road but the overpass was deserted. They drove slowly through town, past the school and the tiny hospital and the grocery store, and finally Cyril turned in beside a brand new building that sat complacently between a fast food restaurant and a diner.

"Do you want me to come with you?"

"No." She fumbled blindly with the straps on the infant seat, and got out of the car with the baby and the duffle bag, and walked unevenly across the parking lot into the brightly-lit offices, hallways, and meeting rooms of the County Children's Aid Society.

"God-damned social workers," Cyril said under his breath.

Even taking half-steps one eventually arrives. Esa crossed the parking lot like she was swimming underwater, and she pulled open the heavy door of the low building against a dangerous current.

At the reception desk she said her name, and asked to see a social worker about voluntary care.

After a long hour, she came back out to the car empty-handed except for the white flannel blanket decorated with tiny ladybugs and yellow bees.

Cyril hands were trembling, and he had trouble getting the car started. Esa offered to drive, but he said no, he would manage. She sat beside him in the front seat holding the receiving blanket to her nose, and breathed in deeply all she had left of motherhood.

Cyril could see the empty car seat in the rear-view mirror. The fact that it was empty did not seem to be a trick of his failing eyes.

"I'd like to go home," Esa said.

"We are going home."

"I mean, my house—I want to go home to my house."

"Are you sure?" he asked.

"Yes."

"You got some rags to bind yourself up?" He made a circular motion in the air with his hand, in front of his chest, not looking at her. "It's going to be painful. Old sheet, or something. Make it as tight as you can stand."

A baby, they say, is a spark that jump-starts a battery left too long in the cold. A baby is a glue pot, sticky with liquid substance, binding together the pages of torn lives. Babies could change hot ash into rich, dark, expectant earth. A baby is like hope itself springing from fertile ground, running pure and uncontained through fields and towns, gathering goodness, and emptying at last into the ocean, that river heaven.

Esa never believed any of that. An acorn is only a brown seed, the outer shell a protection against the elements, against existence. The inner nut, made of wood and earth and time, is nothing until it has been tasted or until it has fallen into soft ground wet with rain.

As for the river, it ran over effluent pipes, through wastelands, under rusty bridges, and beside burnt-out houses. It arrived at its destination bound up with the debris of human carelessness and lasting sorrow.

Esa's belly sagged like an ancient grave. Her milk dried up, and the pain of it was like a burning in her heart.

But she remembered the tiny fingers, the finest branches; the thin frame a slender smooth-skinned trunk; the dark hair a curly bird's nest. The quiet cry was like the faintest murmur of new leaves.

Her baby was not the colour of oak, but of applewood. The tongue a faint pink blossom.

# Chapter 28

*It begins now. It ends now. It begins now:*

*Esa is on the beach, watching the moonlight weep on the shimmering surface of the water. It is her own reflection, distant, bright, immutable. She recognizes it, at last: the true map of a dark path through the endless sky.*

*The tide turns, for a moment going neither in nor out, like the spaces between breaths, or the breaths between words, or the moment between life and death. In front of her the barnacle-covered pillars of the absent wharf sparkle with myriad tiny mouths. They call and call her, as they always have. She picks up a piece of driftwood and scratches long letters in the sand below the high tide line:*

Whatever we can imagine, more is possible.

*Esa looks up at the new little house silhouetted on the rise. Her arms are clasped across her empty belly, the stick dropped at her bare feet. Her own mouth is open in a piercing, silent cry; she breathes raggedly the stinging, salty air. Stirred with the salt is a thick soup of flesh and bone and blood. A human feast that tastes of despair, compassion, sorrow, hope, forgiveness, love:*

*Flour-covered, ink-stained, oak-coloured, fire-ravaged, sun-bristled, charcoal-wooled, long-boned, soft-skinned, moonlit.*

*The fire burns.*

# Acknowledgements

I would like to thank members of my writing groups, Sophie Bérubé, Frances Boyle, Judith Love, Susan Rogers, and Cheryl Sutherland, and also Jeanette Auger, who all provided much early encouragement for this project.

I would like to thank all the people who have told me their stories over the years; particular thanks go to Valda Leighteizer and Sabine Richter, who may recognize the seeds of some stories here, and to Hughie Tom MacDonald and Cyril Davidson, who taught me that old maritime men speak eloquently in ways other than words.

I would like to thank caseworker Mike Mansfield, of Dartmouth District Community Services, for his generosity in meeting with me and answering my many questions.

I would like to thank the Regional Municipality of Ottawa-Carleton for the Individual Artist Project Grant awarded near the beginning of this work.

I would like to thank my readers, Ann Archer, Ceilidh Auger-Day, Ellen Cray, Deb Harvey, Roger Meagher, Tove Morigan, Beaty Popescu, Mary Thomson, and Donna Truesdale, who read the manuscript in development and provided invaluable feedback. I was truly blessed by their dedication and faith, and I would not have completed this book without them.

I would like to thank my agent, Margaret Hart, for her continued support and admonitions for patience, and my editor at Inanna

Publications, Luciana Ricciutelli, for her unbounded enthusiasm about this story.

I would like to thank dear Fern for all those companionable walks through the woods and along the beach.

I would like to thank Nathalie Ladouceur for learning to embrace a writing life.

*Thank you. Words will never be enough. More is possible.*